P9-CBN-342

She was in a state of exaltation close to ecstasy.

She had not eaten for three days. She had walked the last ten miles, burrowing into the interior of the island like an animal seeking shelter. Her mind rang like a bell: I have nothing; I am bereft of friends, food, shelter. The thought brought an emaciated smile to the white face. She looked a little like one of El Greco's saints—her face all bones and sublimity. And a little insanity. Dear God, she whispered, thank you for my solitude and my poverty, your greatest gifts.

She felt in her leather handbag to see if her .38 was ready to hand. Guns were no good if it took you five minutes to get them out.

Geraldine, alias Saint Theresa—pursued by police, the FBI and her companions of revolutionary days. She stands upon a mountain top in Majorca. A sanctuary, but only a temporary one, for no place in the world is safe for this woman who has rioted, robbed, murdered—and loved.

Books by John Crosby

Nightfall
An Affair of Strangers

Published by
WARNER BOOKS

Nightfall

A NOVEL

JOHN CROSBY

WARNER BOOKS

A Warner Communications Company

WARNER BOOKS EDITION

Copyright © 1976 by John Crosby
All rights reserved

Library of Congress Catalog Card Number: 76-12602

ISBN 0-446-89354-4

This Warner Books Edition is published by
arrangement with Stein and Day Publishers

Cover design by Gene Light

Cover art by Morgan Kane

Warner Books, Inc., 75 Rockefeller Plaza, New York, N.Y. 10019

 A Warner Communications Company

Printed in the United States of America

Not associated with Warner Press, Inc. of Anderson, Indiana

First Printing: September, 1977

10 9 8 7 6 5 4 3 2 1

Nightfall

Only in logic are contradictions unable to coexist. In feelings they quite happily continue alongside each other.

SIGMUND FREUD

CHAPTER

1

The great arch clung to heaven for support. Over
the centuries the wall on one side of it had crumbled away, leaving only two huge stones to support
it. It swam a little in her exhausted gaze like a
mirage. Was it an ancient Moorish palace? Fort?
Whatever it was it shrieked of abandonment, which
was what had beckoned her across the valley. The
long climb up from the valley had strained the young
body to its uttermost limits, and now she leaned
against the stones of the topmost *bancal*, the highest
of a series of ascending terraces, on which the
Moors had built these vast structures, and turned
her fierce gaze on the edifice, asking unsuitable questions: *Is God an illusion or is he not the sole reality?
Does God exist only because I want him to?*

She was in a state of exaltation close to ecstasy.
Hunger and exhaustion mostly. She had not eaten
for three days. She had walked the last ten miles,
burrowing into the interior of the island like an
animal seeking shelter. Her mind rang like a bell:

I have nothing: I am bereft of friends, food, shelter.
The thought brought an emaciated smile to the white
face, and she lifted her fierce blue eyes to heaven,
seeking benediction, looking a little like one of El
Greco's saints—her face all bones and sublimity.

And a little insanity.

The tinkle of a distant bell brought her around
to her predicament. That would be the bells on
those mangy sheep she had passed on the white dirt
road. There'd been a shepherd tending them—a
primeval brown face out of the Middle Ages gazing
at her with intense hostility.

There was always someone.

Leaning heavily against the warm stones of the
bancal, the girl swept the valley with a slow blue-
eyed gaze from end to end like radar, searching for
pursuers, for witnesses, for anyone at all.

She found nothing except green hills and orange
trees and the white ribbon of road on which she'd
come. A mile from where she stood, the white road
vanished into a sea of orange trees, and the valley
closed in entirely.

She closed her eyes and felt her aloneness clear
to her toes—a vagabond without friends or possessions. Tears welled from between the closed eyelids,
violating her deepest wishes. No time for tears. She
brushed them aside impatiently and looked for steps
to climb up to the last *bancal*. No steps. Only a
sort of stone ladder they made in Majorca in the
fifteenth century—and still made in the twentieth
century, as if nothing had changed.

The girl forced her screaming legs to propel her

8

up the stone ladder to the summit—even five minutes' rest had stiffened her legs alarmingly—and strode like a wooden doll under the crumbling Moorish arch into the cobblestone courtyard.

Squaaaaaa!

The raucous cry sent her reeling back against the stone wall, clutching at her breast. She'd almost stepped on a brown hen with bedraggled feathers, and it had uttered a cry that scared the wits out of her. She leaned against the stone wall, heart thudding. The hen glared at her indignantly and she smiled back. Another living soul, she was thinking. Me and God and one chicken. No, many chickens. The cobblestone courtyard was alive with chickens, dozens of them, preening, pecking.

Chickens!

That meant people. Chickens didn't occur in the wild. What have I got myself into? Instantly alert, as only a girl on the run could be alert, the eyes darting up, back, around, in one quick, all-encompassing gaze.

No, there was nobody. She could smell her aloneness, taste it. She'd not been on the run for a year without developing *that* gift. The second sight of the fugitive.

Still, people must come here. Chickens needed care. They couldn't subsist on the love of God, as could fugitives and religious nuts. Her gaze circled the courtyard, evaluating every stone. The huge edifice looked a thousand years old, untended for the last five hundred. Immense. Imposing. Regal. A shutter hung askew from a single hinge, as if it had

9

hung there for centuries. The cobblestones cried out
their antiquity, their surfaces rounded by generations
of footsteps. At the center of the courtyard stood
a large square ornamental door, and at its center
a bronze lion, its mouth open in a Moorish snarl.

The girl walked across the court, the cobblestones
sending squirts of pain up her stiff legs, and tried
the door. Locked. Did people live here then? She
couldn't find another hideout. Not that night. The
sun was already preparing to slide beneath the hills.
In an hour it would be dark. She steadied herself
against the wall and forced herself to think. Where
were the people? What time was it? She had no
watch but she guessed—five-thirty. Shouldn't there
be a farm wife, preparing dinner? Perhaps it was
the abode of that solitary shepherd. No, not him.
That shepherd lived in a one-room cottage. She'd
bet her revolutionary soul on it. This place was
immense. The dwelling place of princes, not shep-
herds. And what am I doing in a dwelling place of
princes—me, a woman of the people—a woman in
search of her God and her own soul? Aaah, but
the princes have departed, sanctifying the place by
their absence. At least she hoped so.

At right angles to the wall in which stood the
great ornamental front door was another wall, four
feet thick, much of which had fallen into ruin, exposing a set of stone stairs that leaned crazily against
an inner wall. The steps were ominously clean,
clearly in use. She climbed the crazy steps warily
to the second story. On the landing was a small

closed door. The knob turned easily and she stepped into a dim room with straw-covered floor.

Whoooooosh!

This time she wasn't as startled as she had been the first time. Too exhausted for that. It was a pigeon she'd startled off its perch. It had flown across the room and settled on a windowsill. No, not a pigeon. A white dove. Clearly very domesticated. There were a score of others on perches, all looking with round eyes. Against the walls were hutches full of rabbits, all looking at her questioningly. And trustingly. Clearly well cared for.

On the opposite wall from the door were two large symmetrical windows. It was an exquisitely proportioned room, high-ceilinged, gloriously mathematical. What was it doing housing rabbits and doves? The girl crossed the room, sending the dove whooshing back to its perch. The windows offered a marvelous view of the valley, its greens darkening, as the sun touched the hilltop. What a lovely hideout, thought the girl. She sank to her knees, pressing her palms together and closing her eyes, thankfulness flooding her. I am thanking God for less and less, she thought wryly. But I do love it, dear God, and one must love one's hideout. She'd had six hideouts in the last year and loved all but the last one.

The last one!

She began to laugh, startling the doves, because it was a manic laugh, tears running down her cheeks. I'm getting star-headed—Strick's word for it. Oh, if he were here, he'd slap me out of it, but he's not

11

here: he's in the cold ground with a bullet in his lovely black heart and I'm all alone and broke and three thousand miles from anywhere in a strange land I know nothing about and I'm wanted in all fifty states of America for everything from bank robbery to murder, and God is indeed testing my devotion to the uttermost. She stopped laughing abruptly, partly because she hadn't the energy to continue, but mostly because her severe logic brought her face to face with the implausibility of laughter. I am too intelligent to be properly *religieuse*, she thought humbly, or properly revolutionary. My intellectual standards are so high that no one has yet passed my scrutiny, including myself. Especially myself. I am a Jesus freak with a sense of humor—a contradiction in terms.

She was shivering with cold now. The manic laughter had burned up what little warmth there was in her bony body. She scrabbled about in her big leather handbag for her black sweater, the only spare garment she had. The rest of her luggage was at the hotel and they could make of that what they would. Even with the sweater on she suffered from cold. The sun had slipped behind the hills altogether and blackness was coming on fast. I've got to find covering, she thought, her mind refreshed by hysteria.

She rose briskly. At the door, she smiled at the doves. "We'll get to know each other," she whispered aloud, her voice strange from disuse.

Outside, darkness was falling fast. The girl went down the crazy steps and crossed the courtyard to an opening where a door had once stood. Inside were barnyard smells and that meant hay. She walked through the opening and then stopped, panic-stricken. A big black shape moved terrifyingly toward her—and then thrust a muzzle into her hand, expecting a carrot. A big black white-muzzled mule! The girl gave a croak of relief and stroked the feathery nose. In the darkness, it had looked like the Devil himself. She hugged him as if he were an old friend. "I'm a city girl, mule," she whispered, "unaccustomed to mules in the living room. You must forgive me."

She kissed the silky muzzle and stepped past the mule into the blackness. A girl on the run acquired a love of blackness. A girl was harder to find in the dark. It was the womb. The state of grace of the fugitive.

She was groping now, arms raised in front of her, her feet probing before taking a step. The floor was covered with fresh-smelling hay, an uneasy footing. A very large room, she felt, a room that had seen better days. Once—like the entire crazy place—a residence of princes, now of mules. An edifice down on its luck—like herself. Both of us reduced to penury, she thought, purified by poverty. We belong together, you and I—and I won't give you up easily.

The haystack struck her full in the face, smelling of autumn. She burrowed into it expertly! In her time on the run she'd slept in many haystacks and she knew how to get maximum warmth from one. It was better with a lover to cling to.

Dear God, she whispered, thank you for my solitude and my poverty, your greatest gifts. She sealed the prayer with a kiss and sent it aloft to her multifarious God, who was Christian, Muslim, Buddhist, Hindu, Taoist, Protestant, Catholic, Albigensian, Manichean—in fact, all the religions, all the heresies, past and present. There was only One God up there.

Lastly, she felt in her leather handbag to see if her .38 was at the top of the pile, ready to hand. Guns were no good if it took you five minutes to get them out.

She fell asleep.

CHAPTER

2

Hawkins slammed on his brakes in the nick of time. Or perhaps not quite in the nick of time. The Ford skidded on the wet snow straight into the car ahead. Gently. A very gentle bump indeed. Still, the car window rolled down and a furious face projected out of it. Just for a moment! Then the light changed and the head vanished. The car moved away and Hawkins gently eased the Ford back into motion down the slippery street.

At the next traffic light, the car he'd hit pulled up next to him. Deliberately, of course. The window went down and Hawkins found himself studying a furious face. Fury! Over a little bump? No, a fury like that must have a long and distinguished ancestry, going clear back to his childhood. Looking at that face, Hawkins thought: This man lives in a state of perpetual anger—the tiniest deviation from the established order would be cause enough for eruption into anger.

"You were out of control!" emitted the face—like a blast of steam. "I should call a cop!"

"Easy, man," said Hawkins soothingly. If the man only knew he was a cop, what would he say? Why, he'd erupt again, of course, denouncing the forces of law and order and western civilization itself. Why was civilized man in such a state of irritability? He hadn't always been.

Hawkins smiled sadly at his own query. The Philosopher. That's what they called him at the bureau. Well, he was fifty-five, and after fifty, he liked to say, one got more concerned with the why of things and less upset by the whatness of things. Of course, people killed each other and stole and raped and blew each other up in the most savage ways. Of course. But why? The wrong questions for an FBI man.

The snow was really coming down—so thick, so white, so tumultuous that he could barely see the car ahead. Oh, there'd be some lovely crashes in Washington that day! And missed appointments! And traffic snarls. And trains delayed or canceled. And lost tempers! The FBI man grinned boyishly for his fifty-five years and almost instantly asked himself again—why? Why do I get such pleasure out of chaos?

Hawkins' desk was in what he called the Swampland part of the FBI, the Land That Time Forgot. He was, he told his wife, the man in charge of cold trails. Old trails. "The FBI," he told his wife, "never throws anything away. It just puts it on my desk.

16

That is the Bureau's way of burying the body."

Hawkins undid the ribbons binding together the thick envelope—gently, as he did most things today. His fingers lingered on the ribbons, making the act itself important, a moment in time. He found himself doing this sort of thing more and more, trying to give the most mundane acts—like lifting a cup of coffee to his lips—importance and dignity and meaning, as if he might not ever do it again. That's what fifty-five had done to him—made him treasure each moment, as if it might be his last. What had Tolstoy said in *War and Peace:* one should greet each morning, thanking God for one more day? Enjoy each minute because there might not be another.

Hawkins stared out the window at the falling snow, experiencing an exquisite pleasure at the whiteness and exuberance of it. Slowly, as if he were undressing a woman, he opened the stiff 14-by-9-inch envelope and, almost reverently, spilled out the contents. A gush of old reports, memoranda, old photographs. The old trail, the cold trail of Geraldine Colt—only now she called herself Theresa —after the saint. They all changed their names. Wish fulfillment. Or not fulfillment. Wish expression, rather than fulfillment.

Saint Theresa! A joke? Geraldine Colt was a joky girl. Or had been.

Hawkins picked up the photograph, once one of the most famous in the United States, of Saint Theresa with an automatic pistol in her arms, trying to look ferocious but looking instead only teenage.

17

She looked sixteen although when that picture was taken she was nineteen. Young for her age. Theresa Colt—immature bank robber, killer, kidnapper, and arsonist.

Hawkins pursed his lips and examined his own feelings—as he did these days about everything. What did he feel about this girl whose life he knew better than she did herself? Too much. Too much, he thought.

He picked up the phone and called the agent in Missoula, Montana. "She's been sighted out there," he said neutrally. "We'll have to check it out. Try the bus station, and then ask around the usual places." He was getting a lot of skepticism on the other end. "The last place she was sighted was Mexico—but that was six months ago. I'm surprised anyone remembers the girl any more. The very fact that they do *might* mean there's something in it." He didn't believe it and neither did the agent on the other end. But that was what police work was. Endless, mostly unsuccessful ploddings and questionings.

The Missoula agent was confused and no wonder. "No, you're thinking of the wrong girl," said Hawkins gently. "*That* girl's name was Mary Lou Pierce and she called herself Flower and she hailed from San Francisco. She's even more lost than this one. No one has reported Flower for six years, and I think she's dead."

That had been the fashionable belief, not only among police officers but in the press, for a long

time about all these girls. That they were resting at
the bottom of unknown lakes. Wish fulfillment—
or wish expression—of police officers and press and
public to get rid of the emotional debris left by forgotten runaway girls.

"Geraldine Colt is a different girl—altogether.
She was—" Was? Why am I using past tense?—"is
a New York girl. Came from a very good family."
As did most of them. "She was part of the Black
Torrent." That had to be explained. "Well, they
were Maoist splinter militants—and they bombed
. . . banks and other capitalist institutions." It was
hard to explain to agents in Missoula, and the terrible thing, the most terrible thing of all, was that
Hawkins felt he understood the Black Torrent very
well.

Hawkins still held the photograph in his hand,
the famous photograph that had once blazed on all
the front pages, and he thought, Imagine having to
explain all this to this lug in Missoula. How old is
he? Twelve? But there it was—Geraldine Colt, once
a household name, was no longer a household name.
Other militants, other atrocities, had pushed her
clear out of mind.

"Could we have a report on it," said Hawkins,
masking the command in his gentlest tone, "within
forty-eight hours?"

Hawkins hung up. Then, before he restored the
girl to the oblivion of the file, he rustled through
the photographs—there were a lot of them, over a
period of five years—and lined them up by dates
across the desk. Theresa—at graduation from Bryn

19

Mawr. (So many of them had gone to that famous
girls' college.) Theresa after the bank robbery in
Des Moines—a snapshot her black lover had taken,
found in their room when the trail was red hot.
Theresa—in her black Maoist outfit, a snap defiantly
sent to the newspapers after the bombing of the Bell
Telephone Building in Dallas. Theresa leading the
grape pickers in their strike at Sacramento—the
earliest photo of all.

Hawkins was arranging the photographs chrono-
logically when Rodgers walked in without knocking,
as he always did. Annoyingly.

"Are you mooning over that girl again? She's an
old lady now—twenty-two."

Hawkins didn't look up. He and Rodgers were
old friends—at least they went through the forms
of friendship because they had both been in the
Bureau a very long time. The younger agents called
them the Gunslingers and teased them about being
in on the Dillinger shooting, although neither of
them had been in the Bureau then. Hawkins had
never fired a gun at anything except a target in his
life.

Both men had joined the FBI in the Great
Depression, when J. Edgar Hoover was recruiting
out-of-work lawyers by the hundreds to man the sub-
machine guns; back when belonging to the FBI was
almost the most glamorous job in the world. Then
they were the Good Guys. They'd become the Bad
Guys—all in one generation. But they had nothing
at all in common apart from that. Rodgers gloried
in his FBIhood. Hawkins didn't.

"What's with Theresa then?" Rodgers bent over the photographs, seeking whatever significance Hawkins found in this array. It was Rodgers who had tagged Hawkins with that epithet Philosopher—and teased him about it. Actually Rodgers was always a little in awe of the quiet agent.

"What's the time sequence?" inquired Rodgers. "Five years? She's changed her hair color, and the shape of the hair, too. Also the costume has gone from Maoist to Ho Chi Minh to urban guerrilla."

Hawkins smiled gently. Rodgers would notice these things. What *he*, Hawkins, noticed and worried about in this chronological layout of photographs was a steady and alarming loss of weight. In five years his Theresa (*his* Theresa, what's the matter with me?) had lost twenty-five pounds—and she didn't have twenty-five pounds to lose. She's deliberately not eating, he guessed. Part of some new change in the direction of her life. There had been a great many changes of direction—from grape-picking strikes to urban terror to—what? He didn't confide any of this to Rodgers.

"What's on your mind, Joe?" he asked politely.

"I'm looking for a little fatherly ideology, Philosopher," said Rodgers breezily. He pulled up a chair and placed a photograph of a hot-eyed young girl over that of Geraldine Colt. Very pretty girl. Elf James. Adorable uptilted nose. At last count, she'd killed five people, including two cops. She was a much hotter, higher-rated and more recent fugitive on the FBI Ten Most Wanted list than poor Geraldine, who had fallen off the list altogether—

though she had been number three once. Elf was the household name Theresa had once been.

Hawkins looked sadly at the fresh smile and up-tilted nose of the young murderess. If you elude capture for another five years, you'll be all mine, Elf James. When everyone else forgets about you, I'll start worrying about whether you're eating often enough. The Sargasso Sea of the FBI, that's me. Keeper of the rotting hulks of forgotten atrocities.

"What do you know about the Black Torrent, Philosopher?"

Hawkins winced at his nickname. Lately they came to him for ideological instruction. It was only very recently the Bureau had taken the nuances of ideology all that seriously as an aid to detection. It had come around to the view that you couldn't bust a freak until you could find him—and increasingly you couldn't find him unless you knew what wheels went around in his head. Hawkins, a man on the shelf, had been given the task of studying the Movements. He'd studied too deeply. With study came sympathy. He kept it strictly to himself.

"The Black Torrent is dead. Finished," said Hawkins shortly. "It died when young Strickland got himself shot in Oakland three years ago. It was always Strick's baby. When he died, nobody cared."

"I don't think so," said Rodgers. He handed Hawkins a letter.

There was no salutation:

Farewell should always be brief. Otherwise there is misunderstanding about its finality. I am fleeing quite simply to save my own soul, my own sacred self. I have a horror of collective dogma—all collective dogma from the collective wisdom of the Church to the collective anathema of Karl Marx—not because I am strong but because I am weak. I have been too much and too deeply influenced by your passionate advocacy in directions which increasingly horrify me.

God keep you.

The letter was signed by the mocking, obscene trademark of the Black Torrent that Hawkins had seen many times before. It was a phallus with a snake's head.

"Where did you find this?"

"A farmhouse in Wenceslas, Pennsylvania. They left in a hurry, leaving a lot behind—Elf's fingerprints, food, books . . ."

"What's Elf reading these days?"

"Marcuse, Lao Tse, Hegel, some Palestinian thinker whose name I can't pronounce. Very tough reading."

"How old is this writing?"

"The lab says not more than three months."

Hawkins scowled at the missive, both puzzled and alarmed. That snake's-head phallus had been invented by Theresa—as a joke more than anything else. She was a joky girl. The message was in her handwriting. But the thoughts, the style, were of an altogether different personality.

CHAPTER

3

She was awakened by the gobbledy-gobbledy of the chickens. Not screeching this time. A sort of cooing. Someone was feeding them, she guessed. They sounded petulant with hunger. Immediately she herself felt a stab of hunger that pierced her to the very bottom. She hadn't felt hunger for a long time. Sometimes she went without food for days, not missing it. Now she was famished.

She opened her eyes carefully. Even deep in the haystack, she felt the brightness of the sun pouring through the doorway. She felt rested, alert. Above all, together. Her mind worked—springy, tense. She lay there unmoving, feeling the first twinge of apprehension, that familiar ache of the fugitive. She wasn't going to risk a movement until she knew the score a little better. It was very quiet. Only the contented gabble-babble of the chickens.

Then she heard the voice. *"Buena, buena, buena,"* cooed the voice. Talking to the chickens, she guessed. People didn't talk to each other in that

tone. That was the tone one used on chickens—or
children. She knew a bit of Spanish, a very little bit,
but suddenly the voice was making harsh noises,
the like of which she'd never heard. Mallorquin?
Probably. It was a grating noise, Mallorquin. She
didn't know a word of Mallorquin, and neither did
anyone else—except another Mallorquin.

She stretched her neck under the covering of hay,
carefully, so as not to make any sound. She could
see a bit through the hay. A few chickens pecking.
A brown hand resting motionless close to the ground.
A man squatting, arm resting on his leg. That was
a guess. The hand disappeared. A moment later
the door frame darkened momentarily, as a shape
passed through. She froze, hardly drawing breath.
The shepherd. That taut, dark face. She narrowed
her eyes and prayed for invisibility. But the Mallorquin went directly to the mule, grating Mallorquin,
one hand caressing the velvety nose. Soothingly.
She could see the shepherd clearly framed in her
narrowed lids, patting the mule, murmuring that
outlandish language. And with such passion!

Now he was untying the mule—it was the first
time she had realized the mule had been tied—and
then led the animal out into the cobblestoned courtyard, the hooves clomp-clomping a clear message
on the stones. She could estimate to the yard how
far they were—and when the sound was a clear fifty
yards away, the girl slithered out of the hay and
crept to the doorway. She put one eye only to a
crack in the stones. Across the courtyard, the shepherd stood, back to her, slipping a harness on the

mule. She could smell the leather—old, much-sweated leather. It gave her a stab of delight, that sharp smell.

The shepherd finished his harnessing, and took the long reins in his two brown hands and clucked. The two of them, man and mule, passed through the great Moorish archway and out of sight, the man walking behind the mule.

She turned on her ears full strength. She could hear the clucking of the hens, the clomping of the mule's hooves and, far down the valley, the tinkling of the bells on the sheep. Then came the smells of spring—the hot sun smell on stone, on grass, on orange blossoms. Spring! It was February. But then, of course, that was spring in Majorca. The smell of fresh air.

If only I weren't so hungry, thought the girl. And thirsty.

There were things to do before thinking about that. She looked and listened, listened and looked. No, nothing. She sped out into the courtyard, tried the great door with the massive bronze lion hanging on it. Locked.

She shot up the crazy exposed stairway, noise-lessly, then paused at the door on the landing. Must not send the doves into an outcry. She opened the door slowly, and poked her head in, very slowly indeed. The doves looked at her gravely with their round eyes, making dove noises, throatily. The rabbits chomped on their food, scarcely looking up. The shepherd must have fed them, too. And the doves.

She crossed the straw-covered floor to the marvelous windows—what a grand bedroom it must once have been!—and looked out, standing well back in the shadows. The valley stretched in front of her, drenched in spring sunshine.

She inspected it minutely. From one end to the other. A good five miles of green fields, orange groves, dark-green slopes covered thickly with eucalyptus and pine.

The shepherd and the mule were going down the white ribbon of road now. The only human figure in this landscape. Surely there must be other people in this big beautiful valley. In the clear morning light she saw other houses she'd missed the night before. Were they all ruins—like this one? She didn't know. She watched the man and mule until they disappeared into the greenery. Where did that man live? Not here surely.

Urgent questions gnawed in her stomach. She went down the crazy stone steps again, straight to the great square well standing in the shadow of the stout walls. In her exhaustion she had not noticed it the night before. A bucket on a chain stood on its square stone sides, the whole apparatus connected to a wheel and pulley in an arch of massive wood. She drew up a pail of cold water and drank for minutes, slurping like a horse.

That only made the hunger worse. She stared thoughtfully at the chickens pecking away at their corn. Chickens! Where there were chickens there were eggs. Behind the ruined wall on the far side were the nests, a half dozen of them, fixed on the

stone wall. She reached a hand in experimentally—
she'd never had experience with eggs outside their
plastic boxes before—and her hand closed on . . .
three. She gazed down at them in her cupped hands,
as if they were emeralds.

Three eggs! But what to do with them? She hadn't
even a match. To say nothing of a frying pan. She
stared at them baffled. They might just as well be
emeralds—or banknotes. Raw? Snakes ate them
raw. Swallowed them whole and crushed them in
their tummies. She'd read it somewhere. Or seen
it on television. One of those nature programs. I
should have seen more of those nature programs.
I'm going to need a lot of nature.

She placed two of the eggs on the wall and
cracked the third egg. Gently. Then, head back on
the stones, she let the raw egg slip into her mouth.
It tasted like a man having an orgasm in her mouth,
and with a mighty effort of will, her eyes tightly
closed, clutching her mouth with both hands, she
swallowed the raw egg.

Then she leaned against the warm stone, eyes
closed, for a long moment. I mustn't be sick! I
mustn't be sick! Actually, it wasn't at all bad. She
even felt her hunger abate. After a bit she opened
her eyes, swimming with tears, and contemplated
the other two eggs. Quickly, she broke them and ate
them. Two more orgasms in her mouth. Well, she'd
had plenty of experience with that.

She sat down and waited for nausea to strike. It
didn't. She leaned her head back against the stone
and closed her eyes and felt the hot sun soaking

28

into her brow. Little by little her hunger receded, diminished, finally vanished. She felt uncommonly well.

It made her uneasy, all this rude health. Pain is my natural habitat. Desperation is my milieu. I am at peace, she thought, an element as foreign to my nature as dry land to a fish. It will take a little getting used to.

CHAPTER

4

"The thing you must understand about Theresa . . ."
Hawkins didn't say *Saint* Theresa because Rodgers
would never understand. He hated even discussing
Theresa with Rodgers. But how could he not? Saint
Theresa wasn't, after all, his private property, was
she? Yet he had to fight constantly against the feeling that she *was* his private property, that she was
none of Rodgers' damned business. What the devil
was the matter with him? Theresa was a fugitive
from justice like any other—except that she *wasn't*
like any other. ". . . is her extraordinary precosity.
She went to Bryn Mawr at fifteen."

"Too young for college," said Rodgers.

"She was very bright. Very quick," said Hawkins
tonelessly. Why did he have to share all this with
Rodgers? He hated it. Theresa—Geraldine Colt as
she then was—had been the brightest girl in her
class, only missing *summa cum laude* by a tenth of
a point, and only because she hardly studied at all.
Even then she was deep in the Movement. Studying

Theresa's college records, Hawkins became convinced that the American university system didn't demand nearly enough of its most brilliant students to keep them occupied. He'd become an educational elitist, a weakening of his liberal scruples. It's because I'm fifty-five, he thought. After fifty-five everyone should become an elitist.

Hawkins picked up the Bryn Mawr photograph of Saint Theresa. "She called herself Geraldine Colt then," he said, "because that's what her parents called her. You will never understand these young people—and Theresa in particular—unless you realize that revolt against parenthood is very much at the bottom of it. In Argentina, the revolutionary group, the Montañeros, have a final exam you must take for full membership. One question is 'What action would you take if your mother was in the hands of the enemy?' The correct answer is: 'None.'

"Changing your name is fundamentally an act of rebellion against parents—by denying their existence. A lot of this stems from the teaching of Wilhelm Reich. Do you know about Reich?"

"The orgasm man?"

Hawkins winced. "He was a bit more than that, Joe. Orgasm worship was just part of it. Essentially Reich preached revolution against *all* the bosses—and the original boss of all is Old Dad. When Geraldine cast aside her name, she was rejecting her father. And her mother. Her whole parentage. She became rootless—in order to open herself to her primary instincts, which Reich preached. She was very primary."

He picked up the other photograph, the most recent photograph, and held the two together, Bryn Mawr and six years after. The difference was vast. "Whoo!" exclaimed Rodgers.

Theresa had had a lot of orgasms—with boys, girls, blacks, browns. Hawkins was not going to share that information with Rodgers, though. Theresa's sex life was not to be exposed to Rodgers' prurient gaze because he would never understand that with Theresa it was the giving that was uppermost. She gave herself freely, always had, and sex was a form of giving. Instead he said: "She was an Eastern peace freak. They were very different in life style from the California freaks like Elf— emotionally, psychologically, every way."

He began to gather together the memorabilia of Theresa's life scattered across his desk—psychiatric reports, confidential college reports, intimate talks with friends and enemies (Theresa had made lots of enemies with her brilliance and her sharp tongue), letters, diaries. I know more about Theresa than about my own wife, Amanda, thought Hawkins, much more. I don't even know how well Amanda did in school, come to think of it. Very little about her sex life. How very odd that I should know a fugitive from justice I've never met more intimately than my own wife. Is that why I'm so obsessional?

Aloud, he said, "There were dozens of outfits like the Black Torrent—White Panthers, Red Guerrillas, Progressive Serpents—all tiny deviations in a big radical student movement that today seems ancient history. The Black Torrent wasn't all that black or very much of a torrent. There were never more than twenty activists in it.

"Theresa started the movement when jokes were in style. Back when Jerry Rubin was dressing up like Santa Claus and trying to break his way into testifying before the House Un-American Activities Committee, which radicals had always previously been scared to death of. Fighting the Establishment by making a joke of it. Causing a panic on the New York Stock Exchange floor by throwing dollar bills off the balcony. Exhibitionism for its own sake. Idiot children making faces at the grownups for a laugh. Gestural freaks, they called themselves."

Hawkins picked up the photograph of Elf James and scrutinized it. Altogether different girl from Theresa. She'd killed a cop only the week before.

"I doubt this girl has a spark of humor in her. She came out of the top Red school of them all— the Berkeley campus—not out of Bryn Mawr. She came much later in the radical student movement, when the humor had fled and the viciousness had come in."

Hawkins pointed at the curious farewell note, scowling. "Well, it *looks* like Theresa's handwriting." Why was he saying it like that? It *was* Theresa's handwriting. He knew it well. "But that doesn't mean very much. There's no salutation. We don't know who the note was written to. I very much doubt that Elf and Theresa ever met. If they had they'd have hated each other."

"You're dead wrong, Philosopher," said Rodgers

triumphantly. "They not only met—they were lovers."

"Never," said Hawkins, shocked to the core.

"Want to bet?"

CHAPTER

5

Elf was flat on her back, her mouth open, in a rooming house in Euclid, Colorado. Stark naked. Thinking. She always thought with her mouth open. Always had. The mind darting like swallows on six topics. None of them pleasant.

The bank.

She could see the plate-glass window. Bullet proof. It had better be. For this caper. Turning the Beast's own tricks back on himself. Elf planned to use it as a shield. If they didn't fuck it up. Which they often did lately. She glanced at the sleeping girl next to her. A tangle of filthy matted brown hair. Lovely thighs. No brains at all. No fucking backbone either. Seventeen. Christ. Revolutionary vomit. That's all she got. Lucky to get that.

The Berkeley campus flashed into her mind. The Little Red Schoolhouse. Back when *she* was seventeen. Brains, she had. Too many brains. They all had brains. My God, the brainpower! Robin, the

beautiful boy. Dead. Jerry. So ugly he was beautiful.
In the slam.

Jesus!

The girl next to her woke and smiled, the light
of love in her eyes. Elf didn't smile back. She gazed
back steadily, not quite contemptuously. The seventeen-year-old was kissing her breasts now. All she
was good for, really. Kissing games. Still, one had
to take the troops one could get these days. In the
old days, aah, sweet Jesus, we could fuck all night,
turn on all day, and burn down the Bank of America, bust a honky—all in one piece.

The seventeen-year-old was making love to her in
earnest now and Elf let her, her mind on the bank
job. Counting the troops. Torrance, who wasn't bad,
and this idiot child who was sucking her cunt, and
Lisa, who was as brainless as the seventeen-year-old
between her legs. Elf would have liked a little more
firepower but where was it? In the slam. Or dead.

Elf closed her eyes, shutting out the scabrous,
peeling ceiling, and let herself succumb to the
urgency between her thighs. Freedom from male
pigs. Elf had been one of the first at *that* barricade.
A finger or tongue would do the trick. The great
psychological breakthrough. Body politics.

She came.

Within a minute, even before she opened her eyes,
Elf's mind was flicking over the problems: Did
this idiot child have enough sense to check the gaso-
line supply on any car she stole? No, she didn't.
Remind her. Wipe the place clean of prints. Elf
would do that herself, because last time her dear

black soul brother, Elijah Ali, had not paid proper attention, which was why he languished now in the federal slam in Atlanta. Elf herself had barely got over the wall and out of town.

Elf smiled. The seventeen-year-old, whose chosen name was Bandit, thought she was being smiled on and smiled back eagerly. But Elf's mind was on other things: "Never to fear danger." Well, she didn't. Welcomed it. Better than acid for turning on. Elf's quick mind stopped abruptly from pursuing *that* thought. She didn't want to pursue the way of that thought. It wouldn't square with Herbert Marcuse, that thought.

"Never to fear danger. To behave the same by day as by night. Not to act impetuously. To have unlimited patience. To remain calm and cool in the worst conditions and situations." From the *Minimanual of the Urban Guerrilla* by Carlos Marighela.

"Never to leave track or trail." Elf's smile vanished. Elf had taught Theresa that a little too well. Theresa had not left track or trail.

Theresa had vanished from the underground so completely that not a whisper came through that extraordinary network wherein usually every urban guerrilla knew pretty well what the others were up to. And where.

Theresa!

CHAPTER

6

Theresa walked slowly down the vast room, counting windows—fourteen, each of them enormous and all different. What an outburst of architectural exuberance was Moorish design. Such an extravagance of architectural emotion. What do I know about the Moors? They brought a high culture to the barbaric Europeans and stayed five hundred years. That's all I know.

At the far end of the great chamber was an immense fireplace with massive stone lions supporting the mantelpiece. Theresa leaned against the rampant Moorish lion, surveying the vastness of the room. It looked like the kind of room her mother had gone to debutante parties in in Philadelphia in 1938. She'd seen photographs of those massive ballrooms. Theresa herself had never been to a debutante party in her life. If, indeed, they still had them. Her generation had had sharper amusements. In the winter of her seventeenth birthday, at an age when her mother had been coming out, Theresa had carried a red banner in the grape pickers' strike in the Sacramento Valley and had landed in jail for it. *Her* coming-out party! The first time she had rubbed elbows with poverty. She had come alive at that moment. It was her baptism. Ever since, she had felt poverty was her calling, her vocation. A difficult calling to explain to rich parents.

Theresa sat on a windowsill overlooking the green valley and surveyed the immense room. What on earth did the Moors want with so huge a chamber? Was it an audience room? She had only the vaguest idea what an audience was. The peasants pleading for their lives with the king. More probably the caliph.

And where did he sit while saying, "Off with their heads"? There wasn't a stick of furniture in the great hall. Or anywhere. She'd been exploring the edifice for an hour. It was even bigger than she had thought. She'd counted thirty-two rooms already, all huge—though none of the others as huge as this—all empty.

An emptiness of inconceivable grandeur. Would New York look like this in three hundred years? The Empire State Building—huge and empty. No, in New York they tore everything down before it grew old. All this vastness and all mine! Theresa leaned her head against a carved stone pilaster, twisted in the shape of a corkscrew, and laughed merrily aloud, the laughter echoing eerily in the great chamber. Because this was exactly what she had run away from. Useless material abundance. She had once argued with her mother about why

39

on earth they needed twenty-six bedrooms in the country place at Purchase, New York, when there were only three in the family. Yet here were thirty-two rooms and nobody in any of them—except rabbits and chickens and doves and one mule. And herself.

Why do I love this place? asked Theresa of herself. I should hate it. But I love it. Because it's five hundred years old, that's why. One must be practical. One cannot go on feeling guilty about mankind's transgressions five hundred years ago or where would it end? I would wind up accusing God of inventing capitalism and all the other sins. No, after five hundred years, this place is purified by the centuries. It belongs to the landscape—like the trees.

It was part of the reality of the world with which, increasingly, Theresa felt she had to come to terms. You cannot spend all your emotional energy hating the world. You must save a little for loving it. This was the new revised Theresa. She'd fled from hatred.

Well, then.

What had passed through this great hall once the caliphs and the archdukes had departed? Goats, maybe. Some of the rooms had been used for stabling horses. Some had housed peasants. They'd left little bits of their personalities clinging to the walls. Then they'd departed—after how many centuries—leaving nothing but emptiness. Why did the Mallorquins go away and leave a palace to molder like this? Didn't someone own it? The only part she'd not been able to get into was the central bit with the great front door with its Moorish bronze lion on it. That might be used. The rest was open, some of it to the wind and rain, where the walls had fallen in. Whose chickens, whose mule were they? That peasant's with the brown taut face? She doubted it. A peasant like that, she thought fiercely, owned nothing except his poverty.

A flame of hatred coursed through her at the thought—and immediately she forced it to subside. Hatred was a sin. She'd had enough of hatred. She stared fixedly at the rectangle of golden sunshine that splashed the floor. Golden fire! She felt it on her back, in her bones, in her soul, the hatred slipping away. Leaping off the ledge, she fell into the Lotus position and then bowed her slender bony frame till her forehead touched the floor.

She rose to her feet in one movement the way Martha Graham had taught, bowed low to the right, then to the left, palms outward, arms held back of her. She stretched out both arms then in that sweeping gesture that begged forgiveness. For my sins. My many sins. One must practice humility like tennis, and I'm far behind. She did a bit of her Arab dance—part Middle Eastern mysticism, part Jerome Robbins, around the vast tiled floor. She swooped about—doing a bit of pure ballet she'd learned at Miss Wright's dancing school when she was seven years old, mixed with a bit of Yoga dancing they used to do in the commune in Idaho when she had been a peace freak, interspersed with some of Strick's incredibly agile movements (what a dancer he'd been)—in fact, running through her life from childhood, to her half-dozen phases as a

41

revolutionary—and in the end reverting to the Lotus position, exhausted and exhilarated, both at the same time.

I am alone, she thought. I have always been alone, but it took me twenty-two years to realize the splendor of my solitude. In ancient Rome, the slaves said a man loses half his soul when he becomes a slave. And slave I was—to the Movement.

And to Elf.

CHAPTER

7

The idiot child babbled away. Elf kissed her to shut her up. Little radical masochist. She was fed up with radical masochism, the American disease. Defeatist.

They'd have to steal another car, a standby, and switch after the job if they were to get clean out of Colorado. My soul brothers are going to hate my guts because the pigs will hit the communes again. All my fault. But she couldn't help it because she needed money. Money had priority over ideology, much as Marcuse would have that thought. Motion politics. Don't get caught.

That was the greatest mistake—getting caught. Like Patty Hearst, that little nothing. Elf fought down a sneer at Patty. We were all brothers once. And sisters. Lately, the hatred and the sneers had got intramural, incestuous. Elf was far too intelligent not to be aware some of her soul sisters hated her.

Why? Because I'm successful, that's why. Every revolutionary of real genius finds at some stage that the pressure of events requires him to take action inconsistent with his ideology. To make an omelet one must crack eggs. Lenin himself, the High Priest, said that. I practice it—and they hate me for it. Including Theresa. Theresa flared in her mind—emotional indulgence. Not now.

Elf rose from the bed and picked up the little snub-nosed machine pistol. Check the weaponry. "To shoot a genocidal robot policeman in the defense of life is a sacred act." Tim Leary. That nincompoop. Still, maybe she'd kill another genocidal robot policeman today. Elf had killed two. One more didn't matter. She rather enjoyed killing pigs—and that thought had better not be pursued either. No radical thinker—not Lenin, not Tim Leary, not anyone—ever suggested you should *enjoy* killing pigs.

"Get up, Bandit."

"I'm scared, Elf."

"You won't feel anything once it starts."

What a lie! She was telling more lies now and that bothered her. The very first thing that had attracted her to the radical movement was the idea that she could get away from the bourgeois lies—Establishment lies, media lies, parental lies, honky lies. All that fucking bourgeois hypocrisy. She had worshiped once at the shrine of absolute truth—the rap sessions in California—when you spit it out, no matter how it hurt. Now, telling lies to this idiot child to whip her up onto the barricades, where they'd shoot her down as they shot everyone down.

But she didn't have time for proper indoctrination to banish fear properly. And honestly.

She told lies, just like the honkies. Because there wasn't enough time to tell the truth. And that was pretty ridiculous, too, because another thing that had repelled Elf from the straight world was hurry hurry hurry. Rush rush rush. Now what else was she doing? Hurry hurry hurry. "Get up, Bandit. We've got a bank to bust. At nine-oh-two—promptly." And was that any different from catching the eight-fifty-two out of Scarsdale? Well, yes, it was because you could get killed. By bullets. Instead of by ulcers. Lately, though, Elf was not at all sure but that she had an ulcer—just like a banker. Those sharp pains in her guts. My God, I'm catching their fucking diseases as well as sharing the hurry hurry hurry.

Elf studied her nakedness in the filthy mirror the management had put next to the bed to give the squares a thrill when they were fucking. The famous upturned nose that had been on so many front pages. "General Custer!" her black soul brothers called Elf. Contemptuously. They accused her of ego-tripping. Getting her name in the papers for personal satisfaction. And it wasn't true! It wasn't! She was as dedicated as any of those black bastards. As willing to die!

I'm just too damned good, thought Elf sadly. Too bright. Too capable. My problem is I'm too successful. "Nothing fails like success," she said to herself. Because who else was there to talk to? This moron she was sleeping with had barely brains enough to say hello. When Theresa was around, oh, God, the conversation went on all night. Theresa was as bright, as well read, as . . . aah.

"Get up, Bandit."

CHAPTER

8

At the further end of the vast audience chamber Theresa found a staircase, choked with debris and dark as sin. She picked her way delicately among the crumbled stones, downward, the blackness getting blacker at every step, feeling ahead of her with an exploratory toe before making each step. Good place to hide. When They came. As They always did.

The staircase turned unexpectedly and she bumped her nose. She'd have to remember that. Go back and count the steps and practice so you can fly while the pursuer gropes. Her urban guerrilla training bubbling up through her new religiosity. Well, they must learn to get along together.

She groped her way downward, along a very straight wall. Suppose she slipped down a well! The thought stopped her in her tracks, panic-stricken. Every fugitive's secret dread. Landing in a well where no one would ever find her! The thought made her grimace in the blackness. That would be the final solitude—too much altogether.

After that, she proceeded on all fours, reaching ahead with her fingers to make sure that something lay ahead, to be quite sure she wasn't stepping off a precipice. Another flight of stairs, another 180-degree turn to the right—and then there was light, enough at least to see by. Still another flight of stairs—another 180-degree turn—and now there was lots of light. Brilliant sunshine. Another five steps and she was in a small room, the smallest she'd seen so far. Light flooded through slits—nine inches wide, two feet high. There were four of them —two on one wall, two on another. A corner room. What was it for? She peered out one of the slits and found herself looking up the valley to the north. The other faced sidewise to the valley—the same angle as the great room. It must have been a watch room for the sentry, only eight by ten feet in size.

Nobody is going to find this room. Not easily. It had taken her an hour—give or take twenty minutes. She had no watch and had to guess, but she was not bad at guessing time.

The place just needed a bed. A few chairs.

She turned on her heel and went back up the stairs, more confidently this time, now that she knew there were no wells to fall down. Counting all the way. Five steps up. Turn 180-degree angle. Five more steps, hugging right wall. She retraced in three minutes a route it had taken her ten minutes to negotiate the first time. Next time would be faster yet. Through the great hall at her swift stride that few men could keep up with and on through twelve of the rooms, down the spiral stone staircase that she loved and then she was rounding past the rabbit room and down that crazily leaning staircase. A quick look before venturing out on the cobblestoned court. Finally into the mule's chamber. The mule would have to find another bed companion. Poor mule! She gathered the biggest armload of hay she could manage and took it back to the sentry room.

Four times more she made the trip, each time with a load of hay. Each time, she improved her running time in the pitch-black corridor and on the stairs, which, at the end, she was bounding down as confidently as if she could see. Well, almost. It became a fairly thick bed. Enough hay, she hoped. It got cold at night and the hay was both mattress and covering. The chairs would have to wait for another time.

She slipped out the Moorish gate and into the orange grove, keeping her eyes peeled. But there was no one. She made luncheon out of a dozen oranges. If I slim any more I'm going to become altogether invisible. The FBI would complain, of course. It's probably against the law for a fugitive to become invisible. That is, if the FBI was still looking for her. Which she doubted. I'm unwanted even by the FBI.

She started to cry silently, great tears rolling down her cheeks. Mouth slightly open, eyes wide open, back against a tree, smitten with a loneliness more piercing than anything she had ever known. Three thousand miles from home. And where's home? Nowhere. The sky.

I didn't know it would be like this. I hate it. Her solitude, which she had blessed only an hour ago. Oh, it's going to be harder than I thought, God, much harder than I had imagined. My great problem is I am twenty-seven women all rolled into one bony body, too small to accommodate the vastness and complexity of my own nature.

She cried on for twenty minutes, reviling her womanhood, her weakness, torn by loneliness, impaled by solitude sharp as a blade.

She stopped crying abruptly.

Footfalls. Plod. Plod. The mule. She went flat on the ground behind an orange tree, which provided very thin cover. But the taut-faced peasant paid no attention to her. He was clucking to his mule. Probably someone else's mule at that. She was still revolutionary enough to know the peasants never owned the mule.

Flat on the springy orchard floor, she watched until he was well past her. Then she ducked after him, hiding behind the trunks. When he drove the mule through the Moorish arch, she sped around the corner of the wall to a point where it had crumbled away. She climbed it there to the top. Four feet wide. They didn't care how they squandered stone back there in the fifteenth century! There, lying flat, she could watch him untie the mule and bring him feed. Barley mash. So that's where he kept it. She might have to dip into it herself.

She watched while the peasant collected the eggs and, oh, dear God, counted them. She'd have to be careful. If too many were missing! But then how could he know with that many chickens?

Later the man went up the crazy staircase to feed the rabbits and doves. When he came down the staircase, he was carrying a squirming rabbit. By the ears. He killed it with one blow at the base of the neck. Poor bunny! Was that his dinner then? Or somebody else's dinner? The absentee landlord's maybe.

The peasant went down the road, swinging the dead rabbit. Theresa turned on her back on the high stone wall, put her hands under her head, and contemplated the sky.

Her loneliness had vanished, her own problems forgotten.

She was absorbed by the peasant totally. It had always been like that since her earliest experience with the grape pickers in the Sacramento Valley. That peasant labored so that he might eat and ate so that he might labor all day, every day, and so on to death. It was so basic, so primordial, so like the life of the insect, that it both outraged her— and dazzled her. For it was clearly God's wish, wasn't it? since every house fly, every living thing— except a few lucky capitalists—did the same thing, labored from dawn to dusk until it died.

There was no escape—except eternity.

Eternity. It horrified her still. When I find eternity comforting, dearest God, then I shall be truly free. Not yet.

CHAPTER

9

"Basically," said Eleanora Colt coldly, "we taught Geraldine to love life and above all not to waste it. Basically . . ." That's the twelfth time she has said "basically," thought Hawkins. They have about a twelve-word vocabulary, these old-time liberals—basically, fundamentally, essentially—and the one thing you could be sure of when they said "basically" was that it was anything but basic—just as the one thing you could count on every time a man said "in all sincerity" was that he was about to tell a big lie.

Hawkins had had a terrible time persuading Eleanora Colt to talk to him at all. The FBI was a dirty word to these old liberals. Old? This woman was forty-five—ten years younger than he was. Still a famous beauty and as out-of-date as a Franklin stove. She'd brought Saint Theresa into the world in 1951, when the world was bright with promise and the old liberal clichés sounded as permanent as the Tablets of Moses. She had raised her daugh-

ter—or *not* raised her but let her raise herself—
according to the theology of Spock and Harry Tru-
man, and now the daughter was wanted for murder
and a few other things. Far, far worse, she'd fled
the nest. All that permissiveness, all that understanding, had not created a bond between mother and
daughter; it had created instead a vacuum—and
nature abhors a vacuum. The girl had fled liberalism
as Eleanora, the mother, had fled the Republican
clichés of her own parents. The mother had embraced liberalism. The daughter, anarchy. And what
would Saint Theresa's daughter (if she ever had
one) embrace? Probably Oliver Cromwell, thought
Hawkins. The swinging thing for the next generation
would be Puritanism.

"We wish an end to this harassment by the
FBI," said Eleanora Colt icily. "And if we don't
get it we will take legal steps. My husband is a
lawyer."

"I know," said Hawkins. Her husband was John
Colt, the most famous lawyer for liberal causes.
His money came from Wall Street; the energy went
into the American Civil Liberties Union, despised
by the New Left, including his own daughter.

"We have told the FBI again and again we have
not heard one word from Geraldine since she left
this house six . . . no, seven years ago."

And if you had heard from the girl, you still
wouldn't tell us, said Hawkins to himself. Aloud,
he said, "Mrs. Colt, I'm convinced you are telling
the truth." About that, anyway. "But there are other
things you could help us with."

"I don't think so, Mr. Hawkins. If we could find Geraldine we would have found her ourselves. Long ago."

Hawkins looked at the granite face and felt an outpouring of pity. She was bleeding inside because the daughter had fled her emotionally, as well as physically, and she knew it.

"Your daughter had her own money, left her by her grandmother. The money's in trust and you are a trustee of that fund. If the girl has drawn any money recently, you could—"

"Geraldine has not drawn a penny since she left us." Hawkins didn't believe it. "And even if she had I would not tell you. It's none of your business prying into my daughter's finances."

Liberal as she was, Eleanora Colt still exhibited aristocratic outrage at the very thought of the police nosing about her money. Or her daughter's. In her circle it was all right to discuss who was committing adultery with whom. Money was as private a matter as one's bowel movements.

"This is a murder investigation." Hawkins hated reminding her. "We could get a court order. We don't want to."

"My husband will fight you every foot of the way. My daughter never murdered anyone."

Hawkins didn't believe Theresa was a murderer either. Not even in face of the evidence. He tried another tack.

"Mrs. Colt, this case has been on the back burner for a number of years—although a murder investi-

54

gation, as you know, is never closed. But what brought me to you now is something else."

He hesitated because he didn't want to add this worry to her others. The Colts had woe enough, God knows. But the woman was so unyielding, so hostile, he could see no other way.

"The fact is, Mrs. Colt, I think your daughter is in very great danger. The best thing that could happen to your daughter is to be arrested. For her own protection."

Rodgers had shaken him to the core with his information. Elf James was a terror next to which the old FBI nemeses like Dillinger or the Communist underground were children. You could figure the old-time mobsters and the old-time Marxists. But the dragon children of the Maoist revolutionary youth lived in jungles the FBI couldn't penetrate and couldn't even find. The New Left killers were worse than ruthless; they were casual about killing. Elf James literally didn't give a damn. She was fearless and brilliant, and as dangerous as a pregnant cobra.

He couldn't tell Theresa's mother about Elf James. There were limits. He took refuge in generalities. "The revolutionary youth movement, Mrs. Colt, is in a state of disintegration. It's turning inward—eating itself up, you might say. One set of militants is at war with another—in fact, with many others. We have information that Saint Ther . . . that Geraldine has overstepped the rules—their own rules."

Hawkins waved his gentle hands helplessly. He

could not bear even to say it. Not to the girl's mother.

"I don't believe you." Eleanora Colt rose to her feet. She was very tall, beautiful, and as obsolete as El Morocco. "You're trying to frighten me into telling you . . . things I don't know anyway. Even if I could, I wouldn't."

Hawkins rose, too, because he would not remain seated while this aristocratic and outraged woman stood. They were by the fireplace on one of two facing settees, and there were flowers everywhere in that well-bred living room. Flowers and chintz and space and a painting of a horse over the mantelpiece. This was what Theresa had fled from—all this order and neatness. You could almost taste the cleanliness, to say nothing of the money it cost to put fresh flowers in every vase every day.

"Mrs. Colt, we don't want to have to go to court to get an order to examine Geraldine's trust because . . . well, it would get into the papers."

His real fear he couldn't tell her. Among other things, there were FBI considerations. You didn't say these things. They might not be true and then they'd return to haunt you. But Hawkins was sure of his ground. The girl was broke, flat broke, wherever she was. If this line of inquiry got into the papers, well, Elf read the papers.

"We'll fight you in court. You have no right . . ."

Hawkins stared at her in disbelief. As he had stared at so many of them. None of them had helped, these aristocratic mamas, who had spawned the children who formed the backbone of Weatherman,

and before them the Motherfuckers, and before that
the Radical Orphans—the bombers and bank burn-
ers who had raised such hell and many of whom
came from such good families and every last one
of whom was the brightest in his class or almost the
brightest. The parents they'd deserted and betrayed,
and in some cases even attempted to murder, stuck
by them to the end, cooperated not at all with the
police. Under the delusion that they, their children
who spit upon them, would return to them and say:
"Mother, how wonderful you are! How steadfast!
How loyal! You're one of us!" But none of them
did or ever would. Even the few of the revolutionary
youth who threw it all up and came back to the
straight world did not go back to mother. Or even
think about her.

The worst thing these parents could have done
was to try to understand and sympathize, because
what fun was it to revolt against that? The very
extent to which Eleanora Colt showed love and
loyalty to her daughter was the exact measure of
her daughter's rebellion. If she had been less understanding, Theresa would not have had to rebel quite
so extensively. That was Hawkins' law of the generation gap, which he had formulated after a decade
of studying the revolutionary young. He didn't dare
even tell anyone his law—so shattering was it to
the conventional wisdom.

"Mrs. Colt, when will your husband be home?"

"John won't tell you any more than I will—because he doesn't know."

"When will he be home, Mrs. Colt? Or where

can I find him now? He's not at the office because I tried there."

She stared at him coldly and he stared back, not giving an inch. She's my daughter now, he thought, a very reluctant thought because you shouldn't have thoughts like that. Theresa's thrown you over, Mrs. C. She's mine, all mine. My God, I'm getting senile.

"He's at the Yale Club for lunch," the woman said finally. And turned her back on him.

Nobody is happy to see us anymore, thought Hawkins. People used to fight to get to us with their misinformation. Now we're treated like germs. We have taken the place of Internal Revenue as the least welcome visitor to the home of Fortress America. I'm trying to save her daughter's life and she treats me like the bottom of the sewer. It gave duty an extra hard edge, which was not altogether unpleasant. I'm enjoying martyrdom, Hawkins was thinking, because I'm fifty-five. The thought so intrigued him he forgot to say "Goodbye" and "Thank you for your total lack of cooperation" to Mrs. Colt, an inconceivable breach of manners to the gentle FBI man.

CHAPTER

10

Elf's eyes gleamed. The bank lay there in the splash of yellow morning sunshine like a fat zebra before a waiting lion. If I had a tail, I'd be twitching it, side to side. My salivary glands are already hyperactive. With others danger dries up the mouth. I salivate. What would Professor Marcuse make of that?

She stared through narrowed eyes, mouth open, at the bank and tried to put it in a revolutionary context. Her prey. She'd rip it open and out would flow money like entrails. But the kicks were all wrong. Marxist emotional decadence. Elf was acutely conscious of the fact she was one part Marxist revolutionary to nine parts Women's Liberationist. She'd been the first on the Berkeley campus to spit out the uncomfortable question: Who washes the dishes in the socialist paradise? Fuck Ho Chi Minh, she'd said, which had caused quite a stir among her fellow Marxists. When Elf busted a bank she was, firstly, sticking her knife into the disgusting underbelly of male chauvinism, and lastly—very lastly—into the soft underbelly of capitalism—and this bothered her. Ideologically. I think too much. Especially lately. I was more primary, more instinctual, two years ago.

It was a very small bank because Euclid, Colorado, was a very small town. The bank looked like a Grant Wood painting, shining in the sun, square and rather appealing in its frontier innocence. Still, it had an alarm system, and time locks, and most of the modern gadgets more comforting to insurance companies than distressing to bank robbers. Banks were meant to be robbed, thought Elf, like zebras were made to be eaten by lions. That's what they were for, yea, verily, clear back to Stalin, who busted banks before he became the biggest beast of all— and the worst male chauvinist pig. Almost the only part of Stalin Elf approved of was his bank busting.

The chief cashier was now coming down the too-wide main street of Euclid, Colorado: eight-fifty-eight, right on time. Elf glanced at Bandit in the rear seat to be sure the idiot child was awake, conscious, and in her right mind if that was not stretching the word. Christ, I shouldn't enjoy it so much! What will I do for kicks *after* the Revolution?

She waited till the chief cashier had passed the stolen car—across the street from the bank—and then swung out of the car, gracefully. Style was important in bank robbing, Elf thought; I am a very stylish buster of banks because otherwise it is a low pursuit of felons and I'm not a felon but a revolutionary. All these thoughts thudding through her brain, as she bounded across the street, the little snub-nosed machine pistol under her blouse. She could hear Bandit scuffling along behind her—and she wished she couldn't hear it because if she could hear it, so could he.

He did. The chief cashier turned questioningly, wondering who was on the main street of Euclid, Colorado, at 8:58 A.M., and what met his eyes was Elf James in her black Ho Chi Minh pajamas with her black, closely cropped hair and her famous *retroussé* nose—just as she pulled her machine pistol out from under her blouse. And smiling. That was another thing that the newspapers made much of: that Elf James had a marvelous open-faced smile while bank robbing. They just didn't know, thought Elf, the smile busting all over her face like spring, just how much I enjoy pulling a gun on a man! Even on this rabbity, whey-faced shithead, who is about to piss in his pants with sheer terror. Elf's smile broadened. Christ, I'm practically coming, she thought. Greatest sex thrill of all, pulling a gun on a man. Except, of course, actually killing one.

"Just open the door as usual," whispered Elf throatily, sexily, smiling her famous smile at the terrified cashier. "I'm Elf James."

"Yes, I know," said the cashier. Imagine meeting Elf James! The girl who'd killed . . . He felt the machine pistol nudging his spine, pulled out his keys, and opened the bank.

The three of them, cashier, Elf, and Bandit, slipped in. The bank had a clean, mountain smell, unlike the smell of Eastern banks. Elf was a connoisseur of bank smells. Not much bread, thought

Elf, but enough. Where were Torrance and Lisa?

The pair slipped in then, having walked down the side street as Elf had ordered, partly to case the town, keeping their ears open, partly not to have four in a car, which would attract attention. Torrance was big, black, and inscrutable. Lisa looked as if she were going to burst into tears. Was she going to hold together?

"Just go along with my friend," whispered Elf to the cashier, smiling. Torrance marched him down to the vault, due to open in five minutes. Lisa eyed Bandit, communicating her terror. Any minute these two will bust up.

"In here, Lisa, behind the counter," said Elf, concealing her exasperation. The tiniest bit of anger against these two and they'd come unstuck. "You, too, Bandit."

Elf took the door. There was only one bank pig and he was late. Always late, according to her research. Elf pulled out the cosh. Of hemlock, six inches, shaped like a man's cock. She'd carved it herself. It was going against the book to hit the bank dicks with coshes, especially wooden ones. But he'd be armed. It was always best to stun the man with a gun, Elf thought, to quell the arrogance a gun gave the pigs. If I write my own little Red Book, that will be in it. Hit the pricks—or they get ideas.

The wait seemed interminable in the quiet bank. Only two minutes, actually, but two minutes is a long time when waiting for a bank guard. Elf was behind the main door, which would stay open all day in banking hours. She could hear the sniffling behind the bank counter. Bandit? Or Lisa?

Elf hit him behind the ear in exactly the right place—but too hard. It was the wait that had tensed her too much. The blood spurted. She hadn't intended that. He was an elderly man, fat, out of condition, and he hit the floor like a sack of wet cement. Christ, thought Elf. She tugged at the heavy body—was he dead?—to get it clear of the door because the two women cashiers would be right on his heels within a matter of minutes. Strong as she was, Elf couldn't move the man.

"Bandit! Lisa!" whispered Elf. "Help me."

The two idiot children sprang out from behind the bank counter and then everything started going wrong. The three girls were tugging the bank dick across the floor when the first of the women cashiers, a gray-faced older lady, walked in, using her own key.

To face three unarmed girl bank robbers. Elf had laid down the machine pistol when she started tugging the bank guard. The two idiot children had left their .38s on the floor behind the bank counter when they came out to help her.

Style, thought Elf furiously. The gray-haired lady had figured the situation instantly—probably had worked the bank for thirty years—and she wasn't cowed by three unarmed girls.

Elf recovered first. She plucked the guard's .45 from his holster and aimed it right at the gray-faced lady's eyes. "This is a stickup," she said, not smiling.

63

The gray-faced lady sneered openly. "It's not loaded," she said contemptuously. "That gun hasn't been loaded in years."

Elf sighted down the blue steel barrel and pulled the trigger. Click. "You're right," said Elf and lucky for the old party or she'd have blown her head off. Instead, she hit her with the .45—and instantly regretted it. What am I doing? What am I *doing* hitting old ladies?

The gray-faced lady went down, spouting blood like a fountain right in front of the door, and again Elf had to tug her away. She weighed about ninety pounds, this one, blood spurting all over Elf's black pajamas.

Then the other woman cashier, a young one, entered. And screamed. All very understandable because the place was a welter of gore. Stylish bank robbery, my ass, thought Elf—and hit the young one with the heavy .45 to stop the screaming. It stopped abruptly. More blood. My God, what a fuckup! And who fucked it up—me!

Lisa and Bandit verged on hysteria.

"Get her out of the doorway," said Elf—to give them something to do. She rescued her machine pistol. "Now get your guns, you two." She could hardly reprimand them. She'd been just as bad. Leaving my gun leaning against a post. I'm losing my mind.

She looked at her watch. Nine-oh-two. The bourgeois halfwits would be here any minute, drawing out their rotten dollars. "Bandit, go down and help Torrance. Lisa, stay here with me."

Changing the plans. The worst thing you could do in a bank job.

But no one had touched off the alarm yet. The only thing that had not gone wrong. Lisa whimpered. "Shut up, Lisa," said Elf. A mistake. The girl whinnied like a horse, gushing tears of panic. Elf fought back a desire to hit the girl. Why do I want to hit everyone?

With the great oak doors closed, Elf had no way of knowing what was happening outside. She pulled a stool out from behind the counter and peered out the high windows. Like a fucking church, this bank. Depositors, six of them, three men, three women, were already on the pavement, waiting for the bank to open.

Then Elf saw the police car, approaching fast down the main street from the direction of the police station. No siren. Trying to catch us right on the job. The alarm must have gone off, thought Elf. In the police station. No sound here. The cameras clicking away silently. Oh, I've fucked this up royally. How many pigs? Two. Well, that was Euclid's entire pig population at any one time of day. The entire police force, Elf knew, was only four, half off duty.

Elf leaped from the stool.

How can I break it to this sniveling child? She'll dissolve altogether. Torrance emerged then from the bowels of the bank, bearing one thin canvas money bag.

"Pigs!" said Elf. "We'll have to shoot our way out."

"Jesus!" said Torrance.

Elf took the canvas sack. "Is this *all*?"

"You picked the wrong moment to bust this bank, baby. Every payroll in town was yesterday."

The classic mistake in bank robbery, thought Elf. Almost the first lesson in Fucillo's classic treatise on bank robbery: first, be sure the bank has something in it worth busting it for and, above all, find out when the town's payday is. Busting a bank the day after payday was as brainless as screwing.

Elf sipped at the cup of humiliation for only a few seconds. Later, she'd suffer agonies. Now there was no time. She stuffed the limp canvas bag in her blouse. (There was *something* in there. But what? Twenties? C notes?)

"In a minute they'll be coming in, probably with tear gas. We've got to go out shooting. I'll go first."

Goddamn cameras clicking away. They've caught all the farce. I must give myself a decent exit.

The two idiot girls, Lisa and Bandit, had stopped sniveling; the sheer awfulness of the situation had stiffened them. Or paralyzed them. In extremity, one never quite knew what individuals would do. The cowards burst out laughing. The lions burst out crying. That was what made the game interesting, thought Elf.

She herself was smiling again. Why? What have I to smile about? I'm about to get killed. Radical masochism. She despised it.

Lisa and Bandit threw open the great oak doors, one on each side, and—smiling, Elf burst out, the machine pistol spraying bullets and noise, both effective. In a situation like this, the noise—and it was deafening—made the pigs duck, threw off their aim, cast fear into their hearts—no matter how well trained. That was what all the scholars of terrorism taught—from Thibaut to Marighela.

The two policemen had shotguns. A serious mistake. Elf shot out of the door so fast and so explosively that the first blast went behind her into the oak door. The second blast never came because the splatter of bullets from Elf's gun made both pigs duck behind the police car. The classic pig's refuge.

Short bursts now, just enough to keep their heads down, keep them off balance. She streaked across the street—where were the depositors? gone home to mother!—and leaped into the stolen car, the key still in it. A proper bank heist would have a driver waiting with the engine running—to say nothing of a lookout who would have warned of approaching police. But I haven't the troops, Fucillo. What am I to do?

One eye caught the pig, shotgun raised—pump gun, he's got five more in there, thought Elf—and she hit the floor of the car. The shot shattered the windshield. Keep moving, thought Elf. She opened the curbside door and threw herself out, firing as she went—that caught them by surprise. She had outflanked them now. Torn away the screen of metal between her machine pistol and their fat pigs' bodies —and it demoralized them. The two police fled to the protection of the front of the car, and in that precious moment, Elf leaped into the stolen Ford,

started the engine and—again the classic maneuver
—aimed the car right at the defenders of law and
order.

Where the hell were the others? She was fighting
the war all by herself! Elf expected nothing from the
girls, but where in hell was Torrance?

The Ford, in first gear at about 9,000 rpm,
which would give the poor engine permanent heart
trouble, tore down on the front of the police car,
and half of Euclid's police force again ducked away
—to the curbside of their car, their shotguns dangling uselessly from their immobilized arms, just
as Elf intended—and as the Good Book said. She
straightened the stolen Ford, not quite in time to
avoid the police car. It careened off the other car,
and screamed forward.

Then Elf committed the greatest revolutionary
sin of all. She accelerated out of Euclid, Colorado,
deserting her fellow guerrillas, her soul brothers,
without wheels in the Great Wild West, where to be
without wheels was to be naked.

Why hadn't they come out of the bank? Where
were they? The Ford was doing a hundred now, but
the thoughts flooded. I'll never be forgiven for this,
not even by myself. I should go back and get myself
ritually killed in defense of my brothers, my sisters.
What kind of motivation will I have left in this
rotten life if I leave those three behind to fry in
that honkoid hell? I should go back! I should go
back!

The standby car was in a wood two miles away
by a high-banked mountain stream. Elf perched

the Ford on the lip of the bank and released the handbrake. The car sprang down the bank and leaped into the deep stream like a country boy on a summer day. You could see the car clearly by standing on the embankment, but who would be standing there? They'd find it in a few days, but that would be time enough.

Now they'd be looking for a closely cropped, black-haired girl with the famous *retroussé* nose driving a Ford station wagon. Elf stepped into the Chevrolet with the faked number plates that no one was looking for. The great square handbag was on the floor of the front seat. Elf pulled out the blond wig and pulled it on. Next, the fake straight nose covering her own famous turned-up one. She stripped off the bloodstained Ho Chi Minh pajamas and threw them into the mountain stream. There goes my radical youth, she thought, as she watched the pajamas sink. I'm an onion without a skin. Out of the square bag came blue jeans and a black sweater, the most anonymous protective coloration on earth.

She drove unhurriedly to Denver, an hour away, just another long-haired blonde girl in jeans, of which the world was so full.

CHAPTER

11

Theresa dressed carefully. Or as carefully as a girl with only a single costume can dress. She pulled the crinkly blue-and-white striped blouse as taut as she could, trying to eliminate the wrinkles, trying to make it look a little less slept-in. The black trousers she shook vigorously, hard as she could, to get the dust out—and there was so much dust she choked in the little lookout room—and then she swabbed the cloth carefully with cold water on her only rag, to get out the stains, the dust, the sweat. She had to pass. That's all. Just pass.

It took an hour, making lower and upper garments presentable, and then Theresa—naked from the waist down—skipped up to her audience room and laid the trousers in a patch of hot sunshine under one of the great windows to dry. Now her face. She got a pail of cold water from the well, took it to a dark—but not too dark—part of the room, and looked in. It was her only mirror.

The blue eyes gazed back—serene. When have

I ever craved serenity? Her life had been one long flight from serenity. Still, there it was. The face astonished her—still gaunt and haunted but not demonic. She remembered the last time she'd looked into a real mirror—in the women's john on that awful tourist airplane—Charter Flight to Paradise 235, all included. The face then white, taut, terrified, demented. The face now tanned, rested, above all unterrified. Her calm bothered her a little. It would not do to become too relaxed. I must not fall under the spell of fresh air and sunshine. She was still a fugitive from the FBI—and from Elf. Especially Elf.

She massaged the brown face with cold water, thinking wryly: Once it was a famous face. Once one of the Ten Most Wanted. She wondered if the FBI had a list for the Ten Least Wanted—and if she was on it. The thought made her laugh—and the laughter reflected back from the clear water delighted her. I haven't had a real laugh (as opposed to manic laughter, which didn't count) since when? I am full of the beauty of the world. Instead of its despair. Why not?

She combed the long blond hair, matted with dirt, as best she could. She had no soap to wash it with. Soap would be one of the first things she'd buy in Palma. Then matches. A pot to boil an egg in. Or potato. Some clothes that blended into the landscape a little better than the ones she was wearing.

She put her scarf over the tangled blond hair and the dark glasses over the candid blue eyes. She looked now not unlike a thousand other tanned blonde girls on holiday in Majorca. Finally, the shoulder bag. She took out of it all but her comb and her money—$45—that she hadn't dared change to pesetas at the airport, her faked passport she'd bought in San Francisco, her gun.

Gun! What would she need a gun for? She tucked the snub-nosed .38 deep in the straw.

Making no effort at concealment, she walked down the center of the white road. Skulking was the biggest mistake; that was what Thibaut had taught in his classic manual *Flight and Concealment*. Anyway she was not in a mood for skulking or for Thibaut.

She thought instead about Saint Francis. He reveled in the beauty of the world. Vagabondage and poverty were poetry with him, Simone Weil had written; he stripped himself naked in order to have contact with the beauty of the world. Well, then. Enjoy! Enjoy! Far from being a sin, it was a sin not to enjoy the world.

She strode down the center of the road, bursting with good spirits. Around a bend the greenery stopped abruptly to make way for a tiny vegetable patch on the valley floor. The shepherd was ploughing it with the mule.

"Buena día," sang out Teresa, leaving off the "s" the way the Mallorquins did.

The taut, brown face didn't reply. Just looked at her. The way a forest beast might look. Warily. Not sullenly or with any hostility. Just watchful. A nice face, thought Theresa. How old? Hard to tell. The face didn't smile back but the eyes stayed on her until she passed out of the range of his vision. It left her breathless, that gaze.

Two miles further on, the white road joined the main highway right in the center of the little village of Cuesta, which wasn't even on the map of Majorca. There she waited for a bus to Palma. Within five minutes she knew she'd made a mistake. The children playing in the gutter with their sticks, their only toy, were staring at her with the total lack of self-consciousness of children. Certainly they'd seen tourists in Cuesta before. They'd even seen tourists on buses—Majorca was full of them—but what they had not seen before was a tourist *catching* a bus in Cuesta. The tourists would arrive on a bus and leave on the same bus, if they stopped at all, which was unlikely. Either that or they arrived in their own cars. A person such as herself wouldn't be *waiting* for a bus in a village like Cuesta unless disaster had struck of some sort—a car breakdown, a quarrel with a lover—and, if so, what delicious gossip! All this was in the dark brown staring eyes of the three boys.

Presently there were more eyes. Two fat old ladies put their chairs on the pavement and commenced sewing. Theresa could feel the heat of their curiosity. Another needlewoman joined the two fat Mallorquin women, a very much younger woman, quite pretty, who put her chair next to the other two, her gaze on Theresa, sizing her up, wondering what she was doing there—all as obvious as if she had yelled it aloud.

I don't even know when the bus is coming. Or for that matter what time it is. Theresa looked straight at the pretty young woman and sang out: "*A qué hora viene el autobus a Palma?*"

"*A las diez menos cuarto.*" The young woman looked at her boldly, smiling. Then she made that little crooked waggle of her right hand which is a universal language in the Latin countries and which means that sometimes the autobus arrives at quarter to ten and sometimes at quarter after ten, depending on how it felt. The three Mallorquin women laughed. Theresa laughed with them. Tension was broken.

Quarter to ten, eh? Well, that was not far away from right now. She had no watch but nine-thirty was what she guessed the time to be. Theresa looked up and down the road. Empty. Emptiness was its normal condition, unlike the roads where she came from. Lovely in its emptiness. Theresa decided that the bus wasn't coming that minute and walked over to the three ladies. She smiled at the pretty young Mallorquin woman and pointed to the embroidery, red flowers on white linen, beautifully stitched.

"Very pretty," she said in English. The women all seemed to understand. A compliment was international coinage. "*Por comprar?*" All three women shook their heads vigorously. The needlework definitely was not for sale. A trousseau, perhaps? Imagine a world where they still have such a thing. Marriage itself was pretty quaint in Theresa's world. She felt as if she'd moved backward into the eighteenth century.

The Mallorquin ladies, emboldened by her own

74

boldness, were showering her with questions. "*No comprende*," said Theresa, smiling. She did *comprende* very well, actually. What, they were asking, was she doing in Cuesta at nine-thirty in the morning? An *Inglesa*? She heard *Inglesa* several times and she was not going to disabuse them of the idea she was English.

The bus proclaimed itself half a mile away, screeching and complaining. A rattletrap of incredible antiquity. Theresa stepped aboard, waving a smiling goodbye, singing out "*Adiós*." Keep the natives friendly. You never know when you might need them. More wisdom from the underground. It would be far better if they hadn't even suspected her existence.

She paid the bus driver with the hundred-peseta note she'd stolen from the handbag an American tourist had left open and unguarded for the five seconds it took her to plunge her face in a towel in the ladies' room. An old underground trick. A woman at her most vulnerable with her face in a towel and her handbag open because that's where the face cream and lipstick were. The hundred-peseta note was her only Spanish money. She got very little change from the bus driver.

An hour later she was in Palma.

She walked down the paseo marítimo with scarcely a glance at the huge sparkling bay, full of an extravagance of yachts that would ordinarily have aroused her revolutionary ire. But she had other things on her mind. She strode up to the *cambio* with the arrogance of the born tourist. It was one of those street *cambios* where they paid only the scantiest attention to currency regulations. She thrust her $45, all of it, through the cage and flashed her fake passport, which the man barely glanced at. She didn't even bother to fill out the form and he didn't ask for it. He counted out the pesetas, 2,975 of them, swiftly and contemptuously. More accustomed to hundred-dollar bills, the bastard.

Theresa swept the wad into her great leather handbag without bothering to count it, although it was all the money she had, and got out of there. She walked more easily now, under the great palms on Palma's sea front, past the great seventeenth-century palaces built by the Mallorquin aristocracy in the long-ago heyday now full of bankers and bureaucrats, of whom the world was so full, past the enormous cathedral. Shrine of the great Christian conformity, thought Theresa fiercely. She was a Jesus freak who hated churches and the whole priestly establishment. She loathed the exclusiveness of the Catholic Church. I am a believer, she cried in her heart, who loves the unbeliever as much as the believer. In fact, more, because he needs it more. She despised dogma; she fiercely asserted her right to walk with the multitude, the blessed, the un-blessed, those in God's grace, and those *not* in God's grace. Especially them. I am a loner, she thought, patron saint of the outcast, the friendless, the alone.

Oh, hell! People were staring. Everything shows on my damned face! Every last emotion. Even through the dark glasses, her intensity blazed like a beacon. She hurried on, settling into her disguise.

76

A tourist, me. Past the great cathedral she strode, feeling her way by instinct toward that sanctuary she headed for in all the cities she'd fled in—Woolworth's—where the common folk and the down-at-heel could buy a few things the fugitive couldn't do without.

She could smell out Woolworth's—even when it was called something else—anywhere in the world. Palma's Woolworth was a very big one in the heart of the Old City. There Theresa bought a frying pan, a pot, one plastic plate, one plastic cup, one tin knife, one tin fork, one tin spoon. She felt the pity of the salesgirl on her singleness. Oh, pity me not, she thought merrily, I am Saint Theresa, patron saint of single girls and quite accustomed to martyrdom. I am about to undergo my greatest deprivation. They are about to take my sainthood from me. That was the gossip from Rome. How will I manage, unsainted? Saint Francis had stripped himself naked —but could he have managed without sainthood itself? That was what modern sainthood was all about—you had to do without sainthood to be sainted. All these thoughts chasing fiercely through her brain pan—as she bought matches, soap, shampoo, candles, a small flashlight.

After Woolworth's, she strolled slowly down the main boulevard of Palma, with its great central plaza lined with small kiosks where they sell ice cream and newspapers and studded with park benches where the stroller can sit and eat his ice cream and read his newspaper. She would have liked an ice cream and a newspaper—but not yet. There were things to do.

She strolled along the great *paseo* under the enormous plane trees hundreds of years old, her eyes missing nothing. There was Pan American, and there American Express, the two citadels of the American expatriate. The post office couldn't be far away because expatriates lived for the daily letters. She found it directly around the corner—an immense, very Spanish, very square edifice that looked strong enough to withstand siege guns.

At the cable desk, she picked up the form and wrote a very simple baffling message. The cable address was Admas. Message: Patricia Jenkins. Signature: 126.

The post-office clerk was a square, sleepy-eyed, sad-faced man who looked at this curious message a long, long time, shaking his head. "*Señora*," he said. Then a gentle torrent of Spanish, not one word of which Theresa understood. "*Comme ça! Comme ça!*" said Theresa, thinking mistakenly he might speak French. A vain hope. Presently he summoned a superior, who spoke roughly twenty words of English.

"I want the message to go just like that," said Theresa.

"No, *señora*, is forbidden coda."

No codes. Oh, hell. "It's not a code," said Theresa, smiling her most helpless smile, and telling a great lie because, of course, it was a code.

"Is forbidden the *numeros*, plain English," said the post-office man stubbornly.

Already the argument was attracting attention. An Englishman, dark glasses, scarf at the throat, blue yachting jacket with brass buttons, expatriate type number one, in Theresa's book, tried to come to the rescue. "Can I be of assistance! I speak Spanish."

"No, thank you," said Theresa politely. "I think I can manage." The last thing in the world she wanted to get mixed up with was an English remittance man. He retreated only a little way down the counter, watching carefully because, thought Theresa, what else has he to do?

"Permitame!" She took back the message and altered it to read: "Patricia Jenkins suffers. Liz." Mitchell would understand Liz as an alternate to 126, her code name at the Massachusetts Trust, but he wouldn't like it. He was a very proper, humorless, totally secretive trust executive and he had always told Theresa that a number was absolute. Only one person to each number. It could be no other. Whereas there might be a lot of Lizes. But long ago she had said: If an unexplained Liz message arrived, it was almost certainly she and no other. "Patricia Jenkins suffers" in place of simple "Patricia Jenkins" he would certainly work out. The post office would supply the word Palma for free. So he would know where to send the money. But would he send Geraldine Colt's money to a Liz who might not be Geraldine Colt? That very correct, totally dedicated trust officer to whom money was indeed a sacred trust?

The post-office official scrutinized the revised

message, lips pursed. He ached to say No again. Saying No is what bureaucrats live for, their tiny moment of glory in their dreary underpaid existence. He yearned to say that most favorite and overworked word in the bureaucratic world—"Impossible." "Is impossible!" is a phrase understood and hated by travelers the world over.

Unfortunately, he couldn't find anything the matter with the message. He stamped it sourly and handed it back to the other post-office man. Theresa paid 586 of her precious pesetas. She hoped it was worth it.

Now to get rid of this idiot Englishman, who was trying hard to move in.

Theresa sailed through the door marked *Damas*— the classic ploy and still the best. Since she was there, she might as well use it. She had been accustomed to dangling her bottom over a hole. This lavatory had three lovely chambers, almost as commodious as small bedrooms, with immense old-fashioned toilets. She'd almost forgotten how to sit on one. It was extraordinary how quickly one got accustomed to not sitting on one. After all they were fairly recent in the long march of history, weren't they? How many of the world's population sat on them to this very day? They ought to be against the law, she thought fiercely. Flushing the glorious shit into the ocean, which it poisons, instead of restoring it to the land, which it enriches.

She took a long time and when she came out the Englishman had left.

Theresa's next stop was the open market, and

she found it easily, directly down the main boulevard, near the sea. There in the covered market stalls, you could find anything you wanted, from vegetables to lamp shades. It would be cheap. Theresa bought a pair of blue baggy trousers exactly like those she saw on the peasant and a blue cotton worker's blouse. Very anonymous, very useful. She couldn't get the clothes in her brown bag so she had them wrapped in newspaper and tied with string.

That ended her shopping. Now for a little self-indulgence. She walked back up the promenade, past the great fountain with its stone lions, and back under the shade of the towering plane trees. On the way she passed the sidewalk café she'd spotted on the way down. That's where they'd all sit, having their apéritifs, after they'd got their checks at the post office and cashed them at American Express, and there they all were, the international types—the blond English lady, well covered in English woolens, who'd lived abroad since the war had brought in all those terrible socialist governments with their confiscatory taxes; next to her the thin, well-brushed gray-haired Austrian with the exquisite manners and the little dog, who'd been there since World War I, sitting in the same chair; and next to him the Englishman who had tried to pick her up in the post office; and, on the far side of him, the American in the white duck trousers and blue-and-white striped fisherman's jersey, probably from California, who would have a lovely yacht in the harbor—all these and many more she saw while standing in the shade of the central plaza. A place to avoid at all costs, that café, where expatriates of all nations sat away half the day and would sit until the capitalist system crumbled around their ears.

Theresa sauntered down the center of the plaza, looking through her dark glasses at the people. Almost tasting them. That handsome Mallorquin in the T-shirt. She felt a stab of lust for that one. It had been a long time since she'd had a man between her legs. What did such a one do? He was eating an ice cream, totally self-absorbed. Her glance then flicked over a dark Spanish girl with huge brown eyes, seated on one of the stone benches reading a newspaper. I wouldn't mind a fumble with that one either. What is so pretty a girl doing on a park bench? Waiting for her lover? Or was it her lunch hour?

Suddenly, Theresa felt very hungry. Lunch hour. At the end of the plaza were the kiosks. Theresa bought a double ice-cream cone and an *International Herald Tribune* and took them back to an empty park bench. She ate the ice cream first because it took both hands and all her attention. Then she opened the *International Herald Tribune*—and right on the front page was the headline that shattered her day.

ELF GETS AWAY: 3 OTHERS
CAPTURED IN BANK RAID

CHAPTER

12

Hawkins read the typescript, hoping he would find Theresa's name and hoping he wouldn't. He was in Rodgers' office and Rodgers watched him quizzically. Rodgers liked to tell people that studying Hawkins was his only hobby. Infinite permutations like chess.

"She's only seventeen," said Rodgers. "No brain to speak of. She said she never heard the name Theresa mentioned. But then she said——" here Rodgers grinned and scratched the top of his head in a sort of Stan Laurel gesture—"she and Elf never talked much anyhow. Just made love, smoked joints, and stared at the ceiling. After three hours in the company of Bandit, I can well understand why Elf stuck up a bank—to relieve the tedium."

Hawkins put down the typescript of the incredibly boring interview between Rodgers and Bandit. "How long had she been with Elf?

"Three months—more or less."

"What do you mean—more or less?"

"I gather Elf was not all that faithful. There were other girls."

"Other boys too?"

Rodgers shook his head. "I don't think so. Elf has been to bed with men, of course. But she inclines toward girls."

"Was Theresa one of the other girls?" asked Hawkins, as casually as he could manage.

"No. When Theresa and Elf were together, there was no one else in Elf's life. Theresa filled it altogether."

Hawkins blinked. He didn't expect sentiment from Rodgers. "How do you know?"

"Elf wrote poetry about it." Rodgers riffled through his file on Elf. "It isn't as if she wrote poetry all the time, you understand. Theresa was the first— and the last—to drive Elf to poetry." He found what he was looking for and tossed it to Hawkins.

In pencil. On lined paper:

> Theresa
> Is the sound of
> The stars,
> A sibilant
> Whisper of infinity. . . .

Hawkins was shaken by the intensity of it. "Gosh," he said. Hawkins was almost the only man left in the western world who still said "Gosh." There were pages more of the same. It put Elf in a wholly new perspective.

"Was Theresa writing poetry to Elf at the same time?"

Rodgers shook his head. "You should know better than that, John. Theresa is your specialty, not mine. But from what I gather, just working on Elf, Theresa was—" he corrected himself swiftly—"*is* bisexual, the way they all are. But she is fundamentally heterosexual as Elf is fundamentally lesbian. That was the problem. Theresa was the great love of Elf's life. Elf was *not* the great love of Theresa's life."

No, thought Hawkins, the great love of Theresa's life was a slender black revolutionary named Strickland. A man who'd got himself shot in that very puzzling affair in Oakland that the FBI was still blamed for by the underground and a great many leftist lawyers, including Theresa's—or Geraldine Colt's—father.

"Strickland came between them," Rodgers was saying, "again and again."

"Strickland was dead by then."

"His shade came between them," said Rodgers ironically. "Sometimes death just makes it worse."

What are we doing, thought Hawkins helplessly, a couple of veteran FBI guys talking love like Elizabeth Barrett Browning? "She ran away," said Hawkins. A flat statement. "But when?"

"That's what we don't know. Because it wasn't the first time. All the time Theresa had disappeared as far as we knew, she apparently was Elf's girl. A period of two years, maybe. But what makes it confusing is that Theresa took to her heels several times —and Elf took off after her—and found her. Two times at least that we know about. Maybe more. In the intervals Elf found little idiots like Bandit to keep her company while she looked for Theresa."

Hawkins hated all of it. Pure sex, God knows, was not lightly to be dismissed. But the poetry put everything in a different light. Made it, if anything, worse.

"Where is Elf now?" asked Hawkins. As if anyone knew.

Rodgers scowled. "We can't even find the car. And, of course, she had a standby car—we got that out of Bandit, anyway. Fake numbers. She couldn't remember them. Otherwise she'd have told us. There is some advantage to having an accomplice as dumb as Bandit. She can't concentrate long enough to help out the police."

Hawkins stood up, clutching Elf's poetry.

"Could I keep this for a little while? I'll return it."

"Where are you going?"

"Back to my own desk—the Land That Time Forgot. You've given me food for much thought."

Hawkins shambled to the door in his boneless walk, a graying scarecrow.

"John," said Rodgers, "don't you think we ought to work together on this? This is the same investigation. Where you find one of these girls you are likely to find the other—or at least the trail of the other."

Hawkins blinked at him owlishly, mulishly. He didn't want to share Theresa with Rodgers—or, for that matter, with the rest of the Bureau. Theresa was his baby. His private obsession. He fiercely resented Rodgers' encroaching on Theresa—while unable to avoid the thought that Rodgers had every right in the world to do so. Rodgers had, in fact, been far more forthcoming to him than he had been to Rodgers. Hawkins' evasiveness about Theresa's handwriting had come close to withholding evidence, as cardinal a crime as an FBI man could commit. None of this altered the fact that he did not, repeat *not*, want to share Theresa with Rodgers.

"I think we should keep our investigations separate, Joe," said Hawkins politely, "because that way we'll produce twice as many ideas. If we work together, we'll simply block our minds." As phony a bit of rationalizing as he'd ever committed. Rodgers was far too smart a police officer not to know it.

The mask of friendship dropped like lead. "John," said Rodgers harshly, "you *do* want to catch this girl, don't you?"

Hawkins shut the door he'd just opened and leaned against it, facing his old colleague stonily. "What a damn thing to say. What are you suggesting?"

"That you're not being very helpful. God damn it, John, I've given you everything I have. I've gone out of my way. You just sit there—not saying anything. Today. And the other day too. You've been studying this girl for—what, five years? My God, you must have a few ideas. Open up!"

The trouble was, thought Hawkins, this charge was not unjustified. Still, he didn't like it. He let Rodgers wait a long time, unsettling him with a cold scrutiny that had undone a lot of fugitives in his more active years.

When he was good and ready, he let out a soft sigh. "You want the benefit of my thinking, Joe. You won't like it. You won't believe it. And you'll reject it. Nevertheless, here it is since you asked. That Euclid bank job was as badly mangled as a job can be. Yet Elf had planned it as she planned all the others. Why should as good a bank robber as Elf James mess up an operation as thoroughly as that?"

Rodgers shrugged. "Perhaps she wants to get caught. Perhaps she's tired of running." This has been FBI dogma for some time lately, the idea that the militant revolutionary young would tire of the game and come in from the cold of their own accord. Hawkins thought it was nonsense.

"Never," said Hawkins crisply. "Elf James would hate to be caught by the likes of you or me, whom she despises."

"Then what is your theory, Old Philosopher?" said Rodgers, rubbing it in.

"My theory is that Elf was just trying to get her name in the papers—looking vulnerable, looking like a little girl who needed help—from Theresa, who had skipped out on her. I think further—remember you asked for this—that Elf James sabotaged her own bank job subconsciously, unaware what she was doing. A cry for help." Hawkins' face crinkled into a smile. Rodgers clearly hated the whole idea. "I told you you wouldn't like it," he said.

He left Rodgers' office quickly before the man started shooting holes in it. A Pyrrhic victory, he thought. Rodgers would be talking it around—his obsession with Theresa. It would do him no good, and Theresa even less.

He threaded his way back through the labyrinth of offices to his own cubicle and placed a call to the Massachusetts Trust, which wasn't located in Massachusetts but in Wall Street, where all good trusts go when they die. The call took a while. "You do want to catch this girl, don't you?" Rodgers' jeering question bobbed to the surface of his mind like a dead body in the sea. Did he want Theresa caught? Charged with murder, arson, bank robbery, and a dozen other things? A fair question.

What he didn't want was that Theresa be burned alive in a shoot-out like the one in Los Angeles that had fried half the Symbionese Liberation Army. He didn't want that. Do you want to be in the FBI at all, Hawkins? Someday Rodgers would ask that question, but Hawkins wouldn't tell him the right answer to that either. That was Hawkins' own secret. Even Amanda didn't know.

While he waited, he read a bit more of Elf's poetry:

> The flame of you,
> The moth of me
> Is plane geometry.
> Pure space.
> No time! No time!

No time? Hawkins was afraid there wasn't much time.

His call came through. "Mr. Mitchell, Hawkins of the FBI. I have that federal court order. Must I serve it personally?"

The voice from New York was thin, correct, and as emotionless as a rock. "I'm afraid you'll have to, Mr. Hawkins. I've been advised by counsel."

No use asking which counsel. Theresa's father.

"I hope we can keep it out of the papers."

"I don't think we can," said the neutral tones on the other end.

You don't know what you're doing, thought Hawkins furiously. Liberal lawyers! They fought their cases on the front pages of *The New York Times*, as if people were politics. But he couldn't cry out to Mitchell because he was dealing in hunches, in half-formulated intuitions that wouldn't bear the light of day. But every cop had them, and after thirty years in the FBI Hawkins knew his were better than most. And very frightening.

"I'll be in your office by four this afternoon," said Hawkins grimly—and left for the shuttle plane to New York.

CHAPTER

13

Theresa left the bus two stops after Cuesta. She'd had enough of prying eyes for one day. She'd buried herself in the *International Herald Tribune* during the Cuesta stop, during which two old people, wrinkled as prunes, got off. No one got on. There had to be a limit to this talk about the *Inglesa*. People would forget one visit. They might not forget two.

She descended from the bus, the only one to do so, at the very emptiest stretch of road between Andraix and Valdemosa and struck off immediately cross country, following her nose. The valley, she figured, should be over a range of hills a half mile from the road. It was a stiff climb, but she was in excellent condition and she welcomed the exercise as a relief from the mental turmoil.

Elf!

She tried to slam down the curtain in her mind. And succeeded. Partly succeeded. If I'd picked some other day to go to Palma, I'd have missed the damned story altogether! Why today? God is against

me. Or perhaps warning me. She strode forward
aggressively, thrusting her slender muscular legs forward and up, as if she were biting hard on the
ground. Taking it out on the very earth. Presently
she began to puff and that was welcome. It blotted
out thought. But thought would return when she
stopped puffing. It was going to be a long night.

It was growing dusk and she picked up the pace.
Night fell very fast because, while the temperature
in Majorca was springlike, it was still the middle
of winter and days were short. She needed a fix on
where her tumble-down palace was before the light
failed. Just one glimpse. She was pretty sure she
knew precisely where it lay. She wanted a check.
But at the crest of the hill she found herself deep
in piny woods and she could see nothing, the light
going fast. She sped down the hill at a dog trot to
take advantage of what little illumination there was.

At the foot of the hills, the pines gave way to
orange groves, and now Theresa was fairly confident
she knew where she was. Sure enough, the white
road ran alongside the orange grove and, unless
her bump of direction was dead wrong, her palace
lay to the right. She'd gone north of it when she
went two stops past Cuesta.

It was pitch black now, and she strode through
the fragrant evening, savoring the smells, orange
laced with eucalyptus, a heady mixture. I might try
smoking eucalyptus leaf sometime. Any substance
that smelled as vibrant as eucalyptus might very well
turn her on. Or off. Her larky spirits were returning.
Elf lay buried a thousand fathoms deep. For the

moment. The white road gleamed through the blackness, clear as the white line on a highway, but she had to keep her eyes peeled for the little turnoff.

There it was. Theresa swung off the white road onto the slender track, across the little stone bridge, across the very tiny stream, and then through her own patch of orange trees. Or what she considered her very own orange trees. They had sustained her, that patch of orange trees, a little too well. She'd eaten so many she was afraid they'd be missed and had started picking oranges further down the valley.

The Moorish arch loomed above her in the blackness. She clambered up to it and passed through the gate noiselessly. Before climbing the crazy stairs, Theresa made a little detour to say goodnight to the mule. "We don't see enough of each other," murmured Theresa, feeling the softness of the muzzle in her palm. She could see nothing at all. "You are the blackest mule in the whole world," she whispered, and kissed the velvety muzzle.

Then, in the blackness, a hand closed on hers, scaring her almost out of her wits.

Theresa opened her mouth and the scream, if it had come, would have reached Cuesta. It never came. A hand closed over her mouth, and what emerged was a sort of strangled bark, loud enough in the silence to frighten the mule, which whinnied in alarm. Theresa struggled instinctively, frozen with fright, swinging her one free arm around sharply until it hit a bony face.

A yelp of pain. Then she was on the ground, both arms twisted under her. Am I being raped?

She was terrified of rape, and the conditions of rape. *I don't want to be taken. I want to give. Freely. Above all, I don't want to get raped in the dark. Oh, please . . .*

"*Por favor! Por favor!*" she whimpered, an even more ridiculous plea in Spanish than in English.

It worked. She felt the body move away from her. She lay struggling to free her arms, on her back, in the blackness. A match flared.

The shepherd was on his knees next to her recumbent body. The brown taut face accusing. Mallorquin poured forth from the brown lips. Indignant Mallorquin. Theresa didn't know a word of Mallorquin but she knew an angry man in any language.

Something is my fault, she thought, staring at the taut, brown face, streaming with those harsh Mallorquin noises. She burst out laughing. She couldn't help it. *I'm not being raped. I'm being rebuked. He feels* he *is the victim!*

The match went out.

"Allow me," said Theresa. "*Permitame.*" She struck one of her own matches, feeling rich to have such a luxury. The brown shepherd's face flickered in the matchlight, unsmiling. Theresa smiled at him, flooded with relief. And curiosity.

They faced each other, on their knees, she smiling, he disapproving. The second match went out.

"We can't keep lighting matches," said Theresa. "We'll set the haystack on fire." She turned on her flashlight. Regretfully. The batteries would have to last a long while. "I'm not doing any harm, you know. I just sleep in the hay." Aware that he couldn't

understand a word but hoping the voice was reassuring. How had he cottoned onto her? The missing eggs? Missing oranges?

Would he kick her out of her *palacio?* The
thought terrified her. The *palacio* was home, refuge,
companion, temple, cathedral. She smiled achingly
at him.

It only increased his suspicion. He stared at her,
his mouth working, as if seeking words. But there
were no words that they shared. Theresa let the
smile fade and composed her face into simple blank-
ness. Dignity without hauteur. I mustn't frighten
him. Or overawe him.

Still, it was growing ridiculous—the two of them
facing each other on their knees, wordless. "I am
a woman on the run from the police," she said
softly so as not to frighten him, her eyes huge.
Tell him The Truth. The Truth is all I have, and
what's mine is yours. "I am wanted all over America for murder, arson, bank robbery." He wouldn't
know the words but truth, she felt, had a ring of
conviction. Truth had an urgency that bridged language. Everyone understood the fugitive. A peasant
should certainly.

She talked on—of her life, because what else was
there to talk about? "I've been successively student,
revolutionary, *religieuse*, but always I've tried to
pursue the more difficult truths because anything
less demanding would be unbearable weakness."
It sounded elitist and she didn't want to sound that
way at all. "I have made mistakes, many mistakes,
and my presence here you might say is a form of

atonement. I am fleeing crimes not yet committed."
What was she saying? I'm telling him things I didn't
know. Crimes not yet committed! But, of course,
that was exactly why she had fled. She had never
before put it into words.

She fell silent, looking at the brown taciturn
face. Not a stupid face. A dark closed-in face. I bet
he lives alone like me.

That thought gave her courage. She took his hand.

"Come," she said.

She led him by the hand up the crazy stairs and
through the labyrinth she now knew so well, through
the audience chamber, down the cluttered stairs,
finally to her lookout room with its hay-covered
floor.

Sit anywhere, she said with her hands—that universal gesture. He sat against the wall as far from
her as he could get.

He still thinks of me as the intruder. I must talk
on.

"Who did I murder? And why? Let me explain."
It was like a confessional. Cleansing the soul. Theresa herself had nothing but scorn for the ordinary
Catholic confessional surrounded by the *apparat* of
priesthood. Confession to a peasant! How liberating!

"We were robbing a bank," she whispered, eyes
enormous with the recollection. "We needed cash,
you see, to continue the war to liberate . . ." she
smiled . . ."you." Her hand made a graceful dancer's
movement, including him and all other peasants
into the brotherhood of man. "We didn't rob banks
for ourselves. We lived on nothing." The voice low,

musical, enormously persuasive. "Every penny went to our cause."

Her eyes clouded with pain as she remembered. "There was a bank guard we had not counted on. He hit me with his gun. Here." Her hand flew up to the back of her head, where she could feel the blow again. Retrospective shock. "I went down . . . firing my machine pistol, killing him."

She fell silent, tears erupting unexpectedly, shamefully. A cascade down her cheeks.

The effect on the peasant was galvanic. He had listened, uncomprehending, but with a growing awareness of her as a person, even as a woman. The tears unstrung him. He was at her side, offering her a sweat-stained rag, dabbing at her cheek apologetically, as if the tears were his responsibility.

Oh, dear God, thought Theresa, I didn't want this! These damned waterworks. What is the matter with me? She had confessed her crime before to herself. Never aloud. Aloud was so much more shattering. Truly words fly upward. The realization brought another flood of tears. With it, an immense relief, a loosening of the chains that had gripped her insides for months.

She leaned against the peasant's shoulder and let herself cry it out. Nothing else to do. She couldn't stop. Anyway, why? The situation had gone beyond the point of no return. Confession, tears, had shifted the emotional balance between herself and the peasant irretrievably.

The air was pregnant with possibilities. Anything,

everything. There was no going back. Though they shared no language, they both understood that.

Presently Theresa's tears dwindled and stopped.

She smiled at him. He all but smiled back. There was a loosening of the taut muscles on the brown face, a look of repose. Not quite a smile. He didn't smile easily. They were both on their knees, almost touching, eyes on each other, surrounded by silence. But it was a comfortable silence, not agonizing.

Theresa wiped her cheeks with the sweat-stained rag and returned it to him. He put it away.

She opened her handbag and took out the loaf of fresh bread she'd bought in Palma. A bit reluctantly because she'd hoped the loaf would last her a week, and she hadn't planned on sharing it.

She broke off a hunk and offered it to him. He didn't take it immediately. Sharing her bread meant complicity. Both of them knew that. The bread lay in her outstretched palm a very long moment while he thought it over.

Finally, he took it and ate. She broke off a piece of fresh bread—suddenly she was famished from her long walk, her struggle, her bout of tears—and she ate eagerly, not looking at him.

That left nothing to say, and no words to say it in. They sat on their knees in the flickering light of the candle.

Now what? thought Theresa. Seduction. I'm ready. Oh, God, I'm much too ready. She'd not had a man in months. She was famished for sex, but she didn't know how to proceed with this man. In her revolutionary circles, sex had been so easy, so casual, so bisexual, so natural that she'd lost the knack to operate in a more inhibited sexual environment.

If I fling myself on him, he'll vanish. So she sat back on her heels and waited, inviting him with her eyes. Discreetly, not shamelessly.

The candle flickered. The silence grew heavy, much too heavy. She began talking again low, musically. "I was born in Philadelphia but I spent most of my girlhood in New York. I went to all the best schools—Miss Chapin's, Bryn Mawr—and I was always at the very top of my class. I had many gifts—in fact, all of them. Brains, money, and looks. Well, not too bad, my looks. I belong to a generation that is in revolt against the richness of its own heritage. Do you understand that? Neither does anyone else—including myself. That is why I have turned to mysticism—since the rational explanations have failed me altogether. I am a victim of my own intellect."

He listened, understanding only the tone of her emotional need. The small chamber was fraught with sexual deprivation, almost embarrassingly so.

Still, nothing happened. She spoke quietly, softly, for almost half an hour, saying things she had not brought out so openly ever, her mind suddenly bursting with coherence she wanted to share with someone—or at least to utter to someone. Utterance itself was tremendously important. The words pulled her mind together.

After half an hour, the thing came to an end. The peasant rose to his feet with an unmistakable air of finality. *"Buena noche,"* he said in the Mallorquin way.

She felt a stab of disappointment between her legs. She lusted for him, surprised by the force of it. Clearly, it wasn't going to happen. Not yet, anyway.

He extended a hand, in itself a very large lowering of the barriers. She took it, not quite knowing where this would lead. He shook it formally, bowing a little from the waist. Unexpectedly he smiled. Not much of a smile and very brief. Nevertheless the relationship changed immeasurably. He turned to go.

"Oh, you'll never find your way out alone!" cried Theresa, deeply touched by the smile. She reached for the flashlight and held it out to him in both hands. He shook his head. "Oh, please, *por favor!* You can give it back in the morning." She put it firmly into his hand, showing him how to turn it on and off. After a moment, he accepted. *"Gracia,"* he grated uneasily. *"Buena noche."*

He left the room swiftly.

Theresa sank to her knees, ruefully. She had not exactly been spurned. Quite the contrary, she felt she'd made quite a lot of headway. But this was not a commune in Idaho with its instantaneous sex. I'm in the thirteenth century, she thought. Courtship moves at a slower pace. Courtship! The very word was unknown to her generation. She had to summon it out of her overeducated past—a vision of medieval knighthood, jousts, gauntlets thrown, all the nonsense and hypocrisy the young had so successfully got rid of.

Well.

She blew out the candle. We mustn't waste candles in the thirteenth century. She lay there feeling sexy as sin. I could masturbate but it's nicer feeling sexy and romantic. There's always tomorrow. After all, he has to return my flashlight.

It had turned quite cold. She burrowed deep into the hay. The peasant could have helped keep her warm, she thought regretfully. She fell asleep.

CHAPTER

14

Elf stared at the blond face in the mirror and gently rubbed foundation cream, which she loathed, into the area on both sides of her nose. Or rather *not* her celebrated nose, another nose. Straight nose. Straight in all the ways. The early-morning scream of New York! She winced. New York screamed in agony almost twenty-four hours a day. And, Christ, wasn't it ugly? Elf—a California girl, accustomed to ocean sounds, eucalyptus smells, California sunshine.

She finished her face and inspected the whole Elf in the full-length mirror. Brown wool skirt. Brown wool jacket. White blouse. She hated every article of the clothes she wore, which is why she wore them. She was passing. *To conquer the art of dissembling*. She stared at her prettied-up self bleakly. I'm unnoticeable. I hate it. I've always hated being unnoticeable.

When had she last been unnoticeable?

Hollywood High. Unnoticed by the boys, the girls,

many of them children of the Hollywood movie crowd, who noticed you only if you were spectacular —and Elf had not then had the gift of being spectacular. Twelve-year-old Elf had been a little brown mouse unnoticed by anyone except Helene—pronounced Elaine as the French do because Helene was French. Motherly, buxom Helene, who taught her French and told her how pretty she was (what a lie!) and took her to her own home and fed her cookies and asked her about her favorite books (the first person ever to show any interest in what she liked and didn't like) and enfolded her in her motherly embrace, which became—after the third visit—something more than motherly.

Dearest Helene! Helene had smiled and smiled into her eyes and lied to her and seduced her at the age of twelve and Elf had never stopped loving her because a girl never stops loving her first seducer even when she hates him—or her. Rarely had Elf been unnoticeable since Helene. She closed the door on her narrow shelf of a room and went down the wide, once beautiful circular staircase in the old brownstone residence. Her room was in what were once the servants' quarters, but the rooms had been subdivided since the old days. Elf had half the space once allotted an upstairs maid. Progress.

At the corner of West 78th Street and Columbus Avenue she bought *The New York Times* and took it and herself to the diner two steps away, where she climbed onto a stool and ordered coffee and a roll. The slim Puerto Rican girl who put it in front of her must be about eighteen, thought Elf, but I

mustn't go thinking thoughts. I'm straight as a bamboo pole. No girls.

She riffled throught the *Times* expertly. No point
in dwelling on page 1. She was long gone from
page 1. Follow-up stories would be deep inside and
very brief—if any at all. But she wasn't simply
looking for that. Reading the straight press was a
sort of punishment, but also part of her cover to
find out what *They* were thinking. What was going
on in the straight mind. Role playing. She forced
herself to read the conventional wisdom on the
Middle East, on the currency crisis, on the Re-
cession, as an enemy absorbed foreign newspapers.
Part of her cover.

Language itself was a problem. Elf hadn't talked
straight language for so long that she had to police
herself sternly—straining the "fuck" and "shit" out
of her talk. Always before she had run straight to
another part of the forest, where like-minded people
of the underground persuasion, who talked as she
talked and thought as she thought, had taken her
in and given her shelter. But she had ruled herself
off that turf altogether by running out on her companions.

Alone in the big city. She stared at page 17 of
The New York Times through slits of eyes, as if
trying to burn a hole through the filthy rag. She
should be unhappy, despairing. She wasn't. Numb
was the word. Lately even the numbness had begun
to disappear, burned off by her own intelligence.
That's all she had left. Her intelligence. Number two
at Berkeley, she had been—or would have been.

Number two in her class if they still kept count, which they didn't—and one of the reasons they didn't was students like herself screaming down the elitist walls.

Too intelligent for her own good, her famous foster mother had said of her when she was eleven years old. Dear Mama! Bitch goddess of the silver screen. She had beaten Elf black and blue for her intelligence. No one loves a smartass, Mama had said while wielding the dog leash. Elf's eyes glittered, recollecting.

On page 28 of the *Times* the headline struck her like a body blow, driving Mama clear out of her head:

COLT CHARGES FBI WITH VIOLATING
BANK SECRECY LAWS

John Colt, father of Geraldine Colt, the Black Torrent militant who has been missing for six years, filed suit in Federal Court yesterday for a restraining order to prevent the FBI from gaining access to the administration of a trust fund in which Miss Colt is legatee.

Mr. Colt charged that the ultimate beneficiaries of the trust were Miss Colt's unborn children, and that the FBI under law could set aside the Bank Secrecy Law only when they had reason to believe they protected a fugitive from justice. Clearly unborn children could not be fugitives from justice.

U.S. Assistant Attorney Geohagan, on behalf of the FBI, said that Colt's argument was legal semantics, that the true beneficiary of the trust was Geraldine Colt, who is wanted for the murder of Richard Gabin, a bank guard killed in a 1972 bank robbery. Geohagan accused Colt of engaging in delaying tactics, which amounted to little more than legal harassment of the

FBI and came dangerously close to obstruction of justice.

The trust fund that is being argued over was left by Geraldine's grandmother and terminates by law in the next generation. It is administered by the Massachusetts Trust, of Wall Street, under the personal supervision of Denis Mitchell, who the FBI claims is refusing to cooperate.

Federal Judge O'Halloran adjourned the hearing until next Tuesday, over the strong protests of the U.S. Assistant Attorney.

Blessings on you, John Colt. Stone-faced, Elf cut out the news item with the nail scissors she always carried in her handbag, the same ones she'd used on a pig in a Berkeley dustup, sending him to the hospital for two months for major facial surgery. She paid for her coffee with a dollar bill, one of the dwindling hoard of pre-Euclid dollars she had. She'd not spent any of the $7,346 from the bank job because she didn't know how hot the money was. She didn't want anyone looking for her in New York. Not yet.

Denis Mitchell, thought Elf. Denis Mitchell. She caught the crosstown bus for Fifth and took the Fifth Avenue bus to the main library at 42nd Street, which had the most marvelous books in the world on Elf's specialty. At the library she went under her new name, Estelle Parsons. You couldn't get a straighter name than Estelle Parsons. She'd bought Estelle's identity papers in Denver from the underground paper *Scream* for twenty dollars.

In the main reading room, she asked again for Vinogradoff's *Tacticatus*, the most thoroughgoing history of terror tactics in the world. If I were not an urban guerrilla, I would have been a scholar and maybe one day will be one, thought Elf, waiting for the book to be delivered. She loved the huge quiet room, loved burrowing through little-known volumes—no one she was sure had asked for Vinogradoff's book in a hundred years—loved knowing more than anyone else on earth on her chosen subject. Still a smartass, Mama, she thought, eyes glittering. Even the dear sisters at the Convent of the Blessed Virgin had beaten her regularly for asking intelligent questions, especially ones about the Virgin's virginity. She'd paid dearly for intelligence all her life.

Tacticatus arrived and Elf opened it where she had left off—page 277. Chinese persuasion tricks of monstrous subtlety and simplicity from the ninth century B.C. It was very detailed stuff—the exact position of organs and muscles—meant entirely as a manual for practitioners, not simply a record for historians. Elf couldn't imagine doing any of these things. She was not a torturer. Still, she stored it away, her quick mind chewing it up, devouring it. I'm starved, thought Elf. Months on the run with that moron Bandit. My goddamned brain has turned into a marsh.

CHAPTER

15

Hawkins signed the take-out forms and took the thick dusty envelope to an empty table in the *Times* library. Strickland was in the dead file and it took a bit of persuasion to get him exhumed. Hawkins used charm as well as his badge. He had no clear right to the *Times* files, but sometimes simple courtesy performed where court orders didn't. It was a trying time for the FBI. They had been feared like the Devil himself. They had then been hated. They were now going through a period of open derision.

Two years earlier no lawyer would have dared attempt a restraining order on the FBI on such flimsy grounds as John Colt's. But now? The Supreme Court did indeed follow the election returns, thought Hawkins grimly. Judges could interpret law any way they liked, and they followed the fluctuations of public taste far more than they ever admitted. Hawkins had time to kill until the judge made up his mind about the Colt suit and this was why he was in the *Times* library. Theoretically, the FBI file on the Strickland killing in Oakland would have everything the *Times* had—and a good deal that it didn't have. Practically, it didn't work out that way.

Frequently, Hawkins had found, newspaper files provided a fresh point of view, if only by arranging material in a fresh way—without the built-in bias of the law officer. And what was the built-in bias of the law officer? asked Hawkins of himself, meanwhile pouring the clippings out of the envelope onto the table in the quiet recesses of the *Times* morgue, arranging them in neat stacks. Simply that everyone was either guilty—or that they were innocent. After thirty years in law enforcement, Hawkins felt nothing was that simple or that black and white.

Guilty of what? Squeezing a finger? But who squeezed first? That was the nub of the Strickland case. The police had surrounded the house in Oakland, and had notified the FBI, as they had to do because Strickland was wanted on a great many federal counts—from bank robbery to arson. The FBI had got there late, and beyond that, few facts resisted challenge.

It had been an epic gun battle—and that was the trouble. An enormous amount of gunfire had torn the front door almost apart—as well as the rear door and several windows. This made reconstruction difficult. Colt, who had taken over the Black Torrent defense, argued that the police had opened fire because the door clearly showed most of the bullets going *in*, not out. In fact, there were precious few clearly outgoing bullets. Colt claimed there were none at all. But that didn't mean much because the door was such a mess before forensic people got to it that it was difficult to tell. Hawkins was skeptical about forensic in cases like that. Forensic people had been trained to make flat statements—such and such was. A .32-caliber bullet fired at a forty-two-degree angle from this gun and no other. They had to sound like that or the defense would tear them to ribbons. The trouble was one forensic expert would contradict another—both of them absolutely positive. So where was guilt or innocence?

Hawkins read the clippings slowly, starting with the original terribly garbled story, in which it was reported that as many as twelve people might have been killed, one of them Geraldine.

"A gun battle between police and FBI and Black Torrent militants holed up in a wooden frame house in a black section of Oakland raged until the early hours this morning. According to fragmentary reports, twelve persons, including three police, were killed in the battle."

That meant the battle had still been going on when *The Times* had gone to press and no reporter had got anywhere near it.

When the smoke cleared, there was only one dead—Quentin Strickland—and there were three wounded police officers. But then the fog closed in. Rumors were rife that the police had wounded each other in the shooting, and the militant cry arose that the police had done *all* the firing from beginning to end. Strickland had been found dead in bed with a lone bullet in his heart—and no one had ever found the gun that it had been fired from. But then there had been an awful lot of guns there— police, FBI, and—in theory—eight other Black Torrent militants. One of them Saint Theresa. Where were they?

Colt had argued in a press conference in Oakland that no one had been in the frame house except Strickland, and that evidence suggested the police burst in firing and killed Strickland in bed. That was nonsense since Strickland was not one to lie in bed while gunfire roared. His gun had been found emptied. Also, if the police had closed in firing, the body would have been riddled. It wasn't. Only one bullet in the heart—.38 caliber.

Had Theresa been there? Or the other Black Torrent militants? If so, how had they got out of a surrounded house? Hawkins read clipping after clipping, alleging police, to say nothing of FBI, incompetence of a high order. It had been a dark night. That part of Oakland was a black jungle, in which neither police nor FBI got any cooperation or even any answers. It would have been simple enough for the black militants to melt into the neighborhood—if they could get out of a house on which searchlights played. How did they do that? But then the searchlights weren't brought up until early in the morning. Even if the blacks could melt away, a white girl like Theresa couldn't. Could she?

"One witness, Jessica Flame, who lived in the adjoining house, spent three hours pressed to the floor in her kitchen while the guns roared around her. Her window was scarcely twenty feet from the living-room window of the Black Torrent headquarters."

This paragraph buried deep on page 32 of a color story, just one of eight separate news stories the *Times* had on the shooting two days later, was news to Hawkins. Jessica Flame was a name he'd never heard before, and he had a hunch it wasn't one of the 132 witnesses in FBI files. If only because it was such a . . . musical one. Jessica Flame. No, he'd have remembered Jessica Flame. He made a note.

Twenty feet, eh? Hawkins had no idea the next house was so close.

Late that afternoon, he called the field officer in San Francisco and sent him on an errand to Oakland.

BUSINESS REPLY MAIL

No postage necessary if mailed in the United States

POSTAGE WILL BE PAID BY

boston

1050 Park Square Bldg.
Boston, MA 02116

FIRST CLASS
Permit No. 2426
Boston, Mass.

Get Ahead!
1. Get Boston—
the magazine that keeps you on top of all that's going on around these parts

2. Get a bargain.
*40% off regular subscription rate.

6 months of BOSTON for only $3.
(This is an introductory offer for new subscribers only)

Name _____

Address _____

City _____ State _____ Zip Code _____

4LNB

CHAPTER

16

Theresa awoke, the sun glinting through the stone bars of the lookout room. That meant it was late—10 A.M. at least, much later than she usually awoke. She stretched her arms over her head and yawned luxuriously. For the first morning in months there was no knot of fear tightening her stomach muscles.

I am whole again, a living organism, feeling hunger like any other. Fear enslaves me. Still she missed it. Fear is part of my infrastructure, as instinct is to an animal. Without fear I am driven back to thinking every step. I am accustomed to living in fear. Without fear I become someone quite different.

She rose and threw cold water on her face. The peasant swam back into her thoughts. As mysterious as a forest beast with his silences, his closed gaze. I suppose I'm as strange to him.

She made her way to the audience chamber, skipping up through the black staircase with the expertise of long practice. In the audience chamber, she gave way to her lightfooted mood and danced a Martha Graham routine. Not strenuous enough, she thought, and went into a wilder dance from her teenage past, leaping from one end of the great room to the other, breathless and dizzy with rapture.

I am a slave girl! Or princess! One thing or the other!

Elf knelt before her, arms tied behind her back. Head on the block. Theresa swung the great scimitar high over her head, smiling with infinite tenderness, and severed Elf's head from her shoulders with a single swish of the blade. The head rolled skipping across the stone floor like a basketball. The blood flowed from the gaping hole, black as the inside of Lucifer's heart.

Theresa stood erect, vengeful, breathing hard. King Rama slew a man with a stroke of his sword for breaking the law by becoming religious. Immediately the soul of the man appeared at his feet, thanking him for the glory of restoring him to God. I'm doing you a kindness, Elf.

But Elf would never appreciate kindness of that sort. Not Elf.

I'm hungry.

She sped across the audience chamber through six bedrooms to the crazy staircase. Down that akimbo stone she danced a Russian peasant dance.

The mule was gone.

Theresa collected two eggs from the chicken nests, filled her new metal pot with cold water from the well, and retraced her steps to the bedroom she'd selected. The chimney to this bedroom was hidden behind a wing of the building. No telltale smoke, showing off her hiding place to the whole valley.

Theresa put her little Woolworth pot on the iron grill across the stone embrasure. She lit a fire of eucalyptus wood, which hissed like a gas torch. On it she boiled her eggs. She ate them with a little bit of bread—a proper feast.

She knelt before the fire, her eyes huge. I have never actually believed in life after death. In fact, not thought about it at all. Still, that man beheaded by Rama was quite right. That was the moment of ultimate glory—the tiny instant of death. The moment of restoration to original beginnings—to the beauty of the world.

She rose and fetched a big iron pot she'd found in one of the great rooms, filled it with water, and placed it on the grill. Intelligence is a very great burden for one in my vocation. The unintelligent can forgive. Forgiveness is easy. The intelligent must understand and that's not easy. So many enormities. From the Inquisition to those Protestants and Catholics killing one another for the love of God in Belfast. Must I forgive them all? And understand them all as well? Yes, I must.

She stripped herself naked and shampooed her hair in the pot. With the soapy water left from her shampoo she sponged herself from head to foot. I should have bought a towel. Never mind. There was lots of hot sun all the way from *le Bon Dieu* Himself.

Carrying her new denim workman's shirt and

trousers in her hand, she walked, stark naked, back
to the audience chamber and sat on one of the stone
windowsills in the blazing sunshine, wringing out
her hair.

And who is to forgive me? And understand me?

No, not God. God has other things on his mind.
What insufferable ego-tripping to think God was
absorbed in one's tiny transgressions. Salvation was
a personal matter. The priest wouldn't agree. But
then she had little patience with priests. Idiots, most
of them.

She slipped into her new denims and felt reborn.
Theresa, girl peasant. Sing ho for the simple life.
A laborer, me, in pursuit of my labor, the world
newly washed. She set forth barefoot, through the
Moorish arch, in pursuit of the shepherd. She had
a pretty good idea where he was.

"It's like it's some kind of joke," the field officer
in San Francisco was saying to Hawkins across
three thousand miles of telephone wire. "They don't
exactly laugh in your face but you can hear the
laughter loud and clear, while they're looking at
you with a straight face. It's a kind of inside joke,
that name—Jessica Flame."

Very funny, thought Hawkins. But then the FBI
had never yet got a straight answer out of that black
Oakland ghetto. Just jokes. Some pretty good ones.

"Who's in that house now?"

"Nobody. Not now and not two years ago either.
Certainly no Jessica Flame. You think the *Times*
made up Jessica Flame?"

No, thought Hawkins but kept it to himself. "What about the other house where all the shooting took place?"

"Worse than empty. It's dead. It's spooked. That's what the kids tell me. Nobody would rent it in a thousand years. It's got bad luck written on it in letters eight feet high. The kids don't even dare go in it—though when I was a kid an empty house like that was an open invitation."

"Did you go in?"

"All through it. Top to bottom."

"Has it got a cellar?"

"No." But there was a perceptible pause from the other end. As if he weren't all that sure of his ground.

"Mr. Cooke," said Hawkins, "could you see your way clear to going back and tearing up the floor in the living-room?"

Long pause over three thousand miles of wire. "It will take some authorization."

"Get it," said Hawkins politely. And hung up.

Jessica Flame, thought Hawkins, has a musical name. Whoever thought up that name had a feeling for irony and for words. A poet perhaps.

I have foundered in my own ideology. I am at sea. I am adrift. All this clacked away at Elf's mind as the subway screamed at her consciousness. Paranoia, thought Elf. It's the noise does it. I'm a California girl used to the roar of the Pacific Ocean. This scream of metal against metal strikes at the very brain pan. I'm losing my purpose.

All the while hanging from the strap, trying to

settle into her new identity. She'd been shopping in Bonwit's and was looking very smart in a beige coat and handbag and slippers. Beige was the color of the middle class and she had selected it because she loathed it worse than any color she could think of. If she hated it that much, it must be exactly right.

She came out of the hole in the ground into the financial ant heap. The very heart of the capitalist beast, thought Elf, her pulses quickening with the joy of hatred. Her eyes gleamed, her mouth parted as she breasted the maelstrom of pedestrians on the crowded sidewalk. Wall Street! To a Marcuse-trained radical from the Little Red Schoolhouse of Berkeley it was as legendary as Valhalla. Elf half expected it to be bathed in red mist like a surrealist dream.

Forty-four Wall Street proved to be an enormous citadel of money, rising a thousand feet into the unknown—and the very sight of it jarred Elf. Am I out of my depth? No, I'm not. There is nothing beyond my depth. Not any more. She plunged through the glass revolving doors and marched up to the roster of 44 Wall Street's inhabitants, framed in glass and mounted on bronze like a pantheon of capitalist deities—fiduciary trusts, merchant banks, insurance companies, investment firms—all the panoply and power of capitalism was arrayed there in brass lettering. The Massachusetts Trust was on the thirty-seventh floor.

"I wish to speak to Mr. Denis Mitchell," said Elf.

The reception room of the Massachusetts Trust was paneled in golden oak from floor to ceiling, carpeted wall to wall in brown wool, and hung with perfectly awful paintings of Salem fishing boats. It was monstrously quiet.

"Have you an appointment?"

"No, I haven't," said Elf faintly, playing the little rich girl lost in the big city. "I'm from California. Mrs. Wharton told me to go to the Massachusetts Trust with my problem. Mrs. Oscar P. Wharton." Oscar P. Wharton has immense California wealth. A name to conjure with.

"Mr. Mitchell never sees anyone without an appointment," said the receptionist, a gray-haired lady. But already she was picking up her telephone. "Still, if you've come all this way . . ." She smiled at this demure young person, who'd clearly been to the right schools, the ultimate password to inner sanctums anywhere in Wall Street. "There's a Miss Glee here to see Mr. Mitchell. She hasn't an appointment. She says a Mrs. Wharton sent her. From California. Mrs. Oscar P. Wharton."

Silence. What can they do but say No? thought Elf. They can't arrest you for asking to see someone. Still, it was an awful silence, a threat of disaster. I'm losing my cool. After four bank busts, this shouldn't bother me so much. It's because I'm alone. I've never operated alone before.

"Mr. Mitchell will see you in a moment. If you'd just care to wait. . . ."

CHAPTER

17

Hawkins was on the phone to Washington talking to Rodgers. The air crackled with hostility.

"Where was Elf James on the night of October 23, 1972?" Hawkins asked abruptly. No point in pussyfooting around.

Long silence. "Why do you want to know?"

No question at all to ask a fellow agent. Things had got very bad between Joe Rodgers and Hawkins lately. All my fault, thought Hawkins.

"It's important," said Hawkins. No answer to a non-question.

"John, Elf is my girl. Saint Theresa is your girl. If you have any fresh leads on Elf I wish you'd hand them over."

"I haven't," said Hawkins patiently. "I have only a theory—which you'd laugh at. Was Elf in California in '72?"

Another long pause, which was costing the taxpayers money. "Elf was nineteen then," said Rodgers finally, reluctantly. "Still at the Berkeley campus. Very active in all the movements."

"Thanks," blurted Hawkins, fearful Rodgers might hang up. "What was Elf's favorite weaponry?"

Rodgers laughed harshly. "Everything—from pump shotguns to .45s—and she's very good with knives. So don't mess with her. Call a qualified FBI officer, Philosopher."

Hawkins ignored the jeer and pressed forward.

"Did she ever use a .38?"

"She shot a bank guard with a .38 in that San Diego bank job. Why do you want to know?"

Hawkins grimaced. "I'm trying to clarify a line of inquiry." The kind of non-reply FBI agents gave to civilians, not to each other. It wouldn't help relations between himself and Rodgers.

Rodgers hung up angrily.

Hawkins went back to the *Times* morgue and got out the file on Elf James. It bulged with feature stories from Hollywood. Elf had after all been the adopted child of that dazzling film star of the 1930s —and 1940s and 1950s and even 1960s—Clarissa Venable. Clarissa loved children—or said she did. In spite of her five marriages she'd never had any of her own. She'd adopted six, one of them Elf.

Hawkins flipped through the clippings rapidly, looking for he knew not what. Whatever it was he didn't find it.

He asked the library attendant for the file on Clarissa Venable. For two hours he read about that glittering lady.

Late that afternoon he was in the dressing room

of Christopher Fort, former leading man of the films, now playing second leads off Broadway. One of Clarissa's ex-husbands.

"Love children!" rasped Christopher in a professional snarl of a voice. "Clarissa never loved anything except Clarissa. The children were the idea of her press agent. She adopted six at once, you know. One adopted child would have gone unnoticed. They all had adopted kids out there. But six hit the front page."

Christopher Fort penciled a bold black eyebrow where there had been only a white uncertain wisp of hair before, changing his personality altogether. "Clarissa and I were divorced by then. Still the word got around Hollywood. She treated them worse than her husbands and believe me that would be very bad indeed. Chained them to their beds, according to one of the stories."

"And Elf?"

"Oh, Elf was the ringleader. They all hated Mama —but Elf hated her worst and led the others. She was cheerleader you might say, in hating their dear foster mother." Christopher stared at his own face fondly, and added a stroke of character to his nose. "She took Elf back to the orphanage twice, you know."

"No, I didn't know," said Hawkins.

"Oh, yes. The second time was to be permanent. But that bitch Joanna Selwyn—you know who she is, of course."

"Of course." Joanna Selwyn had been a Hearst columnist of enormous power and influence with, according to her own estimate, fifty million readers.

"Joanna cottoned onto the story somehow and she called up Clarissa and said she was going to break the story to her zillion readers that, far from loving children, she hated them—unless Clarissa took back Elf. So Clarissa had to get her back from the orphanage and keep her until she grew up. Elf took off of her own accord when she was sixteen."

Oh, dear God, thought Hawkins. Now I'm going to get emotionally involved with Elf, too. Aloud he asked, "That name Elf . . . where . . ."

"Yeah, that's a laugh, isn't it? The press agent thought that up too. They all had sweet names like that—Elf, Gruntle, Twerp, Twinkle, like that."

Christopher Fort tore himself reluctantly from the contemplation of his own ruined façade and faced Hawkins. "The funny thing to me is that Elf has hung on to that name, unsuitable as it is. She rapidly got rid of the Venable. I think she took the name of James after Jesse James but she's always called herself Elf. Odd, isn't it?"

"Very," said Hawkins.

Elf smiled tremulously, sizing up the trust officer. He could be tough. Those stringy New England beanpoles sometimes were.

"We have never handled the Wharton estate," said Denis Mitchell neutrally. Nobody could be as neutral as Denis Mitchell. His voice faded into the woodwork.

"Mrs. Wharton knew I was moving east," said Elf timidly "and that I was dissatisfied with the

Avon Trust, which has been handling my money
since my mother died. So she suggested you . . ."
She let her voice fade out. Looking out from under
her lashes to case the joint. Where in hell would
he keep the information? Nothing so mundane as
a filing cabinet disgraced Mr. Mitchell's office, which
was solid rosewood and mahogany festooned with
pictures of sailing ships. On the desk were pictures
of the children—but wouldn't they be all grown
up with homes of their own now?

"I don't believe I know the Avon Trust," murmured Mr. Mitchell. "Pardon me a moment. I'll just
have a look." He left her and passed into the little
sanctuary at the rear of his office where Elf caught
the gleam of books. Checking up on the Avon Trust.
Well, he'd find it all right. Elf was not such a fool
as to give him a phony name. He couldn't very
well call and check up on her because it was only
7 A.M. California time and they wouldn't be open.
Elf had seen to that.

Elf leaned over the man's desk as much as she
dared, eyes darting. She'd been through the phone
book and there was no Denis Mitchell. Private
number, probably. To keep from being annoyed
by millionaires wishing him to harbor their money.
He'd even kept his address out of the *Social Register*,
which Elf had consulted at the public library. The
Register had revealed he was a widower.

She straightened up in the nick of time as he
came back into the room.

"Well—uh—yes," said Mr. Mitchell, subsiding
into his chair, neutral as always. "The Avon Trust

is one of the smaller California investment trusts, but it seems to me to have a fairly solid reputation, Miss—uh—Glee. In any case changing from one trust to another is very difficult business—and sometimes impossible, depending on the provisions of the will. I would have to see that before we could . . ."

"Oh, gosh," murmured Elf, stricken. "I should have brought it! I *knew* I should have brought it!" She rose, looking forlorn. "I'll have to go get it and bring it." She sighed a heartfelt sigh. "I do *hate* that subway ride."

"If you'd just put it in the mail . . ."

"Oh, I'd never trust it to the mail! Mummy's *will* . . ."

Mr. Mitchell was deeply sympathetic. Wills, he felt, should be treated like holy scripture. The sympathy remained buried in the depths of him. He was not one for flaunting sympathy.

"If I might just drop it off at your apartment," said Elf tremulously. "It would save me that long, long subway ride."

Mr. Mitchell pursed his lips, and grew even more silent than was his wont, which was silent enough. He hated to reveal his home address. He was a very private person.

Elf threw everything into her pleading glance. Her mouth formed a little O of longing. The silence grew rich with embarrassment.

It was no good.

New England reticence won out. The thin wire of a man simply outwaited her until Elf gave way, boiling inside. "All right then," she whispered. "I'll bring Mummy's will. Tomorrow."

She couldn't provoke him too far. He might make a phone call to California and that would never do. She smiled her tremulous smile. He unbent his thin lips in what he thought was a smile.

Really tough, thought Elf. Just you wait. Just you wait. It inflamed her—this test of wills—stimulated her. Just you wait.

It was a long, cold wait but then Elf was used to long waits—outside banks; National Guard armories, where they had stolen weapons; police stations, where they learned the habits of the fuzz. She was a jungle cat, waiting in the underbrush. For hours.

If he has a limousine, I'm lost, she thought. But I bet he doesn't. Those New England beanpoles are too tight for limousines.

At 5:05 P.M. Mitchell emerged from the revolving door at 44 Wall Street, just one of thousands, hurrying home from the great vault of Wall Street, where little by little all the world's money was being stored.

Mitchell walked stonily to the Lexington Avenue subway, oblivious of the jungle cat in his wake. It was almost too easy a tail. The sidewalks of Wall Street swarmed with capitalists on their way home, concealing one small revolutionary in their midst.

The crowd on the subway platform was so dense that Elf ventured to within twenty feet of her prey, whose gray eyes were glazed with indifference. She even pressed into the same subway car, not ordi-

narily sound surveillance, but in this crush almost
a necessity.

He got off at 59th Street underneath Blooming-
dale's and walked west to Park Avenue. Here Elf
fell well behind, half a block to the rear. Denis
Mitchell separated from his fellow capitalists at
715 Park Avenue.

Seven fifteen Park Avenue. Excellent address.

Hawkins was already in bed in his hotel room
when the call came through at eleven P.M.—eight
o'clock California time.

"We struck oil," said Cooke jubilantly. *We*,
thought Hawkins. "There's not a cellar or we would
have seen the door down to it long ago. But there
is a tunnel between the two houses. That makes
it a whole new ball game. They could all have
gotten out by that tunnel—and just lain low in the
tunnel until the following night. By that time, there
was nobody but one patrolman left at the scene—
and he stayed in the other house where Strickland
was found." There was a longish pause. "Are you
there, Mr. Hawkins?"

"How in hell did you deduce a tunnel, all the way
from Washington?"

"I've been doing some reading," said Hawkins
apologetically. Tunnels were in lots of the underground manuals, especially Thibaut's book on *Flight
and Concealment*.

"Mr. Cooke," said Hawkins politely. "Do you
think you might see your way clear to finding out

who rented that house two years ago—or who rents it now?"

"I've already done that," said Cooke. "But it's just names—black names that are probably phony. The other house where Jessica Flame said she was lying crouched down for three hours and all that, that house was rented to a black girl named—if you'll believe it and I don't—Hortense Frolic."

"Was it rented about the same time as the other house?"

"Same day. I see you and I are on the same wavelength. Both houses were cover houses for the Black Torrent. Where did they get the money for all that real estate?"

"Bank robbery," said Hawkins.

"Anyhow, these people have never been seen again—since the shooting. This is not unknown in that area. Tenants just slip away in the night, so it wasn't considered noteworthy. Strickland caught a stray bullet—and that was the end of Black Torrent. They just slipped out and left him there."

Not necessarily, thought Hawkins. He might have been killed somewhere else and brought back through that tunnel and laid to rest there. For a long time he'd thought that there was something fishy about finding Strickland dead in bed. It was out of character.

CHAPTER

18

Theresa found the peasant irrigating lettuce in a field shaded by orange trees, sensibly protecting it from the full glare of Majorca sunshine. The stream of water came from a stone catchment that looked as old as Majorca and was covered with slime as green as emeralds. A thin rivulet of water ran from the catchment down a long line of lettuce plants, the water sinking slowly into the soil as it reached the end of the row.

The shepherd crouched next to the lettuce and directed the stream of water by making little channels in the soft earth with his hands. When a line of lettuce had had enough water, he simply pushed a tiny dam of earth in front of that channel and, with his hands, made a new channel to the next line of lettuce plants. It was agriculture as old as civilization. Theresa was touched by the smallness of scale. Even on the communes where she'd worked the fields they'd used plows, hoes. Hands were better.

She didn't dare interrupt, even with *Buena día.*
Instead she sat on the stone catchment and watched
the scene as if she were witnessing the Middle Ages.
Love of the beauty of the world, she thought, had
been the wellspring of all civilizations and of all
philosophies—Greek, Chinese, Mesopotamian, Egyp-
tian—until our very own, when the preoccupation
was wholly with the ugliness of life. Why? It takes
enormous intellectual honesty even to ask this question in the climate of anarchy in which we live. The
beauty of the world is finality. It demands no bloodshed. It is purpose incarnate all by itself. I am ac-
complishing my purpose simply by sitting here
breathing—and how many in the world have ever
had a single moment of such accomplishment?

"Buena día."

It startled her. The shepherd had looked up from
his lettuce and said hello.

"Buena día," said Theresa, thrilled that he'd
acknowledged her existence.

His gaze had returned to the water flow now.
How long could he crouch like that over a thin
rivulet of water? All morning, probably. Different
time scale from a city girl, thought Theresa.

The mule was grazing in the next field and Theresa went to him, stroking him and kissing his
velvety muzzle. Then she lay in the thin grass of
the Majorca meadow and felt the sun on her and
thought about her position. I have fled the world.
Now what? I cannot do nothing. I am not made
that way. I am content but I am not content with

my contentment. Anyway, it can't last because nothing does.

An hour later, the peasant had done with his lettuce. She watched him as he rose and went to the high-wheeled cart. He plucked a worn leather pouch from the cart and brought it to her. Out of it came bread and a thick slab of ham, smoked almost black. He cut a chunk from the ham with his knife, sliced off a bit of bread, and handed them to her.

"*Para usted,*" he said.

Well, thought Theresa. He's broken bread with me. Now I'm breaking bread with him. We're getting on.

They ate together, sitting shoulder to shoulder in the grass in the hot sun. He offered her more ham and this time she cut it off herself. She shook her head when he offered her a raw onion. The ham was the strongest and sharpest she'd ever tasted. They drank Majorca's bitter purple wine from a stone jug. All this time saying nothing. What was there that needed saying? thought Theresa. But when do we make love?

Not yet apparently.

After lunch he tugged at her sleeve and led her by the arm almost reverently to the high-wheeled cart, where he indicated that she mount to the driver's seat. He hitched up the mule and handed her the reins. Good heavens, am I expected to drive? She clucked. The mule did nothing at all, whereupon the peasant took his head and led him, Theresa sitting in the driver's seat, the reins in her hand. After a bit the peasant let the mule loose and Theresa drove the cart.

The peasant directed her to the orange grove, where Theresa had been stealing her oranges. Here the peasant climbed up on the cart and began picking oranges from the trees, placing them gently on the floor of the cart so as not to bruise the skins. After a bit Theresa started plucking the oranges too, the two of them working side by side.

It was endless labor, endless monotony. Nobody will ever understand eternity until he suffers monotony, thought Theresa, plucking one monotonous orange after another.

CHAPTER

19

Two A.M. Elf walked from her pad to the subway station at 79th Street, keeping close to the gutter, eyes on the store-front doorways where the muggers lurked, enjoying herself. Why am I frightened in a banker's office and in my element on the most dangerous streets in the world at the most dangerous hour? I am a child of my time. Danger is my element as water is to fishes. She wore sneakers so that any footfall she heard would be someone else's. She kept her sensitive ears turned up to peak attention and the eyes never stopped darting, inspecting every shadow. The March air was bitter and Elf was huddled in her mackinaw, the switchblade in her right hand in her pocket.

She didn't see a soul, not a mugger, not a cop, not a drunk. The noise of the city was muted, distant but still there. But that area of upper Broadway was sound asleep. Still, she trod warily descending into the subway. At the bottom of the steps, she leaned her vulnerable back against a wall and

listened and looked awhile. Very quiet. She fed
a token into the turnstile and sped down the stairway. At the bottom she listened and looked again.
Aah.

The middle steel girder, where the battered candy
vending machine afforded a kind of cover. Where
was the other one? They usually operated in pairs.
There wasn't another soul on the platform. Elf spun
noiselessly to be sure one wasn't coming down the
stairs. She walked noiselessly down the center of
the platform, eyes fixed on that girder—but not
missing any other girders. The knife was open and
in her hand, pressed against the seam of her jeans.

She walked straight past the candy vending machine, turned swiftly, and her arm came up—all
one movement, aiming at the chest. Thrust—and
out, because if there were two, she needed the
knife free. The mugger fell, soundless, like a bundle
of sticks—and almost as thin—at her feet. The other
one squirted out from the other side of the candy
vending machine, thin as a whisper, and ran like
a deer up the staircase.

Elf let her go, flummoxed.

Girls! She didn't enjoy killing girls. In fact, she'd
never killed one before.

The patter of feet, like the beating of wings, of
the other girl dissipated up the stairs and out onto
Broadway. Elf shrugged. It didn't matter. A mugger
would hardly go screaming to the police. The subway platform was totally quiet now. Elf leaned
over the body. A skinny black girl. They were the
most dangerous ones now. Skinny black girls. This

one was maybe fifteen. Eyes open and staring. Looked like she hadn't eaten in years. Elf grimaced. You and I should be on the same side. I could have used you in Euclid.

She picked up the body, weighing eighty pounds at most, and placed it on the bench, arranging it in a sitting position. She closed the dead girl's eyes, wiped her knife clean on the under side of the girl's canvas jacket, and sat down next to her on the bench. The dead one now looked just like a skinny black girl on the nod. Manhattan was full of them.

It was a long wait between subway trains at 2 A.M. New York City was broke. It couldn't afford to go picking up drunks and muggers and murderers at 2 A.M. as frequently as it once had. Elf sat quietly next to the girl she'd killed, listening to the quiet. Quiet as a tomb, the subway at 2 A.M., just as it was the noisiest in the daytime. Not a single soul on either platform. Elf looked at her watch: 2:10 A.M. Only ten minutes had passed since she had left her apartment. One dead.

She let her gaze roam over the ebony skin on the emaciated face of the dead girl. The face reminded her strongly of a rag doll she'd had when she was four or five years old. Skinny as a stick that rag doll had been, and fiercely loved. Elf smiled wryly a seldom smile. Always she liked them emaciated. Theresa, who was just skin and bones. She felt a sudden hot desire to take this black figure in her arms. Am I getting lecherous over a dead girl? There's a word for that. Necrophilia. What is adorable in the child is unnatural in the grownup. Why am I thinking crazy thoughts like these? Because I'm alone and because I'm too intelligent. Intelligence is a terrible thing to be alone with. It would be better to be stupid.

No, it wouldn't. Elf knew she would hate being stupid. Still, where had all the intelligence got her? To a subway station at two-ten in the morning with a dead black girl. So much education, so much self-denial, so much brilliance—for this!

The subway train came in with a roar ten minutes later—a long ten minutes. Elf stepped into the south-bound subway almost reluctantly. As the train pulled out of the station, her gaze was fixed on the skinny black girl. Corpse, she thought. Not a doll. Wake up, Elf, to reality, as dear Mama used to say.

The telephone call had left Hawkins sleepless. He was propped up in bed, hunched over like a question mark, reading Dietrich Bonhoeffer: "The great masquerade of evil has played havoc with all our ethical concepts. For evil to appear disguised as light, charity, historical necessity or social justice is quite bewildering to anyone brought up on our traditional ethical concepts, while for the Christian who bases his life on the Bible it merely confirms the fundamental wickedness of evil."

Hawkins wondered if anyone else in the FBI ever read Bonhoeffer or had even heard of the great theologian. They should. Law was, after all, only an offshoot of theology. We are in an ethical revolution whose consequences stretch beyond the life span of any of us, he was thinking. People killed as a matter of high principle these days and robbed, not for profit, but as a protest *against* profit. Yet the forces of law operated as if nothing had changed.

He read on at 2:30 A.M. because the judge would not hand down his decision until 3 o'clock the following afternoon and he had lots of time to sleep late.

In Majorca, Theresa awoke, the moon shining down on her through the stone bars of her lookout room, every muscle aching from the labor in the orange grove. What time was it? Two A.M. she guessed. I'm awake because I went to bed too early. The peasant had brought her back to the *palacio* when he brought the mule back. She had wanted to go with him to his own house—wherever that was—but he had said *buena noche*. Very courteous. Very kind. Very final. Then he'd walked out of her life, at least for the time being, Theresa watching ruefully. Courtship was very slow indeed in the Middle Ages.

Now here she was, wide awake at 2 A.M. She rose from the hay bed and made her way up to the audience chamber, where she sat on a stone embrasure, staring out at the moonlit valley. I feel timeless, she thought, untouched by yesterday's guilt and tomorrow's hope.

She rolled a cigarette of catalpa leaf and smoked it, inhaling deeply. It gave her not much of a high but enough for her exalted state. I'm no longer alone. I have my God and my peasant. It won't last because it never does.

CHAPTER

20

It was a plate-glass door covered with scrolls of black ironwork, and Elf worked quickly because Park Avenue was patrolled by police cars—and there was nothing on earth so suspicious as a girl in jeans on Park Avenue at 3:30 A.M. It was tough glass but glass cutting was her specialty. One of her specialties. Elf had many. She was through in about ten minutes, and she reached in delicately and unlocked the heavy door from the inside. There would be a night doorman but they slept soundest at 3:30 A.M. If this one had wakened, Elf would have killed him. Fortunately for him, he slept.

She found him in his little cell under the stairs, in a chair, head back, snoring. Over him was a nest of pigeonholes for the letters. Elf scanned the names. Mitchell—3B. She used the stairs because she didn't want the sound of the elevator to echo throughout the house. It was an old-fashioned building with wide stairways and wide corridors. Big apartments, much bigger than they made them now. The locks had been stout when the building went up. They were childishly simple now. Elf opened it with a sheet of plastic in under a minute and stepped into the dark hall.

Very quiet. She lit a pencil flashlight and methodically explored the place. He was a widower and the children had moved away. But were there sleep-in servants? Elf searched the flat from end to end, quietly. No servants and not even a servant room, so one wouldn't be walking in on her.

She slipped into the bedroom and paused a moment, sizing it up. He was on an austere single bed. Expiating his guilt by living like a monk, thought Elf. He was on his stomach, presenting the back of his head like a sacrifice. Very nice, thought Elf. Sound asleep, breathing quietly. He would do everything quietly, this one. Elf coshed him delicately on the right side of the cranium, low but not too low. She didn't want him out for very long.

She bound him with the nylon cord she'd brought in her leather shoulder bag. It contained a little bit of everything, that bag. A .38. Switchblade knife. Money. Burglar tools. False passport. All the things a hot-eyed young revolutionary girl needed. In the bathroom she found an embroidered linen towel. She cut it in thirds and stuffed one piece into the thin mouth, which, she felt, had never been so far open before. She bound the mouth shut with surgical tape then and listened carefully to the breathing through the nose. She didn't want to asphyxiate the man. She put her fingers under the nostrils to be sure a stream of air was going in and out of both of them. The Chinese manual had advised cutting the vocal cords, but Elf felt she couldn't risk it. A tiny slip and she might cut the man's throat—and then where would she be?

However, she followed one Chinese suggestion. One hand, the right one, was left free from the wrist. One had to communicate somehow. The right arm was bound firmly to the body. Only the hand was free. Could he write like that? Well enough, she thought. She only needed a word or two.

Elf closed the window, drew the curtains, and turned on the bedside light. She sat on a little hard chair and contemplated the thin trussed Puritan figure on the bed. Gray locks straggling over the white bony brow. Parchment skin. Disgusting, thought Elf. The skull of capitalism. Am I working myself into revolutionary fury? I don't need that.

The bony body in its white pajamas—wouldn't you know they'd be white? thought Elf—was as skinny as the black girl on the subway platform. The one deprivation, the other Protestant austerity. I'm having a full evening with emaciated flesh.

She listened to the silence, broken only by the man's whiffling nostril breathing. Should I throw a little cold water on him? Wake him up? She looked at her watch. Three-forty-five. Plenty of time. She felt in the shoulder bag and took out the two bits of sharpened bamboo, and looked at them with consuming interest. Would they work as well in the twentieth century as they had in the ninth? Modern torturers used electricity almost exclusively. It was a failing of imagination, though very effective.

Must I do this? A thought she'd avoided all night long.

Yes, I must, she thought. I'd never find it in that office. They don't keep information like that in files any more. They keep it in electronic memory banks I don't know how to operate. It's the barbarity of the twentieth century driving me back to the barbarity of the ninth.

Why am I so bothered by whatever happens to *that* despoiler of widows and orphans?

In search of serenity, she stood on her head and felt the blood rush out of her midriff, the seat of anxiety, and into her brain, the seat of higher learning. Oh, that is the favorite part of me, thought Elf, upside down. That's where I have poured the wisdom of the ages—from Hegelian economics to ninth-century Chinese torture practices. I am nothing if not broadly based.

Still upside down, she saw Mitchell's eyes flick open, dazed, then startled, then horrified, then frightened, each emotion succeeding the other in less than a twinkling of time.

Elf smiled at him an upside-down smile and then, for the sheer hell of it, stuck her tongue out at him. She was sure no one had ever stuck her tongue out at that one before. He needed that.

"I'm Jemima Glee," whispered Elf. "Remember me?"

A rhyme. She frowned on rhyme. As a poet she had rarely used rhyme, thinking it harmed language. Now he's looking angry, thought Elf. Imagine this happening to *him*, he's thinking. She could see the bony arms straining at the nylon cords. He arched his back and almost fell off the bed. I must fasten the body itself to the bed, thought Elf.

She rolled gracefully over on her back, and for thirty seconds assumed the position of contemplation, while the blood rushed out of her head. Then she set about tearing the upper sheet on the bed into strips and binding Denis Mitchell's body to the bed. It would be thrashing around quite a lot, that body.

That done, Elf sat on the bed and looked at the man for a long moment. "Where is Geraldine Colt?" she asked simply.

She let it sink in, gazing at him. He'd be tough, of course. Getting the time of day out of this one would be tough. "You're the one that sends her money. The one who has always sent the money. I know all about that, you see, because Geraldine and I lived together. They came in very handy, all those certified checks, and they seemed to follow wherever we went. If there is anyone in the world who knows where Geraldine is, you do."

Elf took the memo pad off the desk in the room, put her own pencil in his right hand and the memo pad next to it. "You can just write it right there," she said. She didn't expect him to write it and he didn't. An officer of the Massachusetts Trust? Secrecy was his business as revolution was hers. This is what he's for, to keep secrets. This is his profession.

Elf took the two sharpened bamboo stakes in her hands and explained in a whisper what they

were for and what she planned to do with them—
and how it would hurt. Gazing deep into the flinty
gray eyes, now furious. No fear. Not yet. It was
because he had no imagination. She gave a short
historical dissertation on Chinese torture practices—
this one in particular, keeping her eyes fixed steadily
on him. A stirring of fear then. It's the authority of
history. He doesn't respect me: he respects history,
thought Elf.

She inserted the bamboo into his flesh at the
precise spot—and it was almost torn out of her
hand by the arching body. Damn! I've not fastened
him securely enough. She bound him with more
strips from the sheet, being careful to leave exposed
the right parts of the body.

She was panting now and it wasn't exertion. Oh
God, no! It wasn't exertion. She inserted the bamboo again and this time she watched the body
convulse. Beautiful! Every muscle must have re-
sponded. Elf's mouth was open, her breath coming
fast. Jesus, thought Elf, I'm almost coming. And
I haven't even inserted the other bamboo.

She inserted the second bamboo delicately and
watched the explosive agony in the eyes. That time
she did come all the way. She lay back on the bed,
breathing hard, feeling waves of sexual bliss roll up
from her crotch to her brain—which reacted vio-
lently. Why am I enjoying this? I shouldn't! I
shouldn't!

She rolled off the bed and lay on the floor for a
long moment, soaked in sweat. After a bit she got
up and went to the bathroom, where she bathed

her face in cold water. Then she looked at herself a long moment in the mirror. Where's Elf? Where's Elf? She went back to the bed. Mitchell had passed out, the eyes closed. His body reeked.

Elf woke him up with the cold towel. "Where's Geraldine?" she said throatily. I always get that tone when I'm sexy, she thought in a fury. He was still not telling, so she inserted the bamboo stakes—and this time succumbed utterly to the pleasure, mouth open, eyes dilated, her breath coming faster and faster until she had an orgasm while the body arched in torment.

It took half an hour before Mitchell broke. In a spindly hand on the memo pad, he wrote: "*Palma.*" "What name is she going under?" asked Elf. The spindly hand wrote: "Don't know."

"Oh, I think you do," said Elf in her throaty voice, and inserted the bamboo again—and again. It took only a few minutes this time. The spidery hand wrote: "Patricia Jenkins."

"Where is Geraldine staying in Palma?"

Now the flinty eyes flickered with pure fear. "Don't know," wrote the spidery hand.

"Oh, I think you do," said Elf—and even while she was saying it she knew she was lying. He didn't know. Theresa never told Mitchell her address. Only an American Express box. Or a phony name. But it gave her the excuse to continue with the bamboo stakes—toying, experimenting, watching the convulsed muscles and the agonized eyes, abandoning herself totally to the bliss of it.

She came four more times. The last time the

ecstasy was followed by a wave of disgust—against herself, against him, against everything. She stood up sharply, furious at him for her own outrage. "How dare you!" she spat at him. His fault! for tempting her to these enormities.

She was shaken to the core with revulsion. Oh, Christ, you have to pay for everything, she was thinking. She took out the switchblade and thrust it under the man's fifth rib, flat-bladed, into his heart. Dead, the New Englander harbored an expression of surprised indignation.

Sullenly, Elf gathered up her instruments, wiped the place clean of prints, washed her face and hands in cold water in the basin, and let herself out of the apartment. At the foot of the stairs, she listened absently until she heard the snores of the doorman before walking through the lobby and into the street.

She got off Park Avenue as quickly as possible, heading toward Lexington Avenue and the anonymity of the subway. It was after 4 A.M., the darkest hour of the night, when the unimaginable is imagined —then performed. Nothing will ever be the same again, she thought. I have passed a barrier reef and there's no going back. I've tasted the ultimate— and one should never do that. There should always be one corner beyond which one doesn't go—but I went there, and now what is there for me to aspire to?

Heaven and hell are the same place, she thought. A terrible thought.

CHAPTER

21

The gray-haired receptionist pressed a Kleenex against her nose like a talisman against grief. She had really been fond of that dried-up bundle of sticks. "She said her name was Jemima Glee," said the gray-haired woman, choking down a sob. "I should never have let her in! I should have sent her away! It was all my fault!"

"No," said Hawkins wearily. "It wasn't your fault. She'd have found another way if you hadn't let her in."

Jemima Glee, he thought. Jessica Flame. Hortense Frolic. Elf was having great fun with names.

"Such a quiet, well-spoken girl," said the gray-haired lady, pressing the Kleenex. "I can't believe she'd . . ."

"She is pretty hard to believe—in many ways," said Hawkins. Even for him. Ideologically, this latest of Elf's escapades had shaken him. It didn't fit. Elf had left a string of killings behind her but they had all been—until this one—Elf shooting her way out of trouble, killing casually, without premeditation. But this . . . It boded no good.

He'd phoned Rodgers immediately and Rodgers was on his way. Technically, Elf was Rodgers' concern; his was Saint Theresa. Increasingly, though, the trail to the one was the trail to the other, inextricably linked.

"Mr. Colt?" inquired Hawkins. The gray-haired lady just pointed to Mitchell's office and Hawkins let himself in.

John Colt was waiting for him inside, seated in the chair Mitchell reserved for his visitors. Hawkins walked to the desk and sat down in Mitchell's own chair behind Mitchell's desk. For a long moment, he contemplated the famous liberal lawyer, huddled in the wing chair, the celebrated arrogance at very low tide.

About his own age, thought Hawkins. Too young to vote for Roosevelt the first time—but voted for him the other three times. Served in the war in the OSS. One of John F. Kennedy's strategists—an advocate before Wisconsin, which put him in the inner circle. Now that was all down the drain—the belief, the idealism. Convictions that had seemed rocklike and eternal had dissolved like mist. Now his daughter . . .

The distinguished prematurely white hair, very clean, very short (itself dating him as carbon dates rocks), the cut of the clothes, the cut of the politics, all as ossified as a dinosaur's bones. Hawkins let silence drip on the man like acid. John Colt was awash with guilt and showed it like the good liberal he was. Guilt to the twentieth-century liberal was like elegance to an eighteenth-century dandy. He reveled in it.

"If I'd had any idea . . ." muttered John Colt finally. He rubbed his fingers against his brow as if he could make it all go away.

"We tried to tell you," said Hawkins inflexibly. He was not going to offer any comfort at all.

"Why?" asked the horrified liberal. "Why?"

"She wanted the same thing we wanted—Geraldine's whereabouts." Hawkins always privately called the girl Saint Theresa. The family still thought of her as Geraldine. They were talking about two different girls.

"Elf James," muttered John Colt, "and my daughter!"

He didn't believe it, thought Hawkins, but then Hawkins himself had difficulty believing it. The trouble was that the parents of these girls still tried to reconcile the daughter they knew with the one in the newspapers. They comforted themselves that the papers were sensationalizing, romanticizing, making it all up. The terrible truth was that the newspapers were probably far closer to the facts than the parents. The parents were the romantics, clinging to nursery images as plausible as King Arthur.

"Mr. Colt," said Hawkins—brutally, for him, because the time had come when sentimental concern for the feelings of parents was a dangerous luxury, if not lunacy—"you don't know your daughter."

He told him about Saint Theresa, her love life

and her crimes, flat uncontradictable facts that a lawyer could not parry or trifle with. Brutal it was, but Hawkins was tired of obstruction. Also, he felt strongly that these parents of celebrated wayward daughters were actually enjoying the celebrity of their brilliant revolutionary children, much as they would deny it. It put them in the swim. Or so they thought.

"We don't want any more lawsuits," said Hawkins icily. "We have lost the one witness who might have told us where Geraldine is." John Colt, he knew, didn't have a clue. He'd be the last to find out. These girls had cut the umbilical cord all the way, all the way, as the song said. "We now have little enough chance to get to your daughter before Elf does."

"What does Elf want with my daughter?" asked John Colt angrily. He'd issue a writ, thought Hawkins ironically. He'd seek a restraining order preventing Elf getting to his daughter. Oh, yes. These damned liberal lawyers. They played law as if it were a card game, an amusement. Who wins, who loses. It had very little to do with right or wrong—or, for that matter, with law. And nothing at all with order.

He let John Colt wait a good, long time, fixing him with icy gray eyes. Then he said: "I don't know. All I know is that Geraldine is running away as if from the devil—and Elf is so anxious to find her she tortured a man to death, which is not her style. We don't know why Elf wanted to find Geraldine so badly. Perhaps simply to kiss her. But I doubt it. If you have any concern for your daughter's safety you will stop playing legal games and get the hell out of the way."

Colt shrugged his shoulders, defeated. "Anything you want."

Hawkins rang the bell, summoning the gray-haired lady. "I want to go through Mr. Mitchell's files, every single piece of paper he dealt with, including the most secret of secrets. I want to know where he sent money, under whatever name, and to whatever spot in the world. I want to see any communications to him on the subject of money—in any name or code or number."

Whatever name, it would not be Geraldine Colt or Theresa. He'd just have to follow them all up— and he didn't have much time.

CHAPTER

22

He brought her a lettuce, one of those perfect hand-irrigated lettuces she'd watched him tend several days before. "*Muchas gracias*," murmured Theresa, smiling. "But you mustn't!" In English. She'd taken to talking English to him. Though he didn't understand English, he understood what she was saying pretty well. "You needn't. Not every day."

Every day there was some little present. Usually food. A melon. A bag of oranges. A slice of his strong smoked ham. Always he presented it with a little flourish, putting his whole body into it, in the Mallorquin way, bending at the waist, extending the gift in one hand, flourishing the other hand as if it held a cape.

He had nothing, her peasant. But always a little gift. It was a ceremony, a formality. Very dear of him. Nevertheless it made her uncomfortable. She was herself a giving girl. Her greatest pleasure was giving, not taking. She yearned to give him something. Her body, which was all she had. "Carnality

151

is one of God's great gifts," she'd say aloud in English. "It is a sin to spurn it."

But he seemed in no rush to take her and she knew instinctively she mustn't thrust herself on him. He'd fly right into the hills and never come down, she thought. No, she must play out the dance, feel her way back to the Middle Ages.

After the ceremonial gift, she trailed him as a matter of course to the fields and helped. In the orange grove he plucked oranges like a metronome. She couldn't match this, try as she would, and sometimes she grew mutinous, lying on the ground and shouting revolutionary ideology at him.

"You're being exploited," she'd tell him fiercely. "And exploitation is as much a crime of the exploited as of the exploiters. You are the slave of the bourgeoisie—and a slave surrenders half his manhood and all of his soul. It is a sin."

He'd pluck on, paying no heed.

Once she tried to explain economics to him— using sign language. "You should pick only enough oranges for yourself." Going through the motions of eating an orange. "Or your loved ones." Offering him the orange. "Then stop—and make love." Oh, no, she couldn't do *that* in sign language. "Or pray." She knelt, face uplifted, palms together in supplication.

"You shouldn't spend your life picking oranges for *them*—those tourist idiots in the grand hotels. Or to enrich your bosses, whoever they are."

Who are they? Theresa wondered increasingly. Who owned the *palacio?* Who owned Antonio?

That was his *nombre*—Antonio. She'd found that out. And she'd told him her name—Theresa. They were on a first-name basis now—Antonio and Theresa. A huge step forward in the thirteenth century.

At the end of the day she'd ride with him on the high-wheeled cart back to the *palacio* and help him unhitch the mule, and feed him his barley and oats, then feed the chickens and collect the eggs.

Every night she would offer in sign language to cook his supper. Eggs, the ham he'd brought, the vegetables he'd also brought. Smiling, he'd shake his head. "*Otro día*," he'd mutter. Some other day. But when?

Sometimes he'd climb the crazy staircase to the rabbit and dove room, emerging a minute later with a dead dove or dead bunny in his hand.

"*Buena noche*," he'd say, giving her a dark smile. He didn't open his mouth, even to smile. Still, for Antonio that smile represented a very great unbending.

Off he'd go down the white road, swinging the dead carcass. Invariably Theresa sped up to the rabbit and dove room to watch him swing down the road and disappear into the trees. Did he have a wife to return to? She didn't know but she doubted it. He's a loner like me. An outcast.

This was the lonely time. She'd pick up a rabbit to stroke in lieu of her peasant. "I'm a stroker of rabbits and mules," she'd whisper, nuzzling the soft fur—because what else was there to nuzzle?

Without her peasant she never ate supper, never felt the need for food. She'd crouch on her knees watching the blackness creep across the valley, nuzzling the rabbit.

Until the visions shattered her.

Gunfire.

Black hair across her face. Always so innocent when those black eyes were closed. Legs asprawl. Elf always slept as if she were running.

Gunfire.

And fear. Fear eating into her like acid. Strick lying next to her in the tunnel. Dead. Trying to warm herself on a dead body. Oh, my God! my God! I'm so scared!

Gunfire and the fear rising up in her until she was all fear, solid jelly, nuzzling against a corpse. No warmth, no comfort there.

Elf's black eyes opening, looking at her lazily, smiling hungrily—like a shark. In that earthen tunnel already smelling of death.

Elf!

I was the rabbit, rabbit. Transfixing me with those black eyes, wriggling to my side like the snake she was.

I hate you! I hate you! Over the gunfire.

Pushing Strick away and placing herself next to me where he'd been.

I hate you, Elf James! loathe you! despise you! curse you!

She kissed me on the lips, this murderess. Kissed me, smiling.

I hate you! hate you!

Life is very improbable, rabbit. Have you ever read *Richard III*, rabbit? because you should. Very alarming. At the very outset of the play Gloucester proposes over the coffin of the King he has killed to the Queen he's widowed, who hates his deformed guts—and what's more he wins her. The most improbable scene in all literature.

It was because I was so scared, rabbit! So terrified, terror beyond terror! She kept kissing and kissing. Where could I escape in that narrow tunnel? She was so warm and Strick was so cold.

Anyway is it so improbable? I have heard, rabbit, that the best way to seduce a widow is by the coffin of her husband, because she is craving comfort and one thing leads to another. If you take your time. And Elf took her time because where had we to go? The police were everywhere, shooting their guns.

She kissed and kissed and presently I kissed back. I was wooed and won in a tunnel next to the corpse of my lover by the one who shot him. I hated her, rabbit—and succumbed to her. It was because I was so scared. At least I think so. All that noise! Or was it because the situation was unique, or provocative? The trouble with my generation, rabbit, is that we have made love to so many partners in so many various attitudes under so many different moons that a woman yearns to be unique. Was I just straining to be different?

I'll never stop asking.

She made love to me three times in that tunnel, rabbit, and I have never known such bliss and such shame. I've been expiating my bliss and my shame ever since. It will take an eternity of expiation.

If one believes in eternity . . .

CHAPTER

23

The air in Mitchell's office was electric with contention. And official politeness, which was sometimes even worse than hostility. The Homicide Bureau was there now, in the person of a beefy and enormous individual named Tuohy, who had once been a professional prizefighter and looked it.

Tuohy wanted to know why Homicide had been the last to get there.

"A continuing investigation, Lieutenant," said Hawkins politely. "We are in litigation—or *were* in litigation with the victim. We think the killing had something to do with a fugitive from justice named Geraldine Colt."

"Speak for yourself, Philosopher," said Rodgers. But not out loud. He was furious that he'd got there hours after Hawkins. Elf was his baby, not Hawkins'. Still, deep as the conflict was between Hawkins and Rodgers, they kept it out of sight, the two FBI men closing ranks against the local law officer, who hated them both as intruders.

"I see it as a New York City homicide," said Tuohy bluntly. "Unless you gentlemen can give me some reason for not cooperating, I'd appreciate any help you can give."

"Elf is wanted in nine states, has crossed twenty-one state lines, is clearly a federal fugitive," said Rodgers lazily, infuriatingly.

"Who says Elf James is the killer?"

"She answers the description," said Rodgers.

She didn't, thought Hawkins, but he was not going to disagree publicly.

"The name—Jemima Glee," Hawkins threw it in casually. "Elf had a weakness for rather cute names —like her own name Elf."

Rodgers glared furiously. Hawkins was getting all over his turf. Hawkins could feel the heat of his anger from where he stood next to the window looking down on Wall Street, back to both the others. No wonder no one ever gets caught or if caught is unconvicted. The bureaucracies are at war with each other, everyone far more interested in scoring points than in catching criminals. And was that his interest—catching the criminal Geraldine Colt, or saving the life of Saint Theresa? A worthy aim but hardly what he was paid for.

Tuohy and Rodgers were in the other office now, quizzing the gray-haired receptionist. They'd find out nothing. Hawkins had been through every scrap of paper that could conceivably be relevant to Geraldine Colt's trust fund. There'd been nothing at all.

He stared down the Wall Street canyon, from

thirty-seven stories up, the street aswarm with tiny people, bustling about in the sharp wintry light. He had a piercing premonitory vision of the famous street running red with blood—because this is where it would start—Sodom and Gomorrah in the revolutionist's handbook.

"Elf has no vices," Rodgers was telling Tuohy, "except robbing banks and killing people."

Torture, said Hawkins to himself, a brand-new vice. And very alarming. She must have wanted the information very badly.

"Nothing was missing from the apartment," Tuohy told Rodgers. "Nothing at all. That's what makes it so peculiar, because there was plenty to take, including even some money."

"Elf has enough money. She didn't get much out of that bank heist—eight thousand or so. But she doesn't need much."

"Then where's your motive? What was she after?" asked Tuohy.

The whereabouts of her lover, thought Hawkins. He waited for Rodgers to say it. Rodgers didn't. Was he keeping it to himself or didn't he know?

He turned abruptly from the window: "I'll be running along. I'm at the Gotham if you want to get in touch, Joe. Or you, Lieutenant."

He passed the rest of the afternoon in the main public library studying the history of torture. It had, he found, a very long history. Aristotle approved it—well! well! Plato disapproved. So did Voltaire. Good old Voltaire, always ahead of the others. Hawkins was less than surprised to discover that bishops and lawyers had been enthusiasts for torture. Wouldn't you know? Torture had been the conventional wisdom for many more years than it had been frowned on. In Greece, that citadel of democracy, Hawkins discovered, torture was practiced in open court for all the citizens to enjoy. If John Colt had been a lawyer in ancient Greece, he'd have been right in there torturing away, practicing the conventional wisdom, as later he espoused liberalism, not because it took guts but because it was the fashionable thing. Hawkins had little use for lawyers, and none for liberal lawyers who made enormous fortunes keeping rich crooks out of jail where they richly deserved to be. This, despite the fact that he was himself a lawyer.

Hawkins returned the books to the librarian and ate a thinking supper of baked beans and coffee at the Automat. Stalin had said: "They torture— why shouldn't we?" So the Left tortured—at least the Old Left did. The New Left didn't. Unless you called Manson New Left, and no one did.

His most important finding confirmed his worst suspicions. Torture was largely man's sport. In the long, long history of torture almost all torturers were men. Elf has invaded the last male sanctuary, thought Hawkins, a great breakthrough for women —but then she had always been in the front rank.

Did Theresa know about this . . . predilection? Probably. She was very very bright, his Theresa. If I were Theresa, a very bright girl, and I wanted to flee from Elf James, another very very bright

girl . . . I know all the revolutionary hideouts—
but then so does she. So where do I go?

Back at the Gotham he found an urgent message
from Christopher Steel. Associate Deputy Director.
Call immediately. Trouble. Rodgers kicking up a
fuss. Come back. Hawkins scratched his nose quizzically. Damn! If they called him off the case, who
would take care of Theresa?

He smiled his shy smile at the desk clerk. "Put
it back in the box, please."

The desk clerk took the little square of white
paper in his hand without expression.

"If anyone should ring, I haven't come in yet."

The young man nodded and put the message
back into the box, impassive. Nothing bothered
hotel clerks. They'd seen it all.

Lying on his bed, eyes on the ceiling, Hawkins
thought it over. They'd call back, of course. What
did he do now? Why did he care? Theresa was another fugitive. There'd been hundreds—and this
would by no means be the first one he'd not caught.
Or the first case he'd been taken off.

The telephone rang. Hawkins ignored it. It might
not be the Bureau. It might even be Amanda. He
let it ring. Am I the only person in the world who
enjoys *not* answering telephones? No, there must
be others—none of them in the FBI.

What am I doing in the FBI? An unlikelier character could hardly be imagined. I am a lawyer who
believes English law outlived its usefulness in the
seventeenth century and has been going downhill
ever since. He was an FBI man who had never en-

joyed apprehending fugitives, which was what the game was all about.

The telephone rang and rang—and then went dead. Several people were after him—not just Steel. Oh, well . . .

"I'm in the Bureau only because I'm too lazy to get out." He put words around it. He'd long known but he never cloaked it in words. Not until now.

Hawkins had been one of those innumerable young men who'd got out of law school—Willimantic, not even a very good law school—in the middle of the Depression when the world was crawling with unwanted lawyers. That was when J. Edgar Hoover was recruiting bright young lawyers for the Bureau. Hawkins joined the FBI because it was the only job in town.

"As a law officer, I'm an accident," said Hawkins to the ceiling. It didn't bother him enough, really. He'd passed his life doing something he didn't want to do. But then wasn't this the story of civilization? How many men were in jobs they enjoyed? One percent? The FBI had kept him out of the Army during the war. After the war came the Great Prosperity, when lawyers were in great demand—especially ex-FBI men.

Hawkins had stayed on because the alternatives he approved even less than his work at the Bureau. It was his study of the Movements that had made him restless and questioning. He'd never questioned himself before. Me, the master interrogator. But not a self-interrogator. Until recently.

He interrogated himself:

Q. Why are you giving this personal service to Theresa, Mr. Hawkins?

A. What personal service? She is a fugitive from justice I have been assigned to. I'm checking out all leads. . . .

Q. Including her love life?

A. If it has relevance to the apprehension of the fugitive . . .

Q. But does it? Also her reading habits? Her personal idiosyncrasies? Her likes and dislikes in food, clothes, music . . .

A. All relevant to the pursuit and capture of a sophisticated modern revolutionary.

Q. Do you want to go to bed with her?

A. Oh, for heaven's sake, I'm old enough to be her father.

Q. That's not an answer.

The telephone rang, saving him from even more merciless self-interrogation.

Two rings only. Silence.

He had to have something to give them, if he wanted to stay on the case. He fumbled through his address book and phoned Jo Jo Tomkins, an old chum in the passport office, at his home in Washington.

Tomkins listened hard and then thought it over. "If you're pursuing that line, you should look into airline ticket theft. Lot of that going on."

"Brief me, baby," said Hawkins.

"Well, they steal the airline tickets in big batches and sell them where they can for what they can get to get bread for drugs. Sometimes to get bread for bread. Anyone who knows her way around the underground like your Theresa . . ."

Even Jo Jo is calling her *my* Theresa. I must keep the proprietary air out of my voice.

". . . could pick up a blank ticket on the black market—and write it to where she wanted."

"Oh, it can't be *that* easy. There must be all kinds of checks and official stamps."

Tomkins laughed shortly. "These are very bright kids. They steal all the official stamps along with the tickets. They know every angle. Your Theresa— if she wanted to go abroad—probably showed at the airport with her luggage—that kind of freak doesn't travel with much—and just mingled with a big package tour to Tel Aviv or Rome or wherever she wanted to go. There are frequent no-shows on those charters. After all 360 people can't *all* show up. Last-minute sickness. Relative dies. Missed connection. They start paging the no-shows. Will Mrs. John C. Wilson please come to the ticket counter? How many times have you heard that? The third time, your Theresa steps up with a stolen ticket made out to Mrs. John C. Wilson, which she did herself in the ladies' room five minutes before."

"She can't fill out a passport in the name of Mrs. John C. Wilson," Hawkins pointed out.

"She explains—happens all the time—that the name on her passport, which has been stolen or forged or whatever, Jane Doe, is her maiden name or her former married name if it's Mrs. She just got married the day before and hasn't had a chance to change her passport. Well, they're anxious to close the flight and get off and they let her through."

"Thanks, Jo Jo," said Hawkins.

It wasn't much but it was an opening and he needed one. He looked at his watch: 9 P.M. He hunched himself off the bed and went in search of an airline official. He could hear the phone ringing in his room as he went down the hotel corridor.

CHAPTER

24

Theresa knelt in a splash of moonlight pouring through one of the great windows in the audience chamber, blue eyes full of the sharp pain of devotion. I believe in God, the sacraments, the Eucharist, the Gospels . . . redemption. The last pulled out of the bottom of her. I do not believe in the church's special monopoly of these divine favors. I must arrive at these certainties, which the church calls faith, by my own intellectual processes. The Catholic Church wants slaves and I am no slave—not anyway an intellectual slave, though I have been enslaved in other ways, body and soul. Still, if I am to pursue . . . redemption (such a large word!), it must be on my own terms.

Thus she spoke to God, stumbling along. Much of it was extremely painful. Because she had to work out not only her own salvation but her own rigorous orthodoxy, her own severely rational dogma, each shred of which had to pass her own withering intellectual scrutiny. I am an atheist stricken with belief in God as a last resort. I have explored the very outermost reaches of unbelief in God and I have been driven to my knees because I have no place else to go.

Here she was racked with sobs. Always it came at this point. Always! I am capable of any crime, intellectual or physical, and I have already committed too many. I am fleeing crimes not yet committed.

That had become part—the most important part —of her own dogma ever since she had first blurted it out to the peasant.

She found it difficult to go further than that, although each day she tried to break through. There was something on the other side, some divine pasture where she would find, not surcease because surcease was too trivial for a ferocious mystic like herself, but the final total agony wherein lay true redemption. She had always envied Christ the cross.

I'm a Jesus freak seeking not salvation but crucifixion and that is a very great sin indeed, the sin of envy. She wept, torn by the immense contradictions of her nature, which were far too agonizing for one skinny frame to harbor.

"How do you know?" asked Hawkins. The night manager was very young, very smooth, as if all the edges had been rubbed off dealing with travelers. Good looking, casual, well dressed, eager to please; you could find identical models in Rome, Paris, London. They all looked as if they'd been turned out by computer for airline offices the world over.

"They don't show up for the return flight," the young man was saying. "Of course, you expect some no-shows on the original flight. Someone gets sick or—or their father died or something. But, once a passenger gets *on* the holiday, he almost always shows up from there on. After all, he's paid for his hotel—and for the trip home. When a passenger occupies a seat on the outgoing flight, and then fails to show up at the hotel for a room that's booked for him—and further fails to show up for the return flight that has also been booked for him, then you can pretty well conclude he's on a stolen ticket."

"Do you have a lot of that?" asked Hawkins.

"Not a lot," said the young man. "We have some. There's another way to check it out. When you have a no-show, a few days later—or the same day—someone will phone up with an explanation as to why he didn't show. They don't get all the money back but they get some of it back—20 percent, 40 percent. It depends on the kind of charter flight they're making. Well, if we check our roster and discover that, according to our records, Joe Blow did board the plane, then someone has conned us. Sometimes we catch this when the plane's still in the air and we can apprehend the freeloaders at the point of arrival. But not often. The trouble with jets is they're too fast. Usually the plane has got to its destination and unloaded before we can match things up. Of course, if someone is pulling a swindle like that, they don't show up at the hotel. They just vanish."

"Do you keep a record of names and flights and so forth of this kind of thing?"

"Of course. Much good it does us."

"I'd like to see the list," said Hawkins.

"Sure, how far back do you want to go—six days? Six years?"

"Six months."

It was not a big list after the impossibles had been combed out of it. Only six names from six different flights—to Bermuda, to the Virgin Islands, to Miami, to the Canadian Rockies, to the Bahamas, to Majorca. Four of the freeloaders were men, eliminating them. The two women freeloaders went to Miami and Majorca.

Majorca, thought Hawkins. It was the farthest away.

Elf took the train to Boston. The pigs kept too close a watch on the planes. Trains they forgot. She wore her blond wig, the tough boyish body encased in jeans, quite unavoidably sexy. Sometimes the best way to be inconspicuous was to be conspicuous. On the train she read *Daughter of a Revolutionary* by Natalie Herzen, scowling. What a ninny! At Boston Airport she bought a ticket to London—not to *Palma*. She paid cash with bills that had been carefully laundered by being changed at Kennedy Airport for French francs and then changed back to dollars at the Chase Manhattan Bank in New York, an old underground trick for throwing off pursuers of stolen money. Elf doubted whether the Feds had the serial numbers on her bills but she was taking no chances. If they traced the bills to Kennedy Airport, which was unlikely, they'd be looking for her on flights out of New York, not out of Boston.

On the flight to London, she buried herself in Lao-tse. Confucius was not her bag—but it had been Theresa's and Elf wanted to know why. It put her to sleep.

It was a risk. Theresa knew that. But she could not go all the way to Palma for a bottle of olive oil, even if she could afford it. Besides, if she was to live here, they'd have to get used to her.

She slung her leather shoulder bag over her back and walked to Cuesta barefoot. Perhaps, in her blue peasant smock, her baggy trousers, they'd take her for a peasant—now that her face was burnt almost as mahogany-colored as Antonio's. At the *colmado* she bought oil and vinegar, butter, sugar, salt and pepper, and a large loaf of tough, delicious Spanish bread. But she didn't get away with it as she secretly knew she wouldn't. The little boys interrupted their stick game and stared. The women on the pavements interrupted their sewing and stared—stony-faced.

She had lost caste. She felt it in her bones. They knew her exactly for what she was and who she was. But, by becoming one of them or by trying to do so, she'd stepped down in the social scale—and they despised her for it. Hated her even. Oh, why? her heart protested. I am a peasant like yourself! But she knew better. So did they.

She walked out of the village followed by stares as hard as a shower of stones.

169

"This is awfully theoretical, John." Christopher Steel was trying to be a diplomatist. Rodgers bulked large on a leather armchair. You had to rise very high in the FBI before you got such comfortable chairs, thought Hawkins. Steel was very much higher than Hawkins—and very much younger. But then he probably liked his job.

"You haven't any evidence at all that either of these girls is in Majorca."

"One of them is," said Hawkins flatly.

"Which one?"

"Theresa."

"How do you know?" said Steel indifferently. He really wasn't very interested in Theresa. The FBI, like the Supreme Court, followed the election returns. Theresa was forgotten by the public. Therefore the FBI put her on the back burner. Now, if she'd been Patty Hearst . . . But she wasn't.

"M.O.T." said Hawkins distinctly. His thin rambling body leaned against the radiator—like a scarecrow, head hunched into his shoulders, his favorite position in other people's offices. That way you could take flight without lengthy apologies. Just take off.

"Oh, come on, John," said Steel. "M.O.T., my ass. It could be anyone on that stolen ticket—not even an underground girl."

"No, it couldn't." It was idiocy contradicting Steel that flatly, just putting his back up. Hawkins couldn't help it. He'd never given a damn about any fugitive in his thirty years in the Bureau except this one. He was damned if they were going to take her away.

"If you know anything about Elf's whereabouts, I'd be grateful if you'd hand it over," said Rodgers. In Steel's office he was very much politer than he'd been recently.

"I don't," said Hawkins bluntly. Why can't I be nicer to these two idiots? he was thinking. Am I *trying* to alienate Steel?

"I thought you said she was in Majorca," said Steel.

"I think she will be there—if Theresa's there. Just an opinion."

"Perhaps *I* should go to Majorca," said Rodgers, grinning.

"Neither of you is going," barked Steel, tired of this game. "Now get out of here, both of you."

Rodgers moved to the door. Hawkins stayed mulishly where he was, eyes on the floor, chewing the side of his cheek.

"Coming, John?" asked Rodgers.

"No," said Hawkins.

Rodgers shrugged and left. Hawkins digging his grave. None of his affair. The door closed.

"Suppose I went at my own expense? Would the Bureau back me?"

It took special authorization to get sent out of the country. The FBI wasn't supposed to operate overseas. But it *did* operate overseas when it was thought important. Steel didn't think this was. Going overseas at your own expense was unheard of.

Steel leaned back in his chair and fixed Hawkins

with a stare of total disbelief. He said nothing, trying to smoke him out. Hawkins stayed silent. He didn't give a damn. After thirty years, what the hell? It wouldn't do his career any good, but then his career wasn't going anywhere anyhow. That was his strength. He didn't care—and they *did* care.

A long silence.

"Rodgers says you're deeply emotionally involved with this girl."

"I've never even met the girl."

"That makes it even more . . . peculiar. I think you should be taken off this case, John." He was just trying it on for size. A threat—to see how he'd respond.

Hawkins chewed the side of his cheek and let him wait for it. "It's a very interesting case—psychologically."

"I'm not especially interested in psychology, Philosopher."

Hawkins sighed. He was well aware of that. He was also aware that there were even drearier jobs around the FBI than being the keeper of cold trails.

"You know something, Chief," Hawkins smiled. "I don't really give a damn."

"Ten years to retirement. It could be a long ten years, John."

"Not even you can make ten years longer, Chief."

Hawkins couldn't be pushed. Steel saw that and wondered at it. He changed course.

"I don't quite understand your motivation here, John," he said softly.

Nor did Hawkins. "The girl's welfare, Chief."

"Elf's?" An ironic thrust. Steel knew better. Hawkins let it fly past unchallenged.

"I have total recall."

A feint. Hawkins had no intention of washing the Bureau's dirty linen in public. But if Steel was going to throw out these digs about Elf . . .

Steel tacked straight into the wind. "How long has Theresa been on your desk, John?"

"Five years."

"Too long. Perhaps another agent could bring a fresh point of view."

Hawkins' frame grew even more disjointed. "I'd resign. Then I'd have nothing but time on my hands."

To write a book. He didn't say it. He didn't have to.

"Give up your pension, John—after all these years?"

Sardonically: "Perhaps I'd become a very rich author."

The two men eyed each other now for a very long time. Steel had run out of ammunition and they both knew it. How do you threaten a man who doesn't give a damn? Still, he didn't know how to climb down from this particular fence.

Hawkins smoothed the way: "You *do* want these two girls, don't you, Chief?"

"Yes, of course I want these two girls—especially Elf." Bitterly.

"Then sign the piece of paper."

Steel signed.

CHAPTER

25

Voices!

Theresa was climbing the stone staircase on the *bancal*, her shopping bag on her arm, when she first heard them. She scuttled down the stone steps and into the thick cover of vines on the north wall, a reflex action as quick as a rabbit's. Pressing herself against the crumbled stones, she listened to the voices in the courtyard. Antonio's grating Mallorquin. Then another strange voice, more honeyed, talking first Mallorquin, then, unexpectedly, English. Oxford English.

"He says the oranges are early because they had a mild winter."

Another voice, languorous, feminine, foreign: "Darling, ask him to take the bags in, please." Clearly the woman was bored with oranges.

Theresa blazed with fury. Ask him? Who? Antonio? A porter, her Antonio! Capitalist swine! She was livid, astounded by the depth of her feeling.

Under the cover of the vines, Theresa scaled

174

the crumbled wall like a lizard. Flat on her stomach on the high wall, keeping her brown face well behind the camouflage of vine leaves, Theresa looked down into the courtyard.

They were very elegant Spaniards. He was about thirty-five she guessed, well shaped, his clothes fitting like skin. She was blond and slender and looked both expensive and fragrant. So these then were the owners of the *palacio*, these the keepers of the key to that brass-studded great door with its askew Moorish bronze lion? Without a doubt Spain was littered with their palaces. Visited them once a year! If that often!

Antonio was getting the bags out of the trunk of the purple Porsche that stood there. And how did they get that on the island? Fly it in? Or did they just leave spare Porsches at the airport to drive them around?

Antonio took two brown leather bags—Guccis, obviously—to the front door, and then out of his shapeless peasant trousers drew a large elaborate iron key, with which he opened the great central door. So Antonio had a key! Theresa was dazzled by this new surprising fact. She was consumed with curiosity as to what lay behind that great door. The one bit she'd never penetrated. In *her palacio!*

The man and woman were talking Spanish to each other now. Three languages in five minutes. They probably talked a half dozen—English in front of Antonio, because one didn't want to let the servants in on one's thoughts, just one's commands, thought Theresa, her mind hissing with revolutionary

175

sarcasm. Jet-set types. Both beautifully tanned, every inch a golden brown, as if they had been turned on a spit—a matter of great importance in their useless lives, lying about on one fashionable beach after another.

The two elegant Spaniards disappeared through the great door and Theresa was left alone, spitting ideology at the purple Porsche.

She scrambled down from the wall and stole silently across the courtyard, up the crazy steps, and back to her sentinel bedroom. And how safe am I here?

Hawkins faced the Mallorquin police chief across an immensity of ancient oak desk in a vast square room of imperial pretension. He had never dealt with quite such an excess of courtesy imbedded in such layers and layers of skepticism that seemed to stretch clear back to the Armada. The face was gray, deeply lined, almost sacerdotal with propriety. Looking into those eyes was like looking into 1492. How to explain the runaway children of twentieth-century affluent America to a man still deeply encased in the fifteenth century? The Spaniard had never heard of Elf or Theresa or Patricia Hearst or any of it, and if it had not been for his deeply ingrained courtesy, he might, Hawkins thought, have called him a liar and ordered him out of his office.

Instead, being the man he was, he spread his hands in that intensely European gesture that means simply "welcome," pulled down a map of the island, and did the best he could to explain Majorca to

Hawkins. "You understand your own children better than I do," said the Spanish police chief in excellent English that creaked like a seldom-used door. "I would not myself select Majorca as a place to disappear into but . . ." He shrugged. "We have much landscape to choose from. Here are mountains." He tapped the northwest of the island with his pointer, "which look like the mountains of the moon. There is no one there for the very good reason that there is nothing to go there for. No food. You could hide out forever and no one would ever find you—but you would starve to death in short order."

The Spaniard pointed at Palma: "Our city which you are now in is not a good place of refuge. It is a big city, true, but we know each other very well here and it would not be easy to vanish into—as would Paris or even Barcelona. We are insular, Mr. Hawkins, with all the best and all the worst of it— an intense awareness of the foreignness of foreigners. We harbor a very great many foreigners here as permanent residents but they never melt into the population and become one of us. Never! I know them all, where they all come from, how much money they receive from abroad, and I could even give you a pretty good guess as to where it came from and how honestly. No, Palma is very inadvisable. If your two girls settled here I'd know within a month."

The pointer wandered to the center of the island. "This is our great central plain, very flat, very fertile, very hot, and again very hard to disappear into. One knows everything that goes on in this open plain, and I greatly doubt anyone could hide in it long. Especially such . . . spectacular ladies as you describe."

The pointer wandered to the southwest of the island. "Here is where the tourists go, a great chain of hotels, all exactly alike, where the English go to eat English food and look at other English faces just like their own and read English papers and dance to English music from English pop groups. One wonders why they come. Well, the sun! They see very little of that in England. Your girls might very well melt in here, even if they are Americans—because there are enough of those."

"No," said Hawkins. "They would never go near that tourist ghetto."

Silence. The Spanish police chief seemed reluctant to go on. He rubbed his nose, pursed his straight lips. Finally he said, "Well, that leaves the valleys. We have some beautiful valleys that tourists never get into and even permanent foreign residents who have lived here for years don't know exist."

"To conquer the art of dissembling." Elf was pretty well dissembled even before she landed. She'd bought a new blond wig before she left New York, with long hair that curled under page-boy style halfway down her back. It revolted her lesbian revolutionary soul, which was precisely why she bought it. It changed the shape of her head and the color of her personality to such a degree that she even dared to resume her own *retroussé* nose.

After all, hers wasn't the only turned-up nose in the world.

Once in Palma she headed unerringly to the central *paseo* and walked under the huge trees, getting her bearings, casing the travelers, seeing what was what. By the time she had reached the covered shopping esplanade at the end of the *paseo* she had already decided on some severe modifications of her getup. She bought some huge sunglasses that covered half her face. In another shop she bought flaring white duck trousers of French make, very expensive, and a flower-figured Hermes blouse, of enduring chic.

Spectacular, she thought, looking at herself in the full-length mirror. She looked rich, useless, heterosexual, and stupid—none of which she was. She paid with laundered dollars. She didn't want to use her stolen Diners Club card quite yet because she didn't know how long it would take to find Theresa and she didn't want to make any waves. Not yet.

Fully dissembled, Elf walked boldly back to the sidewalk café she'd noticed on her original reconnaissance. This was where it all was. She sat at a table next to a wispy ancient with a little dog in his lap. On the other side were two sad-eyed women, worn to the nub with the continuous depravity of their own existence, Elf thought. With them was a suave German dressed in an English blazer with a silk scarf at the throat. "It depends altogether on the divorce agreement," he was saying. "If you'd just bring it to my office. Spain doesn't like divorce

but they recognize the divorces of other countries."
A lawyer, thought Elf. Just what I don't need.

She ordered a *café solo*, unfolded her *International
Herald Tribune* and, from behind her huge dark
glasses, kept an eye out for what was going on. The
expatriate community came and went unceasingly.
A pair of English geriatrics entered, the man unwrapping the woman, layer after layer of English
woolens, like a mummy. They ordered coffee and
unlimbered their *Daily Telegraph* and *Times* and
read about the collapse in shares in distant England.

An American in white flannel suit, elegantly cut,
came in with a pouting American girl of about
seventeen. Already badly spoiled, thought Elf.
What's left for her? I could make a revolutionary
of that one—if I hadn't other things to do. The pair
quarreled negligently, drank a Pernod (much too
early for that, thought Elf), and left. No one stayed
overly long. The cast changed constantly. Presently
an Englishman in a blue yachting jacket came in.
Dark glasses, blond wavy hair, roving eyes. Hasn't
got a bean, thought Elf.

The eyes roved over her and stopped. The man
sat one table away, which was as close as he could
get, and ordered a *citron pressé*. When it arrived,
he contrived to see that there was no sugar bowl
on his table. He arose and came to her table.

"May I?" he asked.

"Please do," murmured Elf. What does he want—
my money or my body? Both.

He took the sugar bowl back to his own table,

where presently he said—speaking across the wispy ancient with the dog: "You've just arrived."

"Yes," said Elf. Let him work for it.

Presently the wispy ancient with the dog went away and the Englishman moved next to her. "I've lived here three years," he proclaimed. "I threaten to leave every year—but I don't."

Elf smiled. He's going to eat me up, is he? Well, it might come in handy for concealment purposes. He has a seedy lodging somewhere. She let the monologue flow around her, contributing an occasional polysyllable—but smiling as helplessly as she could manage. Helplessness was not Elf's strong suit.

It was not at all seedy, she discovered, when she went to his flat. Tiny, all right, and up a long staircase, but it was behind the cathedral, facing the sea. It had a minute kitchen with a gas ring and a small refrigerator. He brings the girls here, she guessed, and borrows their money. When they get wise, they drift away and he goes back to the sidewalk café for more.

She went to bed with him and felt nothing. I'm like a whore, thought Elf. It is a point of pride that I don't have an orgasm with men or, in fact, feel anything at all. It wasn't unpleasant. It was just nothing. Still, she moaned and sighed and carried on. He would find out soon enough. Let him harbor his male chauvinist illusions a little while. His name, she discovered, was Robin Frost.

They went out for dinner in the Terreno district, the Greenwich Village, Chelsea-type area of Palma, and the Englishman was very amusing about the freaks, the male prostitutes, the hangers-on—and very instructive, too. This is a hiding place, thought Elf, in case I need one. Anything goes here. The Englishman got quite drunk and very merry. When the time came to pay, as Elf suspected all along, he discovered prettily he'd forgotten his wallet. Elf paid, fishing a few bills out of the immense linen bag she'd bought that day. She didn't want him seeing just how much there was.

Then she took him home, paid the cab, and went to bed with him. After a bit of rather messy sex, she outwaited him, which wasn't difficult. Within minutes, he was sound asleep, snoring alcoholically. Elf rose and dug the .38 out of her handbag and put it under the mattress. She didn't mind the Englishman stealing her money, because she could always take it back. She didn't want him fooling around with her gun.

He might hurt himself.

CHAPTER

26

Theresa lay flat on the north wall behind the protective screen of vine leaves in a square of hot morning sun, watching the courtyard below. Antonio was there with his high-wheeled flared cart, the mule already hitched. The Spaniard was talking to him in Mallorquin, pointing here and there, as if giving instructions. The Spaniard was dressed in white canvas trousers and a royal blue turtleneck pullover with blue rope-soled shoes. Dressing down for the peasantry. Quaint!

The Spanish girl in all her blond loveliness came out the great door, tying her hair up in a flowered silk head scarf, probably from Hermes. She too had dressed down. The trousers were blue cotton, a sort of high-fashion version of the worker's trousers Theresa had on. The blouse was a blue-and-white-striped Basque fisherman shirt—turned out by Christian Dior, *not* by a Basque fisherman. Nothing on under it either, thought Theresa. I wouldn't mind kissing what lay underneath. Enough of that. I'm so horny lately. It's because I've had no sex in months. She was used to regular sex. Famished, I am. Food I can do without.

The Spanish girl was helped by her husband and by Antonio to the seat of the cart. The Spaniard jumped up after her, took the reins, and clucked at the mule. The cart moved off, Antonio following on foot. Keeping his place, thought Theresa fiercely. The aristocracy had made its obeisance to democracy by taking the cart, instead of the Porsche, to inspect the estate, but one mustn't let down the bars so far as to ride in the same cart with a peasant. I'm being unfair, she thought. Antonio is walking because he wants to walk. He's too proud to ride in a cart somebody else is driving.

She was too elated to wallow in indignation anyway. No one had locked the great bronze-studded door. She had watched the Spanish woman walk out, her hands busy with the kerchief, and kick the door shut with her foot. Unless it was a spring lock—and Theresa was sure it was not.

She waited until the cart had pulled out of the courtyard. Then she leaped off the wall onto the roof below, ran across the roof tiles, barefoot, and squiggled through the narrow window, dropping down inside the passage leading to the exposed staircase. Before venturing down that, she slipped into the room with the doves and rabbits. She scooped up her pet rabbit—Pedro, she called him— and took him with her to the big window looking down the valley. There was the cart with its load of expensively dressed aristocracy, Antonio plodding along beside the cart now, apparently talking Mallorquin to the Spaniard. Theresa nuzzled the rabbit, savoring the softness of the fur, crooning low. "Pedro! Pedro! Whose rabbit are you? Mine? Or theirs? They don't even know you're alive." It wasn't very good revolutionary doctrine, this fierce possessiveness, but then I'm not a very good revolutionary these days, thought Theresa. I'm a peasant girl and we are the most unyielding reactionaries. Ah, well, I've changed my nature again, shedding another skin. So many skins—religious mystic, revolutionary, bank robber, killer, sex liberationist, Bryn Mawr radical, stretching clear back to . . . Theresa held the rabbit against her face and tried to think of her parents, misty figures in the distant past, a thousand years ago. She couldn't remember their faces.

The great door had an immense bronze handle, which took both hands to turn. Theresa stepped inside a cool dimness. Two inside steps led up to a long corridor with a white marble floor, light pouring forth from the opposite end. Theresa walked down the corridor, feeling the frosty coolness of the marble on her bare toes, eyes fixed on a great painting at the end of the corridor—the famous figure in the famous martyred position, elongated, bony, agonized. Mother of God, thought Theresa, a Caravello. Is it real? Here!

She fell back a step and looked at the long austere canvas, dazzled. Would aristocrats like that have a *fake* Caravello—even in a *palacio* they visited only once in a blue moon? Never! Theresa stared at it, almost sick with the splendor and the uselessness of it. How many Caravellos in private hands were there in the whole world? And this! In her valley! How splendid! How awful! She stared for a long time and then shook herself. She had to get on. But it changed everything—a Caravello. Did anyone else know?

She passed the painting and ascended a circular staircase of marble, incredibly elegant, that led up to what appeared to be the main sitting room. It had two large windows fronting on the courtyard. Nowhere near as good a view as the rabbits had. The floor was of marble and it was simply furnished. Before a great fireplace was a very deep, very long, very Spanish brocaded sofa. On either side of it were deep armchairs of leather, and behind the sofa was a heavily carved oak table, of imposing dimensions, on which stood two bronze lamps shaped like urns and weighing, Theresa guessed, about two hundred pounds apiece. An oak chest, heavily carved, of roughly the same period stood against an opposite wall. That was all. Except for the paintings. Over the oak chest was a Ribera. Over the great stone mantelpiece was another Caravello. If the art thieves found out about this . . . She didn't want to think about it.

Down a corridor at right angles to the sitting room Theresa found a dining room with a refectory table, bearing heavily carved candelabra, high-backed chairs of carved oak. And again the paintings. These were a bit less grand—a Montagnard of a Spanish grandee and his wife, probably ancestors, with heavy ruffed collars and unhappy stares.

186

Getting down to the cheap stuff. Next to the dining room was a kitchen, very simple, with a Frigidaire—almost as stunning in its grandeur as the Caravello—and a sink from the fifteenth century. Who did the cooking? thought Theresa. That Spanish girl! How splendidly democratic of her! Theresa peered into the fridge. Butter. Bacon. Eggs from Antonio's chickens. Lettuce from Antonio's rows. Thieves, thought Theresa fiercely.

At the end of the corridor was the bedroom, and Theresa leaned against the door, awed. It was the most elegant bedroom she had ever seen, stunning in its austerity, its total simplicity. The walls were white, the furniture—what little there was—black. A heavily carved bed against the wall facing the window. A huge armoire, again of oak, heavily carved. A long table against the wall and two high-backed chairs. That was all. The elegance came from the perfect proportions of the room and the proportions of the furniture, which must have been designed and carved to fit the exact spaces they filled in that room. The painting over the table was another Caravello. Only a Spanish aristocrat could have kept the room so breathtakingly simple. Theresa was drunk with the perfection of it. She leaned against the doorway, letting her eyes take it in slowly, moving from object to object—there were very few—absorbing it into her soul. My bourgeois education, she thought. I should be outraged. Instead I'm enchanted. A betrayal of my social principles? Not necessarily. Enjoyment of the beauty

187

of the world was not only a privilege but a sacred duty.

She tore away her eyes at last because there was work to be done. Back at the great brass-studded door, she took out the massive key and examined it closely. Its very size would make the job fairly simple. She put it back in the lock and turned it back and forth. Aah, good! A well-oiled lock that turned easily.

She took out the key and went back upstairs in search of a piece of paper. She found white writing paper on the table, a pen in the table drawer. Placing the big key on the white surface, she traced it carefully. She measured the thickness of each of the indentations in its filigreed teeth, drew the exact circumference of its stem, restored the key to its lock.

Then, a last look at Caravello's painting—the martyred figure on the cross, arms outstretched. She looked at the bony, agonized face, then in the hall mirror at her own face—just as bony, just as agonized. I've always envied Jesus his cross, she thought, humbly, and it is a sin. She flattened herself against the wall, arms outstretched, imagining her own cross, eyes uplifted, filled with rapture.

Oh, my God, what am I doing? Masturbating! She sank to her knees, torn with self-revulsion, chin on her chest, dry-eyed, horrorstruck with the enormity. She was as exhausted as if she'd climbed the great hill with the cross on her shoulder.

Back in her sentinel room, with the knife Antonio had given her, she carved a replica of the

great key out of tough eucalyptus wood. Making
wooden keys had been one of her specialties in the
Black Torrent and she was very good at it. A hiding
place, she was thinking fiercely. In case They come.
As They always did.

Elf woke, alert. Eyes closed she listened to the
padding of the Englishman about the tiny flat.
Elephant, thought Elf. If he couldn't rob a girl with
more finesse than that, he richly deserved . . . She
didn't finish the thought, just lay there breathing
quietly, listening intently. The thin rustle of paper
came to her ears. Elf had wrapped her wad of banknotes in tissue paper—an underground trick she'd
devised her very self—because there simply was
no way to unwrap tissue paper without making a
noise as distinctive as falling water. In a single continuous movement Elf reached under the mattress
near her head, pulled out her gun, and rose to a
sitting position, gun in her hand, naked—and instantly felt a rush of sexuality that almost made her
swoon.

Pointing a gun at a man while *naked*! She'd
pointed guns at a lot of men. This was the first time
naked. A new, thoroughly alarming thrill. Elf felt
her nipples harden, her breathing coming fast as
if she couldn't get enough oxygen. Jesus, I've got
to keep control.

The Englishman had frozen, eyes on the snub-
nosed .38, mouth open. A pretty picture in fright,
thought Elf calming a little. He had her tissue-

paper-wrapped packet of bills in his hands, both hands, caught in the very act of unwrapping.

"Do you always rob girls so early in the morning?" whispered Elf throatily.

"Put that thing down." The Englishman's voice was unnaturally high, taut with fright.

"Never had a gun pointed at you before," whispered Elf, almost faint with pleasure. "The first time always . . . turns the bowels to water." Followed by the famous Elf smile, which was as involuntary as a hiccup when she pointed a gun at a man. She threw the blanket off her lower half. Sexuality was beginning to make her sweat.

The Englishman, naked, stupefied, held the bundle of cash in both hands, eyes on the gun. "It's a fearful amount of money," he blurted unexpectedly.

"Bank robbery," smiled Elf. She pulled her naked legs up under her now and leaned forward, sighting down the barrel, breathing hard, trying to pull herself together.

The Englishman's eyes glazed. Bank robbery! "A little girl like you—robbing a bank." He tried a smile. "How splendid."

"Six banks." Elf's smile as wide as the sky.

The Englishman grew jaunty—or tried. "We could rob a bank together, you and I. I've always . . . wanted to rob a bank. Hasn't everyone?"

It wasn't bad, thought Elf, sighting down the barrel. This terrified English worm was giving it a good try.

"I've killed six . . . no, seven men."

There was a shattering authority in that bare-boned statement—fully supported by the professional ease and athletic stance of the naked girl, gun held fully stretched in both hands, steady as a rock.

"One more wouldn't matter, would it?" murmured Elf in a silky voice.

"Well, then, why bother?" The Englishman was fencing now, coming up with the lightning riposte, ingratiating himself, which was, after all, his profession. "A waste of a bullet, me."

I'm losing initiative, thought Elf. She rose from the bed and stood very straight. "Put the money back in the bag," she whispered, sighting down the barrel to give thrust to the command.

"Absolutely." Frost pushed the cash back into her oversize shoulder bag, still jaunty, still trying. "You must understand I only wanted enough to buy you breakfast. I'm a bit down on my luck."

"Tell me about it," smiled Elf, savoring the bliss in her loins, prolonging it.

"I came here originally with a lady . . . a rich lady . . ."

"I'll bet," she smiled.

"She left me for another."

"I can scarcely believe any woman would do such a thing."

The Englishman paused. "You really shouldn't taunt—not with a gun in your hand. It's hardly fair, is it?"

"Life is very unfair," whispered Elf dreamily, feeling the urgencies of her devouring loins, heaven and hell opening up beneath her.

He misunderstood—both the remark and the dreamy sexuality in Elf's face. "Oh, it is! It is!" He stepped forward, hand outstretched appealingly, to relieve her of her gun as he would relieve a lady of her cloak. "Let me take that—"

It was as far as he got. "Hand me that bag!" exploded Elf—like a revolver shot.

It penetrated to the core of him. She saw a glimmer of foreboding light up his eyes like spectral fire.

He handed over the bag, speechless.

"Lie face down on the bed," whispered Elf, unable to put timbre in her voice.

She saw the stark fear in him now. He's intelligent, she thought, and that will make it worse. Fear has undone the chemistry of him, changed the basic elements of his humanity into a different compound altogether.

He tried one more time. "It's my least attractive aspect, my ass. If you'd just . . ."

"Lie face down or I'll kill you."

He fell on the bed then like a stone face buried in the pillow, as if he might banish the whole scene, change it back to Square One.

Elf knelt warily at the foot of the bed and bound the man's feet with the nylon cord left over from Denis Mitchell. One length was enough. Nobody could break nylon. Binding the arms was dangerous. She would have to lay down the gun and he might try a quick grab for it.

The Englishman raised his head from the pillow: "You don't intend to leave me here, do you?"

She bound the legs tightly to the bed with the sheet, anchoring him so that a grab would fall short.

"The cleaning woman doesn't come until Tuesday. Nobody comes."

Elf made a loop of the remaining nylon cord, slung it around both wrists and pulled it tight in one movement, then bound hands and arms tightly against the body.

The Englishman tried yet once again.

"You're not contemplating going to the police, of course. Because of course you couldn't explain all that money, could you? Anyway, I couldn't believe a nice girl like you would condemn me to the hell of a Spanish jail." Professional charm, diluted by terror.

Elf unbound the legs from the bed and rolled him over, cock up. She gazed at it, licking her lips.

"I'm afraid this situation has unmanned me." The Englishman trying a joke.

"Shut up," said Elf. "We'll talk in a minute."

She put the gun on the floor and sucked the man's cock until she felt it harden in her mouth. She climbed astride him and slipped it into her cunt with a little gasp of pleasure. Female rape! How very nice. She worked her body up and down. The Englishman began to smile. Oh, she wanted to play sex games! She could read it in his eyes—and let him think it.

Lying full length on the man now, her face four inches from him, Elf smiled. "So you seduce all the girls and steal their money!"

193

"What other choice have I? You don't understand my position. . . ."

Elf gurgled with laughter. "Oh, I understand your position very well. You are on top of the girls—at least until now."

A flicker of fear in his eyes. He's catching on, thought Elf. Mustn't have that. Not yet. She went Marilyn Monroe, parting her lips, eyes bright with lust, all female.

"Tell me," she whispered, "in your seductions did you meet a girl who . . ." How to describe Theresa? "Blond. American. Twenty-four years old. Thin. Very thin. With a haunted face."

The question took him by surprise. Elf held her tough little body motionless, trying to get him off sex for a moment.

"An American girl," said the Englishman. "Yes, there was . . . one. At the cable office. But I didn't seduce her. Honestly! She wouldn't even talk to me."

"Thin," whispered Elf. "Very thin. A wraith with a haunted face."

"Oh, that's her, but believe me, I didn't . . ."

"What was she doing at the cable office?" whispered Elf.

"She was trying to send a coded message. And it's against the rules."

"Aah," breathed Elf. Theresa sending her coded plea to Mitchell. "And what happened to the girl?"

"I don't know! She bolted into the ladies'."

Theresa's favorite trick for getting rid of men!

"I haven't seen her since."

Elf kissed him and fucked him until he came inside her. She came, too, thinking of Theresa. Afterward she lay on his body, breathing heavily, spent and a little scared. What now, little girl? What now? The Englishman was getting bolder, confident of his cock's prowess.

"Can't we be friends again?" he said in a very casual voice. "This is terribly painful, with my arms underneath me, you know."

Elf smiled absently and climbed off him. She retrieved her bag and dug into it for her spool of tape. "Don't you like sex games?" she said, her voice normal for the first time.

"If you'll untie me, I can show you sex games you don't even suspect."

"I'll bet," said Elf, smiling. She went into the little bathroom and tore up a hand towel. Back in the bedroom, she acted swiftly. "Open wide," she said, sticking a knuckle in his kidneys. His mouth flew open to utter pain and she popped the towel into it. She taped the mouth firmly shut. Then she smiled down at him, testing his nostrils to be sure he could breathe.

That done, Elf did nothing for a very long time. She sat on the bed, stark naked, not looking at him, her arms hanging down between her legs. There's no need for this, she was thinking, the thought coming against her will. No need! No need! I know what I know. She went to the window and gazed out pensively at the Blue Mediterranean, sparkling in the morning sunshine. She could hear the sounds of Palma waking up, the traffic hotting up on

195

the seaway drive, metal shop windows being flung open. They went to work early in Palma.

Moral imperatives throbbed in her skull. It's because I've come, she thought. Pangs of conscience. If that's what they were. She gazed out to sea, feeling the cool breezes against her naked breasts. My goddamned mind, thought Elf, is sorting this out with the mathematical clarity of a computer. This is altogether different from the other time. You had to wrench information from that New England clam, thought Elf, but this English worm has nothing more to offer in the line of information. I should get out of here while still sated, before my goddamned cunt . . .

She came away from the window and gazed down at the trussed Englishman. I haven't the smallest flicker of feeling for him. It's not him, she thought. It's my immortal soul that's in peril, my sacred revolutionary purpose. This is vice! Sexual depravity! She lashed herself with moral resolve for the simple reason that she was afraid, for almost the first time in her life, of losing her own self-control. "Always before I've held it together," she whispered aloud.

The whisper galvanized the Englishman. She saw a flicker of sheer terror go through the eyes. He's guessed, she thought. He's guessed! The trouble was that the terror in his eyes ignited her like a match. She was engulfed by her sexuality again. For a long minute she stood there, sexual desire consuming her.

"I'm sorry!" she mumbled to him, shamed to the core.

She got the bamboo sticks from her shoulder bag and began the torment. Twenty minutes later, she tore off her blond wig and tortured him in her own hair, in her own name, as it were. Time and again he would pass out. She'd wait for him to come to and she would resume, inventing new delicacies with the bamboo sticks. The bells of the cathedral started to boom forth to the Christian faithful in the middle of the morning and she tortured on, sweat pouring from her body, unable to stop herself, hating it and loving it—and coming again and again. Oh, God, help me, thought Elf, as the bells pealed. Shortly after noon the Englishman expired, and then Elf lay down next to the body, mouth open wide, breathing very hard, waiting for the revulsion. When it came, it was too shattering for tears. No tears. I've been shorn of my tear ducts as punishment.

She rose leadenly from the bed and stared at her face in the bathroom mirror. Haggard. The emptiness of the face horrified her. Or would have horrified her if she had any horror left. I've been drained of horror as well as tears. I am an unperson. All cunt, no soul, no mind, no anything.

The body.

Something had to be done with that goddamned corpse. Elf stirred the remnants of herself. She emptied the little fridge of its few possessions—a half loaf of bread, a sliver of butter, two bottles of tonic, ice cubes. Poor English. He'd been a rotten con man. She felt no pity. Not even for me, thought Elf. Certainly not for that male prick. She took out the shelves of the fridge. It would be just big enough, if she got him in there before the body stiffened.

By myself, thought Elf. That is my problem. I'm too much alone. It's made me unhuman. Also, when need be, superhuman. It took superhuman, or at least superfemale, strength to collapse the body like an accordion, knees up to chin, and push it into the fridge. Elf summoned it up from she knew not where. She stuffed the bloody sheets in with it, though there had not been much blood. Very neat, Chinese torture.

Elf lay on the bed and stared at the ceiling as if it were eternity.

CHAPTER

27

Antonio came to her in the tower sentinel room after he'd finished feeding his animals. She was kneeling in the hay, lost in contemplation.

"*Madrileños,*" said Antonio.

"I know," said Theresa.

He put his fingers to his lips, kneeling next to her. Theresa nodded, mutinously. She was to be quiet. She knew that. She didn't like this skulking. "*No incendio.*" She nodded dumbly. No fire. She mustn't cook.

"May I breathe?" she asked ironically.

Even that bothered him because she had spoken aloud in normal tones. He put his fingers to his lips again, counseling her to be quiet. It aroused her indignation. "Quake, like an animal," she said fiercely. "Not me. Or you either, Antonio. They are bourgeois vermin living off the sweat of your labor! Parasites!" In her fierce social indignation, she put her arms around his neck and looked into his eyes with passion.

"You are worth twenty of them, Antonio! They do nothing! You are a man of earth and fire. You make things grow! You tend the flocks and harvest the oranges. They are useless."

He smelled of sweat and leather and mule, ferociously male, and it turned her on. She'd never had her body pressed against his before. She could feel sexuality throb within her and that turned him on. Almost against his will. She could see him struggling with it. Why struggle? It's as natural as breathing. Her eyes invited, mouth open, body pliant.

I must not do anything further than this, she thought, arms around his neck, eyes large with desire. From here on he must take me—or it will be spoiled for him.

He kissed her finally, almost reverently. I'm to be treated like a madonna, thought Theresa swimming in bliss—because it had been a very long time since a man had kissed her.

They lay side by side in the hay smiling, gazing into each other's eyes. His courtship is as old as his agriculture. I'm in the ninth century. Their bodies were touching and she could feel his cock hardening against her. When it was fully stretched, he took her because he couldn't prevent himself. Very simple, very basic. This was the way it ought to be, thought Theresa, the very last thought she had. After that she was all body.

Hawkins and the Spanish police chief were being driven in the police chief's car with the police chief's chauffeur along the cliff face on the southwestern edge of the island. Hawkins had not wanted the chauffeur—or for that matter the police chief. But then he was in someone else's country. One must observe the conventions. He didn't quite know what the police chief was trying to tell him but, whatever it was, he was taking a circuitous route.

Hawkins looked down the dizzying precipice at the water eight hundred feet below. One of the most beautiful drives in the world, he was thinking, but what had it to do with catching Theresa and Elf? At Banulbufar, the police chief had treated him to a disquisition on the terraces that led the eye in easy curves to the sea, dwelling on their antiquity. All made by slave labor in the ninth century. Yet there they were a thousand years later, not only exquisitely beautiful but also marvelously utilitarian, still performing the function of buttressing the land against wind and water for man to till and grow crops on.

Hawkins admired and listened. It was an editorial, an apologia, an outcry of conservatism—something one didn't hear much in the western world any more. "One shouldn't have to endorse slavery to admire its works, should one?" inquired the Spaniard. "No," said Hawkins, wondering. What sort of position was he being driven into? "I am thinking of your revolutionary children," murmured the police chief. "Revolution! So much bloodshed for so little reform. These things cure themselves. In our country slavery just went away, leaving behind these beautiful terraces. In yours, the Civil War left scars that have not healed to this day."

Hawkins was astounded the Spaniard had even heard of the American Civil War. He felt impelled to some defense. "We are a revolutionary people," he pointed out. "The United States came into existence by revolution."

The Spaniard looked inscrutable. "Are you quite sure that was necessary?" said the Spaniard. "Canada is as free as you are—without all that bloodshed."

"Two hundred years later," said Hawkins.

The Spaniard permitted himself a small gray smile. "You Anglo-Saxons are so impatient. What's two hundred years?"

That's what he's trying to tell me, thought Hawkins, that time scale is all. But what has it to do with my search?

They paused for lunch at Deya, where Robert Graves, the poet, lived. Hawkins ate *paella* and looked at the bearded and sandaled youth walking the streets, lounging in the cafés. "This is the closest thing to St. Germain des Prés Majorca has to offer," said the Spaniard. "Your revolutionary children would fit in very well here."

He called over the bartender, who appeared also to be the owner, and spoke to him for quite a while in Spanish. "They are not here," said the Spaniard with finality, "and they have never been here." Then he added almost grudgingly "They are very well known—your revolutionary children. He has heard them discussed by the writers and artists here. But they are not here and never have been."

Very shrewd, thought Hawkins. Deya would be

the sort of place Theresa would gravitate to. He doubted whether Elf would.

After lunch, the Spaniard drove him to the cliff-side estate of a long-dead archduke and they walked through the trees far above the sea. "His mistress lived here. He lived at another estate up there." He pointed up the cliff. Is he suggesting they might be here, wondered Hawkins, or am I getting another lecture on how pleasant life was in the nineteenth century? A bit of both. "We have many anachronisms like these huge estates on the island," explained the chief. "They might have taken refuge here. Both estates are very big." He spoke to the caretaker who showed visitors through the old house, which reeked of nineteenth-century passion like mothballs.

"She doesn't think anyone is hiding out here. No loss of food, which is the first thing we notice. We might just poke around while we're here." They visited the folly, which hung on the stone cliff like a bird's nest, the sea pounding six hundred feet down, inspected the old stables, where the landaus and carriages still stood ready for the archduke to take his old girl friend for a drive, and sniffed the flowers in the immense old-fashioned greenhouse.

"I didn't know Spain had archdukes," said Hawkins.

"He was a Russian," said the Spaniard. "Spain has dukes, no archdukes. One of the Spanish dukes is in Majorca at this very time. Visiting his estate. He has twenty-six big estates scattered about Spain. Tens of thousands of acres."

Hawkins couldn't resist: "Do you approve of that—one man owning tens of thousands of acres while so many of your people have so little? Or nothing?"

The Spanish police chief pursed his gray lips and stared out to sea, saying nothing. It was like asking if he approved of God.

Days passed. Elf lay on the bed, face upward, sleeping, waking, sometimes—the worst of all—in between sleep and awake, when the demons crawled out of her nostrils, and she thought them real.

I must get out of this room! Why don't I?

She had jailed herself. Voluntary imprisonment. She couldn't move, could scarcely move off the bed. The bed where it had all happened. The bliss, the torment. You must pay for everything. Every last mouthful is paid for.

Awake, naked still because she could not summon the strength to put on her clothes, she would stare out the window at the blue Mediterranean. The cathedral bells drove her almost into shrieking madness.

Mad I am. Shrieking mad not yet.

Why do I care? Another body. That English worm!

Am I going to carry him around my neck for the rest of my life, an albatross?

No, no, it's because I'm alone. I must get out of this room. The room is my punishment. My aloneness! She drank coffee, felt no hunger, felt nothing for hours—then the blackness would descend. This is what hell is like—not flames, just black depression! Just the bottomless pit. No end, no end.

Her face twisted into a savage grimace, the closest thing to a smile she could muster. She was past suicide. Wasn't that truly comical! I should have died hereafter. There would have been a time for such a word. Tomorrow and tomorrow and tomorrow creeps in this petty pace from day to day, to the last syllable of recorded time, which is the precise measure of time I have spent in this God-cursed room. Lady Macbeth, oh, she was an angel of mercy, next to Elf. Canst thou not minister to a mind diseased, pluck from the memory a rooted sorrow, raze out the written troubles of the brain . . .?

Leave me alone, Lady Macbeth. I have my own troubles next to which yours were naught. Throw physic to the dogs. Come put mine armour on. That's the talk. My brain, my damned brain that once learned *Macbeth*, on a bet, from end to end in a weekend.

No brain, no brain, all cunt, me. Hell is just one all-devouring cunt, a word Shakespeare would have relished, would he not?

Antonia carried her blanket, her pail, her cup, her saucer, her two pots, her candles. There wasn't much, after all. She carried her big shoulder bag. That was all. Behind she left two important possessions, because Antonio couldn't be allowed to know about those. Deep in the straw were her .38, and the wooden key to the front door. She'd have to

come and get those another time when Antonio
wasn't there to watch.

"Why are we fleeing in the middle of the night?"
she asked. In English. But he understood the fierce-
ness of the question and perhaps even the sense.

They were passing through the audience chamber
and she seized him and stopped him and put her
arms around his neck. "Flight is my destiny. It's
not yours, Antonio. You should never run away.
Not you."

Proudly. After all, he was her lover now. Her
stance has changed in a twinkling from cool objec-
tive to ferociously possessive.

"*Madrileños*," he said in a whisper as if afraid
they might hear.

"You're afraid they'll catch me in your arms,"
said Theresa laughing. "Am I an object of shame?"
Because of course she knew she wasn't. "I love
you, you mindless, stinking peasant, and I don't
care who knows it—and you shouldn't either."

She kissed him, Antonio struggling but not very
hard. Still, he was in a hurry and he didn't put up
with it long. He broke the embrace and seized her
hand and hurried her along.

"I fall in love much too easily," she whispered as
they felt their way down the crazy steps. "You
must understand you're not the only one. There have
been many others."

That was the nice thing about Antonio. You
could tell him everything, thought Theresa, dazed
with happiness. My forest lover, my man of mystery.

Mystery? She knew Antonio quite well now even

without language—his superstitions, his wisdom. "I even understand this flight," she said as they walked down the white road. "I just don't approve of it. I am like a wife who understands her husband's response to any given situation—without always approving of it."

Antonio grunted.

"We have some marvelous conversations, you and I," said Theresa merrily.

A mile down the white road toward the closed end of the valley, Antonio abruptly turned off and started up the hill through scrub pine and underbrush, Theresa struggling and stumbling behind him. A steep and painful climb. At the crest of the hill was his cottage—small, square whitewashed stone. There was no road to it, hardly even a path. A tethered goat looked at them as they approached. Theresa gave it a passing caress because she could not pass any animal without caressing it.

Suppose I find a wife inside!

There was no one. Her flashlight flickered from one corner to the other. A bed hand-hewn of unpainted pine stood out from the rear windowless wall. It had been neatly made, with a single blanket tucked in all around. He was very neat, her peasant. Nothing was out of order, but then there was little to be out of order. A stone basin with a bucket next to it. A fireplace hung with a few pots. From the rough-hewn beams hung black hams, sausages, and strings of onions. That was all.

Theresa closed her eyes and smelled deeply. The smell of mule and sweat and ham. She put her arms around Antonio and kissed him fiercely. Now that I'm his I can be bold as brass. Now he won't mind.

They clambered into the bed, fully clothed. Malodorous straw. I must change it if I'm to be his wife— if that's what I'm to be. He was fumbling again with her peasant trousers. She took them off and submitted. Submission, she thought, is what I'm for, what I do best. He smelled of mule and sweat and saddle soap, acridly, and she loved the fierce thrust of him. Oh, I'm a mindless peasant too, mindless, mindless, mindless. . . .

Afterward he fell asleep instantly.

She lay awake, mind as sharp as a blade to all the little sharp pricks. In lovemaking one lives entirely in the present. But after? Afterward I become all past and future. I am Theresa, girl fugitive. I wish I hadn't left my gun in the straw. A girl fugitive should never be without her gun.

Money. A night thought. What do I need money for? I have Antonio. Money, the curse of the world.

Still, the thought nagged her as night thoughts always do. The money would be waiting at American Express. . . .

CHAPTER
28

She was alone. Even without opening her eyes she could feel his absence. Ah, well . . . She opened her eyes on sunlight filtering through a very dirty windowpane. There were only two windows, both filthy. They let in little light. That was why she had slept so late. She was accustomed to dazzling sunshine in her sentinel room. She missed it. And the fresh air. The little stone hut smelled of bodies.

Theresa arose, threw open the heavy wooden door, and stepped out into the sunshine and the spring smells of the hilltop. The sun was very high. What time was it? Eleven A.M. at least. She had not slept so late in years. I've been fucked, she thought wryly. It relaxes the muscles of the mind and tires the muscles of the body. She felt so marvelous she felt guilty. I am unworthy of such glorious feeling—and then felt guilty about her guilt. Clearly, it was God's wish that she feel glorious, not guilty.

The goat eyed her from the end of his tether and she caressed him and kissed his nose. She would have preferred the mule and her rabbits, but if a goat was all there was to caress, she caressed that. After a bit she sank to her knees. Carnal love was one of God's blessings or why did it exist? Blessed be my carnal nature. I love not only my peasant but the sunshine, the trees, the fields. She was flooded with love, drenched with it. I am one with my God at this moment and how many moments have I had like that in my whole life? Not one! Not one!

"*Buena día!*"

It was like an explosion, a desecration. Theresa scrambled to her feet, outraged.

The *Madrileño* stood there. Where had he come from? How dare he! In her moment of Godhood! She glared at him with such ferocity that he stepped back a pace.

"*Losiento,*" he stammered. "*Perdóname, por favor.*"

Well! She'd unsettled him then. He looked thoroughly flummoxed at this apparition of a blond wafer-thin girl on her knees. He kept stammering apologies, and Theresa helped him not a jot. She glared truculently. Capitalist vermin, living on the backs of the oppressed peasant, one of them her Antonio! That's what she thought and it all hung out.

He fell into a splutter of Spanish—and then Mallorquin, looking ever more perplexed. He was a very handsome aristocrat and he knew a lot of languages. He tried French, which Theresa understood—full of "*Je m'excuse*" and revolving around the idea that he "*était cherché*" Antonio. She decided not to own up to understanding French or any language at all. The idea so amused her she burst out laughing, full in his face. This was so total a change of mood that it dumbfounded him altogether—and offended him. He gave her a deeply wounded look. Clearly he wasn't accustomed to being laughed at. It touched her, that look, and she stopped laughing abruptly.

"I'm sorry," she said contritely.

Damn! She'd blown her cover. It had just popped out of her like a hiccup. *I'm sorry.* My damned upbringing. In olden times there had been the patrician accent that distinguished peasant from aristocrat. Now, *I'm sorry.* It showed her up—clearly Anglo-Saxon, clearly no peasant. She'd been branded by her damned manners for the cursed bourgeois she was.

His brown eyes widened only a moment. Then he smiled.

"English," he said softly.

Theresa let it pass. English, then. If she couldn't pass as a peasant, she'd at least not revealed her Americanhood. That cover at least remained.

He was looking at her thoughtfully, mouth pursed, smiling a little.

"I am very sorry if I interrupted your . . . devotions," he said. "I was looking for Antonio."

Theresa had a pretty good idea where Antonio was at any hour of the day. She'd learned his habits very well.

"He's in *naranjal norte.*" Antonio's name for it.

They'd been picking oranges there for a week.

He continued to regard her, finger to his lips now, "I didn't know Antonio had a *señora*."

Señora meant wife, woman, the same thing almost in that class.

"You've come since my last visit."

"And when was that?" Scornfully. Theresa couldn't resist. Visited his *palacio* once a year, did he?

He didn't answer. Instead he gazed at her, very thoughtful indeed, for a very long time.

"You're not English," he said. "You're an American. No one but an American says *that* quite so thatly. Like a piece of wood hitting a table!"

His eyes crinkled wryly.

Showing off his cleverness, thought Theresa. He was regarding her very steadily now, chin cupped in his hand, thoroughly assured. He's passed through a dozen moods since he surprised me. I'm beginning to know him very well, damn his eyes. She knew his schools. Certainly English. The Spanish aristocracy was far too clever to send their children to their own rotten Catholic schools. His amusements: shooting certainly. They went around the world slaughtering birds at the precisely fashionable moment—England in the fall, Spain in late summer, South Carolina in—when—February? She even knew pretty well who he'd know in Philadelphia. International jet set. Oh, I know you very well— and I despise you. Except that she didn't. You couldn't possibly despise anyone so self-possessed as he was.

Still he gazed, his self-possession even beginning to unsettle her a bit.

He turned on his heel and walked away from her half a dozen paces, then turned and faced her again, his hand cupping his chin. It would have been rude, that gaze, in almost anyone but him. He gazed, very courteously, she thought wryly, neither undressing her nor prying into her mind. Just gazing.

"I've seen your face before, you know," he said.

Oh, dear God! Alarm skittered through her brain and all over her face. My damned face that shows every last thought!

"Oh, you needn't worry," he said quickly. He'd seen the alarm as clearly as if she'd rung bells. "I don't . . . I wouldn't . . ." He was too courteous to say what he wouldn't do. Blow the whistle! But how well did he know her face?

Her eyes bored into his, trying to find out. He'd seen her face in the papers? How much did he remember?

Terror engulfed her—and it communicated to him immediately. He came to her side. "*Señora*, I assure you you have nothing to fear from me. It is none of my concern. It was all a very long time ago. The only reason I remember your face at all . . ." He hesitated, pursing his lips, as if wondering whether he should tell her. He shrugged, deciding he had no choice.

"I knew your mother. When your face appeared in the papers, I . . ." He made an expressive gesture with his gloved hand. "Otherwise I'd long ago have forgotten. I'm sorry."

213

Sorry! That damned word again. We go around the world stepping on toes and saying we're sorry!

"You have my solemn vow, *señora*, that I will not breathe a word of your whereabouts to anyone."

My solemn vow, thought Theresa. Only a Spanish aristocrat could say the words without bursting out laughing. Still, he'd keep his vow, that one would. Wild horses couldn't drag her secret out of him. He was that kind of person, as antiquated as King Arthur.

"Including Mother," rapped Theresa. "Especially Mother."

"Especially Mother!" He smiled and bowed.

The bow too. Oh, hell, I'm no longer a peasant to him. She couldn't let him get away with it unscathed. She dropped a curtsy to him, a relic of her dancing-school days. If we're going old world, let us by all means go all the way. My larky spirits!

He laughed.

"I must congratulate Antonio on his excellent judgment." He turned and walked off down the hill, whistling "Long Ago and Far Away," a Jerome Kern tune as sentimental and out of date as himself.

CHAPTER

29

Hawkins waited, the telephone cradled between ear and pillow. Steel would ask a lot of questions and he had no answers. He examined the palm of his hand, searching for clues in the life line, the love line—is that what they called them? A fifty-five-year-old man spent too much time alone—friends dying off and no new ones replacing them, wives deep in their own pursuits. Mistresses? What a laugh—his love line! I'm too old to leave the FBI. Even if fresh pastures wanted me, do I want them?

He jiggled the hook, helplessly. Telephoning anywhere in Majorca was an exercise in exasperation that consumed hours of his day. A week! Nothing done. Well, not nothing. He'd eliminated and police work was largely elimination. Negative. Suppose he had Theresa in his . . . grasp (nice word, that, "grasp") at this very moment, what would he do? Question her? Of course. Make love? What an idea!

His real fear—a very great fear—was that when he had Theresa—finally *had* her as he knew that he someday would (no matter what Steel did or tried to do)—his fear was that after all these years he might be disappointed in the girl. I'm expecting too much! Too much! Imagine, an FBI man demanding that his prey live up to his expectations! Did any other FBI man in all history harbor such high expectations of a fugitive from justice? Oh, things have come to a pretty pass when police officers exalt their fugitives. If anyone suspected such a thing, I'd be placed in the hands of a psychiatrist— yet it is not me that needs a psychiatrist, it is society itself. I admire this girl (if admiration defines my feelings correctly), not because I'm insane but because, Your Honor, by most civilized lights she *is* admirable. She is intelligent, selfless, courageous, hard-working, frugal, abstemious, idealistic—all things we once considered admirable—and still a fugitive from justice. Who's loony now?

The call came through.

"Yes, she's definitely here," said Hawkins to Steel without preamble, not letting him get into his complaints. "I need another week. She's been sighted by three people. One more week and I'll have them both." Remembering in the nick of time that Steel's interest was Elf. "Elf's been sighted too."

He hung up with his authorization. Lies, every last bit of it. Theresa had not been sighted. Neither had Elf, but who would know? He'd never told lies before—certainly not to a superior or to anyone else in the FBI.

"This pursuit has changed my personality, my

216

character?" said Hawkins to his love line on his
palm. "For the better? Well, now, who is to say?"

Elf settled at the corner table of the sidewalk
café where all the expatriates hung out. Her first
venture into the outside world. Four days in that
room! The hardest thing she'd ever done in her
activist life was getting dressed, forcing herself to
the street. It was the demons that did it. She'd not
felt hunger, not once. But starvation had made her
intelligence flicker—and that had brought the
demons, the apparitions. I'm losing my mind, my
last possession. That had driven her off the bed,
finally, forced her into putting on her clothes. My
intelligence is slipping away and without my mind
what's left?

The face that confronted her in the mirror would
have horrified her if she had not been well beyond
horror. Gaunt, skull-like, a death's head. She looked
middle-aged, like a figure in one of George Grosz's
savage cartoons of postwar Germany. Well, good!
She'd blend into those rotten expatriate faces as
if she'd never been anywhere else.

She ordered a *café solo* and vanilla ice cream.
Her first food in days. She couldn't swallow much.
She hoped she could hold it down. The best position,
the corner table, her thoughts swimming a little, as
if she were at sea.

She looked about to steady herself, to test her
wits. Aah, yes, there was the post office where
Theresa must have sent her cable, fifty yards up
the street. From this seat one could also cover the

paseo where Theresa would have to go to American Express to pick up her money. Every expatriate in Majorca would sooner or later have to pass this point.

Elf took out the little compact mirror and looked at herself, a loathsome bourgeois act she forced herself to do for the sheer authenticity of it. Blond wig, enormous dark glasses, reddened lips. An abomination of a face. The sheer awfulness of it gave her a crumb of comfort. This was not Elf and if it was not Elf why must I feel this horror? But horror is my condition now. Like a chronic illness I must get used to it as a cripple to his crutch.

Elf stiffened, alarm bells going off in her skull. Two men had walked into the pavement part of the expatriate cage—both shriekingly out of place. These were no expatriates! Fuzz! Elf could smell fuzz in any language! Spanish cop—and he looked very high-up Spanish cop! All that gold braid! The other —plain-clothed cop, but cop as cop could be. American.

She fought the desire to dive behind the *International Herald Tribune*. Instead she stared boldly. The smartest thing to do because everyone in the café was staring, mouth agape. The elderly Austrian with the little dog. The English ancients who came every day. The American rich idiot with the yacht, the others. They all stared at the Spanish police chief and the American FBI man with open-mouthed curiosity because they looked so cop, so normal, so healthy, so official in this expatriate den of degeneracy. In her blond wig, sheltered behind her huge spectacles with her reddened aged-looking lips, Elf stared too, looking just as degenerate as everyone else—sinking into a sea of anonymous degeneracy.

"This is where they all come," said the Spanish police chief. "Eventually."

Not Theresa, thought Hawkins. Not his Theresa—a girl he'd never met.

The two men stood at the entrance, a little passageway, between tubs of shrubbery that separated the café from the rest of the sidewalk. Hawkins looked over the denizens one by one, his gaze lingering for a moment on each one separately—the American boy and his girl companion, the Austrian and the dog, the English, the blonde bedizened one, the mother and submissive daughter from Germany, the enormously fat woman who was supposed to procure girls for rich Englishmen . . .

"There are more tables inside," said the Spanish police chief.

The men went inside. Hawkins resumed his survey. A gaunt man of indeterminate age who looked like a refugee from Dachau, another of those bedizened blonde women who roamed the world looking for men or diversion like that one outside.

The one outside? The face flashed back into Hawkins' mind. Blonde, huge spectacles, reddened lips, *retroussé* nose . . . *Retroussé* nose!

"Wait!" said Hawkins.

He darted back outside. The corner table was empty, pesetas in the saucer to pay for the *café solo*.

The bird had flown. Or had she? There were lots of *retroussé* noses in the world. But why so precipitately?

"Pardon me," said Hawkins to the English ancients. "Did you happen to notice the blonde woman at that table? Which way did she go?"

The ancient pair pointed, as one, toward the *paseo*.

Hawkins strode out of the café into the *paseo*, which was full of passersby of all descriptions— except for a blonde girl with a *retroussé* nose. Back in the café, Hawkins questioned first the English old parties, then everyone else. Did they know the blonde girl with the *retroussé* nose? Had they seen her there before? How many times? Recently arrived? Aah! Been there only twice. Seen to leave with an Englishman who liked to pick girls up. No, they hadn't seen the Englishman again—but it was early for him. Four, no, five days ago, yes, that was when the blonde girl and the Englishman were last seen together.

Where did the Englishman live? Aah, they all laughed. They must find one of his girls to answer that. He never took anyone but the girls there. The girls came and left Majorca by every boat.

Hawkins cursed himself. The damned climate had slowed his reactions. He was sure it was Elf and just as sure that she'd never go back to that café again.

"We can find the Englishman," said the Spanish police chief. "It may take a couple of hours."

Elf would be long gone, thought Hawkins.

After the first disgraceful day, when she had lain long in the straw bed, Theresa sprang up with Antonio—at first light, 6 A.M. usually. She prepared his coffee—all he had for breakfast. But, when he went off to milk the goats, she remained behind to straighten out the stone hut—throwing open door and both windows to air it out, changing the straw of the mattress, washing the windows, scouring the pots, washing Antonio's spare blouse and his best trousers.

Only then did she join him in the field. She irrigated the small garden patch now, letting the water out of the slime-green stone catchment, directing it down the rows of lettuce and carrots and beans, choking it off. Afterward they picked oranges, which were the chief cash crop. Backbreaking toil.

Four days! Married bliss, ho! No ceremony, but Theresa felt connubial. This must be what marriage on the poverty line was like. Part of my education, she thought fiercely. All my thoughts are fierce these days. It defines me—my ferocity. My soul blazes.

"Good morning!"

Oh, dear God! Why does he always catch me on my knees. She was planting melons on a bed of solid horseshit, the best bed for it, in the stone frame —herself smelling to high heaven.

She looked up, swallowing her resentment, smoothing her face. "*Buena día, excelencia!*" She had discovered he was a duke. A duke! She tugged at her forelock in a parody of deference. Peasant, me. Let him make of it what he would! Capitalist beast!

A friend of Mother's! What have I done, dear God, to deserve this? I have fled to the ends of the earth to run into a friend of Mother's!

He looked down on her in quiet amusement. Her playacting didn't bother him as much as she had hoped. "I don't mean to interrupt."

"Oh, but you are interrupting!"

"I'm sorry."

Here we go again. Sorry! Forever apologizing.

She scrambled to her feet wearily. "You're interrupting me making you richer," she observed crisply. "It's your own bank account that's suffering."

If he was going to presume on friendship with her mother, so was she. Cut and thrust is what he wanted and he was damned well going to get it. She glared at him fiercely.

"How long *is* your visit, your grace?" she asked bitterly. A very rude question.

"Oh, we'll be off in a few days. You and Antonio can resume your idyll soon."

"Idyll!" she said bitterly. "Toil and poverty!"

"Self-inflicted," said the duke.

"Not self-inflicted by Antonio!"

"Antonio can have anything he wants. We've known each other since boyhood. I wanted to send him to university. He wants this. I respect his wishes."

The implied rebuke was crystal clear. She, Theresa, did *not* respect his wishes. Except that she did!

222

She knew as well as the duke precisely what Antonio wanted—and what he didn't want.

"I know," she said shortly.

"I respect your wishes, too," observed the duke quietly.

She nodded dumbly because there was no comment she could make on that. He was not responsible for this accident of a meeting. He'd handled it admirably. He was an admirable man in many ways—but then when you were a rich duke being admirable wasn't very hard. It was part of the job—like playing polo well or shooting birds with stunning accuracy. You had lots of practice.

"You're very kind," she said briefly. She didn't want to be in his debt. She especially didn't want to like and admire him. But she *did* like him. Her admiration was limited; still there was more of it than she liked to admit. It conflicted with her severe revolutionary purpose. One shouldn't mingle with the upper classes, she thought bitterly, which was why she had run away from home in the first place.

She stared at this admirable and exasperating aristocrat wryly. "Your Grace, may I continue? I'm falling behind in my daily toil."

"Forgive me," he said and resumed his stroll down the white road. Theresa stared after him, sucking her lower lip wryly. Conversation. She'd enjoyed it. She'd not really had anything resembling conversation since . . . Elf.

Elf!

Hawkins and the Spanish police chief were in

Robin Frost's flat. The Spaniard was examining the place with microscopic thoroughness, looking for prints, for identity, for evidence. Hawkins was already sure enough of identity—and equally sure Elf wouldn't leave prints around. He was inspecting the body, or what part of the hunched frozen figure he could get at, for . . . style.

Most of the wounds were concealed by the legs drawn up to the chin. Except in the lower right- and left-hand abdomen, where the bamboo sticks had delicately tormented the kidneys.

"Elf has been studying anatomy," he murmured.

The Spanish police chief's face was an engraving of fourteenth-century incredulity. "You can be sure," he said stiffly.

"The M.O.T. is identical," said Hawkins tonelessly. "Puncture marks are in identical spots. If it's a different person, they studied the same ninth-century Chinese book—which seems unlikely. Even the shape of the wounds is identical, indicating the same sticks."

"A woman!" The Spaniard spat out the word like a curse.

Hawkins prevented himself from smiling only by extreme interior discipline. These Spanish, he couldn't help thinking, had a history of cruelty that stretched back two thousand years. Even today the disciplinary customs of Spanish prisons could hardly bear inspection by a human rights commission. It wasn't Elf's skill with the bamboo sticks that outraged the police chief—it was her sex. Girls had

no business pushing into these essentially masculine
diversions.

"Women's Liberation," explained Hawkins dryly.
"The women are insisting on not being left out—
of anything."

The police chief looked like one of the carvings
on the Palma cathedral—medieval, thunderous.

Theresa descended from the bus on Palma's *paseo
marítimo* and walked along the shimmering bay,
secure in her peasanthood. The sun had burned
her black. The shapelessness of the blue trousers
and smock concealed the gaunt body fairly well.
There was only her blond hair to betray her—there
was not a native blonde in all Majorca and there
were precious few in all Spain—and she had tucked
her hair into her kerchief so skillfully not a lock
showed. With her market basket on her arm, she
looked entirely peasant.

Theresa had adopted a peasant shuffle in place
of her normal free-swinging stride. Role playing,
she thought, shuffling along. Why do I so enjoy
being someone else? Not just me, my whole generation. All of us. Bluebloods want to be peasants;
the peasants want to be top dogs, the workers reactionaries—everything upside down.

She shuffled past the market, where she should
be selling produce like the other peasant women,
down the *paseo* under the huge trees where the likes
of her were seldom seen. This was the street for
rich *turistas*. The Mallorquins were behind the
counters, selling things, not in front of them buying.

What am I doing here? Money! Who needs money? A peasant exists outside the money economy. Not entirely. Antonio needed a few things. A pot big enough for two, for one thing.

At American Express she smelled danger. The moment she stepped into the coolness of the long, crowded rooms, doubts screamed in her mind. The room was crowded with the usual lot—teenage kids so American they looked like a Walt Disney movie, getting their parents' checks, middle-aged Americans of tremendous girth—why did American middle-classness go so hideously to the waistline?—and elegant aging American females searching Spain for their missing youth (which Ponce de León went looking for in Florida).

In such a company her peasant appearance was all wrong. Theresa calmly pulled off her kerchief, letting loose the fountain of blond hair. She straightened herself, casting off the work-worn look; she smoothed her smock, making herself slim. It made all the difference. Now she was not a peasant but a young girl who had found the right shops for the veritable peasant costume they had all come searching for. The brown face was seen to be the product of lying on the right beaches, not toiling in the vineyards. Role playing! I'm being what I once was, thought Theresa, the biggest lie of all.

She took her place in a very long line, still smelling danger. Why? Because they're Americans. Because I'm exposed to my own countrymen. No, that wouldn't account for the numbing terror that was creeping from her midriff down her thighs and up toward her heart. Why should I be so frightened? Because they're surrounding me—all these conventional, law-abiding, stereotyped Americans, reminding me of my sins. She had shed her past as a snake his skin and here it was thrown back at her. Calm down! Calm down! I must not look the way I feel, said the girl who always looked exactly how she felt.

They're looking! They're looking! Indeed they were. But then she was a striking girl with her gaunt, haunted face, in her peasant clothes—and it was a long queue and there was nothing else to do. Theresa lifted her chin, an old trick she used to rise above the panic at her mother's terrible parties she so much despised. The way to fight back—teenage wisdom—was to stare back, coldly, contemptuously.

Theresa surveyed her fellow Americans from the lofty heights of her uplifted chin. Directly ahead of her in line was a tall, spare, gray-haired character in short-sleeved shirt who looked like a rich cowpoke; ahead of him was one of those blue-rinsed female heads that had become the symbol of American imperialist affluence and depravity, this one pushing seventy, still aggressive. In front of her was a brown-eyed teenage girl as skinny as Theresa in jeans and cotton shirt, as American as apple pie, and probably started sucking cocks at twelve like me, thought Theresa, the terror receding a little as she directed her gaze outward, subjecting *them* to the scrutiny she so feared.

It doesn't matter what they think about me; what's important is what I think about *them*. Changing in one bound from the American to the European point of view. Not caring what they thought, she spun on one heel and surveyed those in line behind her—a bit of massive impudence that thoroughly alarmed the good-looking young man directly behind her. Theresa directed her queenly, comfortless gaze directly at this insecure young man, unstringing him altogether, then behind him at the last one in the line, a wispy ancient in a paisley jacket of the sort Americans hang on themselves abroad; he looked like a New England banker.

Theresa spun around then, facing front again without apology. In the spin, she caught a peripheral glimpse of a figure in a chair. In a chair? Theresa looked again, giving her full, queenly, chin-uplifted look to this character, a grandmotherly old crotchet, seated in a chair by the wall, placidly knitting, eyes downcast. Good heavens! Theresa had never seen anything quite so benevolently matriarchal outside the paintings of Norman Rockwell, which had come back into fashion. This old party seemed to have modeled herself almost exactly after one of Mr. Rockwell's canvases.

The line inched forward and Theresa with it, eyes front now. Only three people ahead of her now. Then she would ask for her mail under the name of . . . what *was* the name she'd cabled? Oh, God in heaven . . . The terror returned in full force, turning her legs to water—and her face. Oh, dear God, the face! It always showed. Patricia Jenkins! Of course. And she had a passport to prove it. The terror receded. But it didn't go away. It was weakening her resolve, this fear, and why should she be fearful?

The queue inchwormed forward once more. Theresa was now one person from the counter.

Grandmother in a chair! Waiting for what? No! The terror smiting again. Theresa swiveled around for another look. The chair was empty. Grandma and her knitting needles had departed.

"*Señora!*"

It was Theresa's turn. The elderly clerk was looking at her. So were the others in the queue.

Grandmother, my ass! thought Theresa, eyes blank with fright.

"*Señora!*"

Theresa stepped out of line and walked rapidly back to the glass door. There she stopped, looking out at the *paseo* in the permanent gloom of the immense shade trees. Not a sign of grandmother. There wouldn't be, of course. If it were . . . I'm being paranoid, thought Theresa. She's four thousand miles from here. Go back! Get the money! But she couldn't. They were all looking at her now. If she went back, she'd blow the name—Patricia Jenkins—now shrouded in blessed obscurity.

Theresa walked out of American Express quickly. Panicking, she thought. Panicking! Doing the worst thing. What would happen now? She had barely enough money for the bus back to Cuesta—and then what? She'd never get back to Palma again unless she walked—thirty kilometers.

She sat on one of the stone benches under the towering trees, trying to conquer her forebodings.

Ridiculous! The word didn't diminish the over-mastering fright by a single particle. She sat huddled under the great plane trees, in the busy *paseo* hundreds of people strolling or seated about her, fearful of each one.

She sat there for half an hour, a big mistake. Never sit still, when action should be taken. She was forgetting all her urban guerrilla training. She got up briskly and walked with her free-swinging stride—she was a very fast walker—to the bus stop on the *paseo marítimo*. There she had to wait an hour for the bus.

It was only when she was on the bus on the way back to Cuesta that she realized. I've made a mistake! I've made a huge mistake! No one took the two-o'clock bus. If a woman went to Palma, she spent the day. She was almost alone on the bus—as conspicuous as a gold tooth.

I should have lost her first, thought Theresa. If one could ever lose Elf. I should have led her a dance through every back alley and waited until dark and then slipped out on the last bus. But she hadn't. She had walked straight back down the *paseo marítimo*. True, she had caught not so much as a glimpse of the grandmother. Or anyone else. But then Elf was very skillful at not being seen. She had been the best at eluding, not only capture, but any kind of surveillance. And Theresa had not really looked until she had actually got to the bus stop. By then, it was much too late.

Now there was this car lying far back that had not left the trail since they quit Palma. Paranoid, thought Theresa. There's only one road. Why shouldn't a car follow the bus? Where else would it go? Why didn't it catch up and pass us? thought Theresa. But then, why should it? The bus didn't stop either to pick up or let down anyone because it was the early bus—and there were no passengers either getting on or getting off. Why should the car catch up? Where would Elf get a car so quickly to follow me? she asked herself—and almost instantly answered herself: steal it, of course. Elf stole cars as easily as most people crossed streets.

Far back the car hovered on the very edge of her vision on the long straight road—neither dropping back nor gaining. Paranoid! Paranoid! I'm making up Elf. Inventing her!

Still she wouldn't be so foolish as to lead her back to her valley palace. Not she! She knew the terrain. Elf didn't. She had the advantage there.

She descended at San Jacinto, five long miles beyond Cuesta. It would be a long, hard slog back. But even longer and harder for Elf—if it was Elf. Theresa waited at the side of the road as the bus left her, looking stonily down the road toward the other car as it approached.

Her eyes narrowed as the car sped by—surely it had speeded up, hadn't it?—and tried to scrutinize the figure at the wheel, whose face was shrouded in a bonnet. Bonnet? Bonnet? Who wore bonnets? Mallorquin women wore them but not the ones who drove cars.

Theresa left the road abruptly and took to the woods, which were piny and very thin cover in that area. Later they'd get much thicker, and then Elf would have her work cut out pursuing her—if it was Elf.

CHAPTER

30

From the crotch of the tallest pine on the crest of the hill, Theresa listened and looked until her ears and eyes ached. Nothing. Not even the song of birds. Silence.

Did I imagine Elf? No, I didn't. About Elf I am second-sighted, sixth-sensed, magicked. Elf is on the island.

For two long hours she stayed up the tree, scanning the empty forest, outwaiting Elf. (Had anyone ever outwaited Elf? She could outwait the stars.)

Still, she couldn't freeze in the crotch of a tree. That would be the worst kind of strategy—doing nothing. When she descended from the tree it was— she estimated—about four-thirty. Perhaps she'd waited a bit too long. A long slog home—and the light would fade altogether at six. The springlike weather in Majorca didn't alter the fact it was still winter with its early sunset—especially in her valley.

She trudged warily, trying to force her mind to think what Elf would do. Had she circled around her and was she waiting somewhere along this forest floor? Elf was very good at ambush—the best there was.

The thought stopped Theresa in her tracks. She leaned against a pine, eyes darting from tree to tree. The worst thing, the absolute worst thing was to be immobilized by fear. Anything was better than that.

She couldn't inspect each tree; she told herself ferociously she'd never get home before dark. Speed would be far better than skulking. Speed would spoil Elf's aim, force her into mistakes. Thus Theresa reasoned with her terror, trying to force her intelligence to master her fright. A difficult business.

She bolted from her protecting tree, forcing herself into action, running at top speed forty yards, then diving behind another tree. Short wait, heart beating like a wild bird's. Another short burst, the breath exploding out of her, exhausted by fear, that most humiliating passion.

An hour later, the light had almost gone and Theresa had still not seen a single familiar landmark. I've tried so hard to lose Elf I've lost my way. That meant climbing another tree. Oh, dear God, I haven't the strength.

But she did. Just. From the top of a tall pine she could see the *palacio* gleaming whitely through the dusk—her *palacio*. She slithered down the pine, mumbling apologies to Antonio. She hadn't the strength to climb the hill to the stone hut, she said in her mind. She doubted even whether she could find it in the darkness. Night in Majorca fell like a thunderclap—and it was almost on her.

She strode more confidently now, feeling the protection of darkness, hoping Antonio might be waiting for her in the mule's room. At the Moorish arch, she stopped and listened for him and heard only the soft gurgle of chickens, already gone to their roosts. She groped her way through the mule's great room, which was much blacker than the courtyard outside, her hand outstretched, feeling for the mule's soft muzzle.

Elf grabbed the outstretched hand, as if she owned it, spun her around, the other arm encircling her waist; Theresa's scream never came because Elf was kissing her—as effective a way of shutting a mouth as any.

Theresa exploded with terror, her heart stopping altogether, blackness engulfing her wits. Rabbitlike, she struck out at Elf, flailing with her one free arm and both legs. Elf tripped her up and fell on top of her—rapacious, erotic, avenging, triumphant.

In the darkness, the mule stopped chomping, paralyzed by the contradictory sounds that punctuated the blackness. Sobs, giggles, sharp screams, and always the continuous crackle of hay as the two bodies thrashed. There were no words. No need of words between these old lovers and enemies.

After the first wild fit of terror, Theresa fought instinctually and brutally and with no holds barred. Her fingers groped for eyeballs, for breasts, for kidneys, for all the weak spots—but in the darkness she got only elbows and shoulders and muscled thighs. Elf fought defensive warfare, keeping her body glued to Theresa's. Blissful. Also, unassailable.

When Theresa savagely kneed her crotch, she was too close to feel anything but delicious pleasure; when the fingers groped for her eyes, her head was stretched clear around Theresa's and buried in her hair. Theresa changed her tactics, beating her fists on Elf's back, her knuckles going for the kidneys.

Instantly Elf grabbed the elbow, and twisted Theresa in a half nelson, turning her dexterously upside down so now Elf was on her back, teeth sunk in her neck, an affectionate not vicious nip, feeling her delicious ass in her crotch, while not neglecting to pinion both Theresa's eyeball-gouging hands underneath their bodies. It was overwhelmingly sexual and Elf lost herself in the pleasure. For a moment too long.

Theresa gathered up all her fury and arched her back, then straightened it—the two movements sending Elf, ass over teakettle, into the hay on her back. Theresa resisted her enraged instinct to fling herself on the girl and continue the fight. Instead, she took to her heels, relying on her greater knowledge of the *palacio*. And on the darkness. She flew out of the mule's chamber, across the cobbled courtyard, up the crazy staircase. In a few seconds she was in the rabbit and dove room. How could Elf find her there in that darkness?

She couldn't have made a bigger mistake. The doves set up a cooing of welcome that could be heard a hundred yards away. Could Elf find that room up that staircase in the dark? Theresa was gasping for breath, her legs weak as sticks. I'm making too much noise with my damned breathing to hear properly, she was thinking frantically. I should get out of here and lose her in the *palacio:* she can't find her way around that.

But she didn't want to run into Elf on that rickety staircase, which had no railing. No place for a battle.

The door opened and Theresa could see Elf outlined against the blue sky. The door closed. The two girls faced each other across the blackness, both sobbing for breath.

"Let's talk," said Elf.

She's winded, thought Theresa vengefully. Elf had barely got the words out.

The door shut, extinguishing that square of dimness. Now there was only the faint glow from the great windows facing down the valley. I must be outlined against one window, thought Theresa. She sat down abruptly and leaned her head against the wall between the windows. She'd have to grope for me—and I could dump her out the window with my feet. Theresa had always been better with her feet than Elf.

Meanwhile, breathing heavily—and listening. Elf couldn't get across that straw-covered floor without her hearing. She listened to the thudding of Elf's heart—or was it her own heart?—and the soft whiffle of her breathing. Otherwise Elf was silent. Letting her heartbeat settle down, thought Theresa. Trying to unsettle me with her calm. But she's not unsettling me at all. I'm cool as spring water. Why? With that damned woman in this room! Still, there it was. After the explosion of violent exertion, in the stillness of the twilit room, Theresa felt a deathlike calm. I knew this moment had to come. I knew it and it has haunted me and now it's here—and *that* part is over.

Silence. And blackness. Elf is really trying to undo me with all this quiet. She doesn't know. It's a new Theresa, dumbfounded by her own repose.

Noiselessly, she leaned over and, with her mouth only an inch from the floor, she whispered in the quietness. "You should have shot me when I was outlined against the window. You missed a chance." It was an old urban guerrilla trick borrowed from the lions. With the voice box that close to the floor the sound seemed to come from all over the room, from behind Elf, from everywhere.

Let Elf wonder where she was in that dark room. Darker now, the last light fading.

Silence.

"I didn't come ten thousand miles to shoot you."

It was a low, thrilling whisper—and it filled the room like Theresa's own whisper. Using my own trick against me, the bitch, thought Theresa wryly. She's exactly where she was. Or is she? Elf had been the best, absolute tops, at this kind of exercise. She could see in the dark, they used to say at urban guerrilla school in that bleak farmhouse in Colorado. Hell!

Theresa had one tiny advantage. She knew the room. There were pigeon droppings everywhere, hard as birdshot, especially under those windows where she lay. She could feel the pellets under her hands. With a single movement, Theresa gathered up a handful and threw a scattershower of the stuff where she knew the doves roosted—tensing her knees for a spring, as she did it.

A volley of indignant cooing from the perches as the grapeshot hit the doves. Then a flutter of wings, the doves resettling themselves. By the time the noise had subsided, Theresa had moved diagonally across the room and was lying, mouth to the floor, next to the rabbit hutches. Let Elf find me now!

Silence again. Outwaiting me, is she? thought Theresa. Had Elf moved with the dove noise? She didn't know. Curiosity overpowered her.

"What *did* you come ten thousand miles for?" whispered Theresa to the floor. "To wrestle?" I shouldn't be making jokes with this demonic female!

"To make love!"

Another thrilling whisper. Elf's throaty whisper, the most nakedly sexual sound Theresa had ever heard. Elf had always said that all women harbored titanic sexual powers—but held them in check. Centuries of male oppression, custom, fear. Only Elf, said Elf, dared to unleash in her voice the full range of her sexual desire—as natural as breathing.

Theresa trembled. So that was the game! Trying to seduce me! Seduce me first, kill me later.

Mouth to the floor, her face wreathed in a manic smile, Theresa whispered—foolishly, as she knew the moment she did it—"I'm in love with a man."

Nothing would enrage Elf more. For Theresa to be in love with anyone but Elf was crime enough. But with a man! Theresa waited for the lightning.

239

Nothing. A long nothing. Trying to suppress her rage.

The reply, when it came, was unexpected.

"Why did you leave me?" No rage in the voice. Only heartbreak.

Bitch! Getting at my womanhood!

The low throaty voice throbbed on. "I wanted to kill myself. I didn't have the strength to pull the trigger."

Sentimental tripe, thought Theresa. She's trying to lay a spell.

"Bullshit!" she whispered. But it came out all wrong. Like a question. Not at all like the malicious gibe she meant. Oh, Christ! Here I am in that tunnel again with the gunfire overhead! Being seduced in the most unlikely circumstances. There's two involved in this. Elf had reveled in the unlikelihood of that earlier seduction, brandished it like a spear ever after. But then didn't I, too? Hadn't I reveled in surrender, damn me? Here she's trying it again.

The throaty whisper, resonant with sex, pulsated around her.

"I love you more even than I did then." In the whisper now there was a sort of overpowering elation, a promise of pleasure undreamt-of in all the tumultuous history of sexuality. The bitch knows how to use that voice on me!

"I love you, Theresa, more than anyone ever loved you—or ever will."

She's attacking my cunt with words, thought Theresa bitterly. I should go tear her eyes out while there's yet time.

Only one possible reply. "I hate you, Elf! I hate you, loathe you, despise you!" A threnody of hate! Putting the same note of glee in it that Elf had put into her love song. Make her mad!

Theresa whispered it as sexily as she knew how—though no one could get into Elf's league in that department. "I behead you every day! And watch the blood flow over the stones! I cut your rotten head off every day—and laugh!"

She'd gone too far. Theresa heard a low giggle through the blackness. All that hatred and all she got was laughter.

"Love! Hate! Passion!" Elf's low, throaty growl. "All the same thing! We're one, you and I. We can't even talk across a pitch-black room without arousing each other."

Not only was that too true; it was also too close. Elf's been crawling up on me under the cover of that sexy whisper. Oh, the bitch! She's going to spring on me in one second and what do I do then? Spring first.

Theresa leaped for the door, counting on her superior knowledge of the room. But Elf had anticipated that. She lifted a leg and Theresa in the darkness tripped and sprawled. Elf was on her, tigress-like, but Theresa brought both knees up sharply, catching Elf amidships and sending her somersaulting over Theresa's head. Toward the door, damn it. She's between me and the door. Theresa made another rush and Elf met her headlong and then the two girls were locked in combat again—Theresa

241

biting, kneeing, elbowing, Elf using bodyholds, hammerlocks, staying close.

She's having an orgasm, thought Theresa, thrashing wildly. Bitch! She threw a kidney punch but it went wrong, hitting only Elf's muscular ass. During her momentary confusion, Elf threw a body block and then the two girls were lying end to end, Elf on top, her head buried in Theresa's groin—laughing and tearing at her clothes. In another moment, she'll have me naked.

Theresa bit Elf's bare thigh, feeling a heady pleasure. She bit it again, and Elf moaned with the pain and the pleasure—let go Theresa's groin—and rolled off her altogether.

Theresa lay on her back, blowing like a horse. She had never been so totally exhausted in her life. Walking five miles, climbing trees. Now two bouts of unarmed combat.

She lay on her back—everything wide open, her eyes, her mouth, her cunt. I'm unbuttoned from head to foot. God help me! Each breath coming in and out as if it were her last. I should flee. Elf's spent. She's finished. But then so am I.

Elf took her time. Theresa waited an eternity for Elf's hot, hungry mouth on hers, and when it came, it sent a charge through her to her toes. I'm undone, thought Theresa. She lay inert while Elf took her clothes off, first the blue peasant trousers, then the tough shirt, and then she was naked in the birdshit, waiting, subdued, seduced, passive, for Elf's tough, muscular body to do with her as she saw fit—loving the submission, the surrender—and

242

she knows it. She knows me inside out and I hate her for knowing me so well and mastering me so easily. . . .

Then Elf was on her, all supple and naked, and light as a moth with her tongue and her hands and her mouth, and Theresa went out of her mind altogether.

CHAPTER

31

"Saint Theresa," Hawkins read to the Spanish police chief, "fell in tears at the feet of the figure of the wounded Christ which had been prepared for a religious festival, and that was the beginning of her visions. There was a violent difference of opinion as to the meaning of these visions even in 1554. One group held them to be of Divine origin, attesting her sainthood; quite another body of opinion attributed the visions to possession by the Devil."

Hawkins' voice became wry at this point. He was greatly amused by Saint Theresa and her sixteenth-century public-relations problem. "Still another group of ecclesiastics held that Theresa was just trying to attract attention to herself—a heretical idea indeed and one that might be directed at all saints from Saint Joan to Saint Joseph. In the sixteenth century it was a new idea—that sainthood might, in fact, be self-indulgence."

Hawkins closed the book. The Spanish police chief was pouring a thimbleful of sherry into a heavily carved glass. Ceremonial, thought Hawkins. Everything the Spanish police chief did was surrounded by this halo of ceremony. Hawkins, himself as American as a Kansas wheatfield, found it deeply poignant, this attachment to form.

"Saint Theresa is one of your bunch," said Hawkins. "From Castile. And she's about to be unsainted by the Vatican—or already has been, I'm not sure which."

The Spanish police chief pursed his lips. He found the whole thing indescribably blasphemous. "Defilement!" he said finally.

They were in the Spanish police chief's home, itself a bit of a joke. The chairs, a throwback to the Inquisition, designed for discomfort, succeeded admirably.

"Theresa's great problem is that she's out of style. Eight years ago, she was a saintly figure; five years ago, she became a Devil figure; today she's forgotten." Except by me, thought Hawkins. "What's interesting is the time span. It took your Spanish Theresa 68 years to sainthood—and 383 years to unsainthood. Our Theresa went from girlhood to sainthood to unsainthood to oblivion in about eight years. This is the wonder of modern communications."

The Spanish police chief looked at him with hooded eyes. Then he said something quite unexpected. "These young revolutionaries worship at the shrine of change. How can they object to change when it comes? Did they think they would be left unchanged?"

245

The two men went out to the waiting limousine and chauffeur. Events had thrown the pair together quite a lot in the last few days. After all, they now shared a murder—Robin Frost's corpse belonging to both of them equally. Englishman found dead in mysterious circumstances. That's how the local press had carried the story. Three paragraphs, deep inside the paper. Nothing about torture or about Elf.

"We'll go have a look at that valley I was telling you about," said the Spanish police chief. He was covering Majorca by process of elimination, valley by valley, methodically. "Even if we find nothing, it's a nice drive. And we can catch a glimpse of the duke's old *palacio*—the one I was telling you about."

"How did you find this place?"

Sun pouring through the stone bars of the sentinel room. Ten o'clock at least.

"Asked a few questions in Cuesta." Elf lay naked in the hay—muscular body tense, unslaked even after hours of voracious lust.

"You don't speak Spanish."

"It doesn't take much. *Donde está Inglesa*? They took me by the hand and led me to the white road and pointed down it. You are very well known in Cuesta."

Theresa stared out at the green valley, sun dappling naked breasts, emaciated body straight as a rod. Elf hadn't followed her through the woods. All that tree climbing had been unnecessary. I've been outwitted. "Why did you pick out *this* ruin—among so many?" Theresa urgently needed to know.

"It was the biggest. I know your romantic nature." Mocking, malign.

Always malign!

"Come back to me." Elf's throaty voice.

"Haven't you had enough?"

"Never!"

"No!"

Theresa picked up her baggy blue peasant trousers and started to slip them on, but Elf was on her instantly, wrestling her down into the hay. Theresa didn't resist. She lay quiescent, like a dead body, while Elf kissed and nuzzled and caressed. After a bit, Elf gave it up.

"Like making love to a pillow. What's the matter?"

Theresa's blue eyes were lost in pain.

She drew her finger very tenderly down Elf's nose, pausing on her lips—a benediction, a forgiveness. "I've simply awakened . . . a transformation impossible to explain to anyone except another *religieuse*. And another *religieuse* wouldn't require an explanation. Go ahead—laugh."

"I'm not laughing!" Elf was convulsed with lust. A *religieuse*! The erotic possibilities! The muscled body went to work on the unresisting wraith of Theresa. Lips, tongue, hands, toes even, exploring the body.

Theresa simply looked up at her—and at these frantic sexual efforts—out of pained blue eyes. Presently Elf gave up, feeling ridiculous, lost.

"It wasn't like that last night!"

"I know!" Theresa smiled a ghost of a smile. "I am the sum of my contradictions. We are held together by our opposite natures, Elf." The pain had vanished from the eyes. The voice was mocking. I'm a dozen women in one. I'm mercury, I'm sulfur, I'm all the colors of the rainbow—and how will Elf cope with that? How will I?

She sprang to her feet, while Elf was still fuddled, and slipped into her trousers. Elf let her, shocked by her own impotence. She lay in the hay, feeling her nakedness as never before, and watched Theresa slip into her blouse, brush her hair, finally sink to her knees.

"I'm going to pray." Theresa laughed at Elf openly. "You may watch if you like—and wonder." Theresa was totally self-confident. Thou has *not* forsaken me after all, dear Lord—but not aloud.

Aloud—hands clasped under her chin, eyes uplifted, a parody of the attitude of devotion—Theresa spoke, clear as spring water: "This existence is an illusion, a form of theater, pure imagination. Under your vast canopy, dear God, I empty myself altogether of false divinity—the greatest of illusions. I surrender my intelligence, my selfhood, my soul, to the one great Truth; that it was You who created me, not I who created You."

Silence. Elf stared open-mouthed. "That's a prayer?"

Theresa was angry. "I was praying for *you*, you dunce. Playing at God! How dare you! Shooting bank guards for their own good! Hah! Revolution,

my ass! Vaudeville! A rotten, self-indulgent vaudeville show that everyone has got tired of. Including
the players. Especially me!"

Elf lay naked in the hay, under this barrage, eyes
agleam. "A Jesus freak! You! On your knees before
the sacred vomit." Voice silken with malevolence.

Theresa's eyes clouded with pain. When she an-
swered, she was breathless as if she'd been running.
"I'm on my knees because I had nowhere else to
go. I didn't want to wind up where the others were—
Ellerbe in a Pennsylvania farmhouse, subsisting.
Janet in Canada living on some oaf's security checks.
The others in jail." She spoke very softly. "On your
knees is better."

Elf's laugh like a knife slash: "Fucking opium!
Blowing your mind with sacred bullshit!"

Theresa blazed right back at the jeering girl: "And
I suppose Marxism isn't a religion, you little fool?
It's religion without God. The dregs of a religion,
and it has been unashamedly used as the opium of
the people for the last fifty years!" The ultimate
impiety.

Theresa expected an outcry of ideology. It didn't
come. Elf just lay there, eyes empty. Not even pain.
Something's happened to her, thought Theresa.
Something awful. No point in asking. She'd just
tell lies.

"Get dressed! You look ridiculous lying there."

"What do I do if I get dressed? Pick oranges?"

"What did you come to do?" Theresa was jeering
now. "Stir up a little revolution? You're in the wrong
century . . . General Custer!" The supreme revo-

lutionary epithet for the showoff revolutionaries. "It's 1322 around here. Come back in six hundred years."

I'm being unkind. Elf looked wretched, lost. When had Elf ever been lost—in her ferocious life. Did it make her more or less dangerous?

Elf was slipping into her black trousers, her black shirt sullenly. She looked Vietcong.

"Where are the rest of your clothes?"

"The car."

Theresa was alarmed: "You haven't left a stolen car lying around here? You haven't got the fuzz on your heels?"

Elf ran her hands through her short black hair, shaking it out: "The fuzz are on somebody's heels—perhaps yours."

"What do you mean?"

"The café on the *paseo*. Two of them. One Spanish *policía*—with gold braid from his ears to his cock." Elf placed her face between the bars and looked down the valley—from one end to the other. "The other one Uncle Sammy himself. I didn't stick around long enough to find out who he was after—you or me. Probably both."

"Where's the car?"

"In a barn. They won't find it for a while."

"Where are your clothes, your things?"

"In the car." Elf was suddenly alert. "Who's that?" Pointing through the bars. Theresa looked.

The duke and duchess, walking toward the white road. Antonio driving the high-wheeled cart toward them from the lower orchard.

"They own this place." Theresa pulled her back. "They mustn't see you."

Elf's black eyes bored into her. "How about you?"

"None of your business."

She didn't feel like explaining Antonio.

She didn't have to. Elf laughed—jarringly. "Oh, that's him, is it? It wouldn't be the fatcat. Not you. It would be . . ." Elf looked out gleefully ". . . that shambling peasant."

Theresa spun her around ferociously. "I'm his woman!"

"Shall we share him?" Elf taunted, eyes aglitter.

Theresa went black with fury. "I'll throttle you, Elf James, if you lay a finger on him. He doesn't know what a lesbian is! He doesn't understand people like us. He's a peasant! He is what you and I were going to liberate—remember?"

"Oh, good. Let's liberate him!"

She laughed and Theresa hit her as hard as she could with her open hand, sending her sprawling in the hay—still laughing.

CHAPTER

32

"Madness," said the Spanish police chief in his creaking gate of a voice. "The odor of sanctity drives some women over the edge."

Well! Well! thought Hawkins. Who would have expected such sentiment from this medieval figure of a police chief? As if reading his mind, the Spaniard explained: "We have things in our nunneries that would widen your eyes. Sometimes the police have to be called."

Now what is the old owl up to? wondered Hawkins. He had learned the Spaniard never threw out observations like this for no reason.

"That's why your Saint Theresa worries me. She could be as dangerous as the other woman."

His Theresa? Never. "The other woman," said Hawkins bluntly, "has her own religious problems. She's a Maoist, a theology as unbending as Savonarola."

They were lunching under a grape arbor in a little house just outside Cuesta, part of the little eliminations that police work all over the world is largely about. The Spaniard summoned the proprietor and for the next ten minutes raked the man with questions. Hawkins understood not a word, but he had got fairly expert at judging the interrogations by their length. The old fellow must be onto something or the questioning wouldn't have lasted so long.

"He says there is an Englishwoman in the valley living with a shepherd."

"Theresa is not English."

The Spaniard suppressed a smile. "English, American—we can't tell them apart."

"*We* can't tell a Mallorquin from a Spaniard," retorted Hawkins.

"Feel the palms of their hands," suggested the Spaniard. "If the palm is horny, it's Mallorquin. We Spanish produce nothing but priests, soldiers—and police." He paid the bill because it was his turn. "Come, we'll investigate her nationality—and her theology."

Elf and Theresa lay behind the thick tangle of vines on the north wall. The best place for observation. "But you must keep quiet. They can hear in the courtyard." She hadn't wanted Elf with her at all. But then what was she to do? She couldn't toss her out. Elf was her revolutionary sister-in-arms, no matter what had happened. To say nothing of her lover. Lying under the cloak of vines, Theresa gave tongue to an irrelevant whisper. She'd been suppressing it all morning.

253

"Who is Bandit?"

"A girl!" Scornful, almost an epithet.

"Your lover?"

Elf shrugged indifferently, admitting the charge and deprecating it, all in one movement. "Brainless cunt!" she mouthed, not uttering it.

Theresa felt a stab of jealousy clear to her toes. Jealous of Elf! Why? My damned womanhood! Theresa was even profoundly jealous of Bandit's participation in a robbery that she herself hopelessly disapproved of. Eaten by jealousy! She closed her eyes in an agony of humiliation.

Elf stabbed her with her elbow, making her eyes jerk open again.

The great police limousine had pulled into the courtyard, where it looked as menacing and inappropriate as a battle cruiser.

The two girls became indivisible, urban guerrillas, conspirators. As inconspicuous as shadows.

The Spanish police chief strode to the massive door and banged the great bronze lion of a knocker. Hawkins followed him out of the car and the two men stood there, chatting—in clearly audible English.

"Savonarola would have understood your revolutionary children very well," the Spaniard was saying.

The two girls under the vines exchanged glances. Revolutionary children!

"Children from ten to twenty years old ran all the way to church to hear him preach. Florence was governed by a monk—and gangs of wayward children operating under a cloak of ideological self-righteousness—just like today." The Spaniard banged again with the bronze lion.

"I don't think anyone's home," said Hawkins. "Shall we have a look around?"

The two police officers mounted the crazy staircase and disappeared.

"Sssh," whispered Theresa. "There's a police chauffeur left behind."

"What do we do?" Elf mouthed it, no sound.

"Wait!"

Hawkins stood at the very center of the vast audience chamber, facing the great stone fireplace. Conspicuous consumption in the fourteenth century. He tried to imagine it bursting with tourists, the huge fireplace converted into a tourist shop selling postcards, small plaster replicas of the *palacio*. Awful thought. It was better off empty.

"Audience chamber," the Spanish police chief was saying. "In the sixteenth century, it was also a court. Trials were held here and, it is said, some executions. It is all in the hall of records in Palma. We are a great people for keeping records of forgotten trials. All bound up neatly in vellum, written down in great detail—these five-hundred-year-old trials and executions. No one has looked at them since they were written and no one ever will." The voice was dry.

The past had its own reasons, Hawkins was thinking. The tremendous chamber filled him with awe. Not its size. Americans were used to size. Its age. Americans were always astonished that anything

NIGHTFALL

was five hundred years old. The world had started
in 1776.

He strolled to the great corner window and looked
down the valley. Up in the hill he could see a shepherd herding sheep. Or perhaps goats.

"No one lives here?" Hawkins had picked up
the stub of a homemade cigarette, and smelled it.

"The duke and duchess are paying their annual
visit. The duke loves the old place; the duchess
doesn't."

Hawkins handed him the cigarette stub and the
Spaniard sniffed it.

"Not marijuana," said the Spanish police chief.

"No," said Hawkins. Catalpa. Had something of
the same effect, he was thinking. But who knew
that? Except American urban guerrilla fighters. Very
exotic information even among them. Should he
share this information with his friend the Spanish
police chief? He didn't.

The Spanish police chief looked at the butt,
puzzled. "The shepherd takes care of the animals
and the house—what care is taken of it." He sniffed
the cigarette butt again, reflectively. "I wouldn't
have imagined the shepherd would come to this
room."

"Perhaps he came to admire the view," suggested
Hawkins.

"Shall we go ask him?" said the Spaniard. "That's
him on the hill."

The two men returned to the limousine in the
cobbled courtyard.

"The Ochillo family is one of the oldest in Spain,"

the police chief was saying. "They are the family who brought Caravello to Spain from Italy—and they still possess more of his paintings than any museum in the world."

Theresa lay under the cover of the vines, listening and hoping Elf wasn't. Vain hope. Elf always listened. She didn't want her knowing anything at all about the Caravellos. Or his grace. Catch her missing a chance like that. Worldwide vaudeville, those priceless paintings could be made into! Elf had always wanted to break onto the world stage. Theresa glanced at Elf lying next to her, eyes narrowed. What in hell was she thinking about?

Oh, hell! Oh, hell!

I should have shot her while she lay asleep in my arms this morning. The gun was there under the hay. Would I be capable of killing Elf, my comrade, my lover, my enemy. Yes, I would. I am capable of all crimes, all of them.

The duke walked into the courtyard with his duchess and his dog, a picture of nineteenth-century capitalism. Stinking of bourgeois wealth, bourgeois romanticism, bourgeois beauty—the pair of them. Theresa could feel Elf's hackles rising, almost smell it.

There was an exchange of high-flown civilities in Spanish. Suddenly English floated up to the girls in maddening bits and pieces.

". . . English gir . . . Have you . . . fug . . . shep . . . merican . . .

Was the word American? They were all standing under the Moorish arch, too far away. The girls could make out only syllables. Now they walked to the big door and the words boomed forth clearly.

"Antonio's wife is neither American nor English," said the duke, casually. "She's an Italian woman who talks a bit of English. Anyone who talks English they think is English down there in Cuesta. She's been Antonio's woman for years."

Theresa's stomach turned over. He was telling *lies* to protect her. Damn! She didn't want to be under his protection or in his debt. He's not doing it for me; he's doing it because he knew Mother—and I don't want to be in her debt either.

CHAPTER

33

The two women made their way down the white road away from the *palacio* toward the end of the valley, where it closed in and the hills became steep and rocky, an area Theresa had never explored. They were moving away from the orange grove, the vegetable patch, the lower meadow—all the areas Theresa knew—away from Cuesta.

They walked well apart, separate as the poles of the earth—tension between them unbearable. They were on the way to the barn where Elf had concealed the stolen car, to get her clothes. That was the spoken purpose of this silent walk—but the air around them shrieked with unutterable conflict.

What's on her mind? What's she want? Thoughts skittering around Theresa's brain like bats. Elf was ahead of her, keeping close to the trees, staying out of sight—her face closed in. What are we picking up besides her clothes? Her gun? Her knife? What does this damned woman plan to do—with her knife, her gun? Theresa looked at the boyish back ahead of her, almost torn in half with totally conflicting emotions. Desire. Hatred. Fear. All those together. Which was the dominant one? It shifted from moment to moment, and the terrible thing was that Theresa didn't want to feel any of them. I don't want to love her. I don't want to hate her. I don't want to fear her. Why must I?

I am all feeling, all emotion. That is my terrible burden. It has always been my curse. She's driving me back into areas of feeling I have abandoned for the love of God.

Elf looked over her shoulder. A glance, blazing with malignity, straight into her eyes—then Elf's eyes flashed front again and Theresa was left with the back to contemplate. The glance stunned her. She doesn't trust *me!* She distrusts me as much as I distrust her. She's wondering what *I'm* planning to do next.

And what am I planning to do? Love her? Or kill her? Oh, dear God, along with my fear of what she will do is my fear of what I will do.

Around the next bend, they ran headlong into Antonio—and his sheep.

She'd forgotten him altogether. No, not altogether. She had thought, when they started down the white road, that at least she would be spared an encounter with Antonio. All of Antonio's haunts—the orange grove, lettuce patch, meadow—were the other direction. But here was Antonio bringing his sheep down from the high meadow. She'd forgotten the high meadow.

The classic confrontation. Wife. Husband. Lover.

The lover a woman, but that changed nothing. Or everything. A threesome. A trio.

Trinity.

I blaspheme.

Theresa turned her emaciated face toward Antonio, as if asking instruction. I am yours, my peasant. Take me out of my dilemma. They were without language, she and Antonio, but he understood a lot. She could feel his mood under her skin. It was thunderous.

"*Donde estaba usted?*" he asked, glowering.

"Palma," she pleaded. "*Por comprar. La noche . . .*" She wanted to say that night had trapped her but she hadn't the words. She stared at him out of her haunted face.

Elf standing there, smiling malevolently, loving it.

Antonio turned his glare now on Elf. He didn't like her. Dislike poured out of him like sweat. He could hardly guess what went on between these two women—but he didn't like it. He was like a dog smelling danger with a sense of smell six hundred times that of the human animal. He could smell Theresa's fear. He could smell Elf's powerful lesbian emanations without understanding them—just disliking them.

"*Yo siento,*" Theresa pleaded.

One of the sheep rescued her. It left the road and started up the hill to nibble at an elderberry bush. She went after it and pulled it back to the others.

"*Hola! Hola!*" commanded Antonio.

The sheep started up again down the road, The-

resa going with them as a matter of course, without
a glance at Elf.

Smiling broadly, savoring the situation, Elf retraced her steps, following sheep and Antonio and
Theresa from a distance.

"*Ella debe marcharse!*" muttered Antonio.

"He says you must go away," said Theresa faintly.

Elf burst out laughing. "Ask him where I should
go. Tell him we're both wanted for the same murder."

"I've already told him."

Elf laughed again, gleeful, holding her arms close
to her sides, casting mischievous flirtatious glances
at Antonio, reveling in the thunderclouds.

"Why don't you go get your clothes?" asked
Theresa angrily.

"I'm a shepherdess—deep down," eyes agleam
with malevolence. "Murder is only a sideline. Like
you."

"You're a fifth-rate vaudeville actor—with the
soul of a whore!"

Elf laughed fiercely. "Does he pray with you, this
shepherd? Bullshit smelling of sheep shit. Doesn't
God complain of the odor?"

They went down the road, the two girls barking
these pleasantries at one another in a language Antonio couldn't understand, Antonio driving the sheep
along, hating all of it.

At the lower meadow, Theresa helped Antonio
tether the sheep to their little bit of allotted grass.
Elf sat on a wall, watching with her secret thoughts.
She's changed her plans, whatever they were, to

something new. Antonio had added an extra dimension to the chessboard and Elf would never miss an opportunity to play every piece on the board.

The merriment had fled now. Elf was blank-faced, watchful, thinking God knows what.

Then the situation got very much worse.

"*Ven conmigo*," said Antonio.

Oh, no! thought Theresa. He was asking her to come along to the stone hut, come along home. She wanted to, oh, God, she wished she had never left. If she had not gone to Palma . . . Enough of that.

Theresa faced Antonio, agonized. The classic confrontation: my lover, my husband. End of the day. Whose arms will I lie in tonight?

Antonio wanted exclusive possession in the stone cottage. He wanted to separate her from Elf, physically and emotionally. And I am torn right down the middle by desire and distrust. I want her body and I hate her soul and I distrust her—oh, God, I distrust her. The thought of Elf left alone to go back to her *palacio*, to find her way—why did I show her the way?—to her tower room, to find her gun and her key. Oh no . . . All this in her agonized, mutinous look.

"No!" said Theresa. The first time she'd ever said No to Antonio.

He hit her a stinging slap on the face, shocking her to the marrow. Her gentle peasant! Theresa put her hand to her cheek, thunderstruck, the tears starting. Oh, he must know about Elf and me. He must know more than I thought. Her head spinning with the force of the blow.

Through her tears she caught a glimpse of Elf sitting on the stone fence, legs crossed. Enjoying her subjugation. Theresa, fourteenth-century chattel. Elf who had enslaved her just as thoroughly but in twentieth-century enslavement—lesbian, urban guerrilla, the very last word in slavery.

Antonio hit her again, very hard, seized her by the wrist and started to drag her up the hill. I can't fight Antonio, tears gushing. And what is Elf going to do—just let me be dragged off like this?

Elf did exactly that. She sat on the stone fence, watching the scene like a spectator at a play. Any minute, thought Theresa, she'll burst into applause.

Meanwhile, she was being dragged along behind Antonio, who was strong as an elephant. Why doesn't he drag me by the hair? Cave girl, me.

A hundred yards up the hill, Theresa jerked her arm so forcefully it stopped Antonio briefly. Theresa swung around to face Elf. Elf had leaped off the stone wall and was striding briskly back toward the *palacio*, her back to both of them, as if she'd wiped Theresa clear out of her mind.

After that Theresa went along meekly, fourteenth-century slave to her lord and master—because what else could she do?

CHAPTER

34

"*Alucinante?*" asked the Spanish police chief. He'd summoned his drug experts at police headquarters, and they were all gathered around the cigarette stub, sniffing and testing.

I should have let it lie, thought Hawkins. It had been a reflex action. A lawman couldn't walk away from evidence.

The three Spaniards were deep in Spanish conversation, not one word of which Hawkins understood. How long would it take for them to diagnose the cigarette stub as catalpa? Catalpa wasn't even native to Majorca. An American plant.

". . . *Americano* . . ."

The one word emerged from the torrent of Spanish—full of menace. *Americano*. Someone had figured out something. Hawkins studied his own palm, trying to work out the secrets of the universe. He was a guest in this country. He couldn't rush around changing the . . . rules. Could he?

The Spanish police chief addressed him: "It's catalpa."

"Indeed!" said Hawkins politely.

"It would not occur to a Mallorquin to smoke catalpa. It doesn't even grow here."

Never underestimate a Spanish police chief, thought Hawkins studying his palm. If this Spaniard collared his Theresa on a drugs charge, she would spend years in a Spanish jail—and Spanish jails were not very nice. Or there might be gunplay. Another Oakland.

"We must pay another visit to the *palacio*," said the Spaniard.

Hawkins looked up from his palm then, pursing his lips quizzically. "Tonight?"

"Tomorrow," said the Spaniard.

Mañana! Saved by the curse of Spain.

"Tomorrow," said Hawkins, smiling. "I'll say goodnight then." He shook hands with the Spaniard formally. A ritual parting they engaged in every night. Feeling like Judas as he did it. "No, I won't need the limousine. I'll walk."

Outside, Hawkins looked at his watch: 11 P.M. He didn't want to get there too early. It would be much better for all concerned if everyone was asleep. If Elf was there . . . Hawkins didn't want to think about that. The Spanish police chief would be angry enough at his plunging in alone . . .

At his hotel, the hired sedan stood ready. Hawkins edged it down the waterfront drive very slowly, to kill a little time. He hoped he remembered the way.

It was not only a violation of all the rules of international police cooperation—and probably of international law as well; it was, even more gravely in his own eyes, flagrantly discourteous to the Spaniard who had been a model of courtesy to him.

Therefore, why am I doing this? And why don't I turn around right now and go back? Because I want to save Theresa from a Spanish jail. Because I am terrified Elf is closing in on Theresa. What would Steel say to that? That I'm obsessed with this girl to a degree that makes my continuance in the FBI deeply questionable—or some such bureaucratic semantics.

He stopped the car at the curb beside the bay, glittering with the lights of yachts, the only light in the moonless night, killed the engine. Were these Steel's questions he was worrying about? Or his own? What lay behind and under this obsession with a girl he'd never met?

"I'm not talking as an FBI man," said Hawkins to Hawkins, "but as an old friend."

A classic line from the kind of movie they don't make any more.

Black as the inside of a bear. An old Yankee expression. Could she see her hand in front of her face. She tried it. Just. Theresa lay in the stinking bed, listening to Antonio's snores. A man's man, she thought tenderly. Fucked me inside out—an old urban guerrilla feminist expression that said everything.

I love him tenderly. I lust after Elf. I love God. I am the sum of my contradictions.

Life is preposterous, mine no more than anyone else's. My carnal nature quarrels with my compassion, which is my true purpose and should be everyone's true purpose.

She was bone tired. Still I cannot lie here, flat on my back, all night long, wondering what Elf is up to. I have obligations. To the duke. And to Mother. No, not to Mother. Whenever I contemplate Mother, I become as a child. It was to escape my childhood that I fled. A person must flee to escape the nursery in bourgeois America. They don't let you out willingly, not my parents, not anyone's parents in the twentieth century. One has to break jail—which is why so many of us are on the loose.

Theresa stepped out of bed carefully, massaging her stiff muscles in the blackness. She didn't have to be too careful about noise. Antonio never woke up. She slipped into her baggy peasant trousers, pulled the blue blouse over her head, groped into her rope-soled shoes. That done, she felt with her fingers for Antonio's face, caressed it lightly.

Outside the stone hut, Theresa leaned against the door a moment, rubbing her eyes, collecting her wits. Not even a star to guide her. She'd never operated in blackness like this, even in guerrilla school. Relax. Let the eyeball adjust, as the instructor used to say. She opened her eyes wide. There was always some light somewhere. Wait. Presently the blackness changed to dimness. She could see the outlines of trees. Very faint.

What time was it? Ten-thirty? Eleven? The night, she felt, was young. She'd fed Antonio the moment they'd returned to the stone cottage—and then sub-mitted. Wifely submission. Very connubial.

She moved off down the hill. Very slowly. Hurry was a waste of time, her instructor had taught. Paradox. Hands in front of her to ward off trees— and the ghosts of my wild and wicked past. Oh, the ghosts are out in full force tonight. It's because I'm wide awake. Because I've been slapped silly. And fucked foolish. It stirs up the bats in a girl's belfry.

So went the monologue. Feeling her way down the hill. Putting out one leg very gently, toes arched in an exploration to see to it that any bumps were gentle ones. Putting down the foot experimentally so she didn't break an ankle if she happened to step into a hole. It took a bit of time.

But then what was time to a woman facing Eter-nity? To say nothing of a murder charge in Phila-delphia.

Murder charge? That thought hadn't crossed her mind for many a long night. Theresa leaned against a tree, closed her eyes, and thought about the Phila-delphia bank bust—breathing deeply to calm her nerves.

I didn't, whispered Theresa. Quiet but still aloud. She'd never before denied the charge. It had been the central core of her guilt, the inescapable, the unutterable experience. Now, in the blackness of this black-as-hell night, there shone this bit of blind-ing light.

I didn't kill him! Elf did!

I've always known it really, always. Why then

have I pretended to be the murderess I wasn't? Because I was then madly, hopelessly besotted by Elf.
I wanted to be part of her, so I took possession of a
murder that didn't rightly belong to me.

Theresa sat down on the steep slope, staring
into the black night, and thought about that bank
heist. Why am I thinking about that distant night I
haven't thought about in months? Because I've been
slapped silly, all the foolishness slapped out of me
by Antonio.

She'd got slapped around the night of the bank
heist, too.

The bank guard had struck her viciously with
his gun—she still had the scar on her scalp—and
she had gone down firing. That had been the legend,
carefully nursed by the group—not least by Theresa
—wearing her murder like a decoration. But she
hadn't fired the gun at all. She'd gone down, not
knocked cold, just knocked silly. The gun wasn't
even in her hand. It had fallen—and Elf had picked
it up and Elf had killed the bank guard.

Why had she thought differently all these years?
Because the mind did funny things when hit by gun
butts. It didn't make any real difference in law.
Anyone taking part in a felony in which someone
got killed was as guilty of murder as the person
who pulled the trigger.

I'm still a murderess—but I didn't kill anyone.
That made a difference, not to the courts, but to
Theresa—and to God. Taking life was . . . an
arrogation of divinity that she was happy she had
never committed.

For minutes she sat stock still, giddy with the relief of it, lighter in mind and soul. Then she started down the hill again, straining her eyes through the dimness for sight of the white road.

CHAPTER

35

Theresa walked down the edge of the road on its edge of thin grass, her dark blue peasant clothes blending into the blackness of the night, using the white road as guide only. Stay off white roads, her senses told her. At the meadow where they'd tethered the sheep, she turned off the road into the lower orange grove. She knew it well, having picked oranges there tree by tree.

Leaning against the first tree, she bound up her blond hair in her blue kerchief. With her tanned face as dark as the rest of her, she was now invisible, even to Elf's sharp eyes. She couldn't see a yard and she was terrified of getting lost in the orange trees, which stretched for acres. On hands and knees she felt her way to the irrigation ditch that led to the *palacio* wall. Gently she eased herself into the ditch, barefoot, her rope-soled sandals in her hand, and crept to the wall, feeling the mud on her toes, making no sound, fearful of Elf and her sharp knives.

She went up the *palacio* wall like a lizard as she'd
done many times before, knowing every toehold. At
the top of the wall, flat on her belly, she listened.
Nothing. Not even the gurgle of chickens. She didn't
want to rouse the animals to whinny or cackle or
coo. Not that. On all fours she crept along the wall,
over the Moorish arch, feeling ahead with exploratory hand for the sharp turn in the wall. The thought
of falling off the thirty-foot wall onto the cobbled
court made her giddy with fear.

I'm afraid of the dark, afraid of high places, des-
perately afraid of Elf and her blade. What am I
doing on this wall in the dark going *toward* Elf. I
should be fleeing from Elf. The sum of my contradictions.

She lowered herself off the wall directly outside
the dove and rabbit room, dropping the last five
feet with a plop on the stone, hoping it wouldn't
alarm the doves to outcry. In the passageway the
blackness was so total Theresa felt her very identity
slipping away. The ultimate terror of the fugitive,
that his chromosomes will change him into some
other vertebrate, lower on the social scale.

At the entrance to the audience chamber, the
blackness turned to dimness. Theresa could see the
lovely rectangles where the great superbly proportioned windows looked out on the valley. The audience chamber where she'd prayed and danced and
cut Elf's head off innumerable times.

The smell stole into her nostrils—faint, subtle,
unmistakable. Elf smell. So faint an emanation from
that tough boylike body Theresa would have missed

it if they had not long lain as lovers. Theresa could smell Elf at a hundred yards. Elf had been there. And gone.

Theresa moved the length of the great chamber, sniffing like a hound dog. She stole down the stairway at the foot of the audience chamber, avoiding the piles of stones at every landing with the expertise of long practice. It took her five minutes to get to the tower room through darkness as Stygian as Dante's imagination.

At the doorway she sniffed for Elf, smelled only hay. Elf wasn't there. Theresa knew it. Elf gave out powerful waves of presence. Many times Theresa had wakened in the dark and felt Elf's presence next to her. Or not next to her. She could always tell. On her knees she explored the room, went through the hay bed inch by inch.

The wooden key was gone. So was her gun. So was the rope she used for tethering the goat.

The wooden key struck something immovable and stopped. Elf framed an obscenity in her brain, not wanting to utter it. The real key was on the other side, of course. Now what?

She turned the great bronze knob. The door opened easily. Elf smiled. How very convenient these aristocrats were. Far from the urban terrors, they hadn't bothered to lock the door. She slipped into the entrance passageway, feeling the marbled floor on her naked toes. Upstairs a hum of languid voices, as she locked the door behind her.

Awake. Would that present difficulties? No, it wouldn't. It might even speed things. She smiled again. Total despair. Girl at the bottom of the well.

She saw now the great Caravello, its agonized martyr on the cross, glowing in the light that tumbled down the staircase. Opiate of the masses. She was thinking less of Christ on the cross than of the great painting itself—and of art altogether. Art she appreciated in reverse—the more valuable, the more to be despised. Religious art in particular she felt to be a sort of bourgeois insanity, millions of dollars in fake values, hanging on the walls of capitalist pigs. A fantasy world, the art scene, with its hypocrisies, its pretense, its cocktail parties, its phony auctions. Art, the ultimate refuge of the Philistines.

Elf went up the staircase in barefoot silence, listening to the soft murmur of Spanish. What were they talking about? Their money? Their paintings? No, probably their dinner. Conversation became trivial in almost exact ratio to how far you were up the social ladder until, when you reached the dukes and duchesses, it attained a degree of triviality unknown even to spiders. So thought Elf. At the bottom of the social scale the talk was of starvation, at the upper that the *marrons glacés* were not quite, quite.

At the top of the stairs, flattened against the curved wall, Elf looked kitty-cornered into the sitting room. The back of the duke's head. Where was the duchess?

Elf walked boldly into the room, her gun outstretched as if it were an invitation.

"Stand up, Your Grace, with your hands over your head," she barked. Very loud. It helped to

275

bark these commands at the beginning to establish dominion, to lay down the ground rules, to define the players. When was the first time I walked into a room with a loaded .38 in my hand? Followed almost immediately by self-admonition. What in hell am I doing thinking irrelevancies like that in the middle of an operation? I'm losing concentration. Flights of rhetoric when action is all!

The gun held steady at eye level, where it cast the most menace—and was also most operational. The duke's head had twisted sharply around, eyes full of surprise. Not fright.

The duchess, Elf now saw, was seated at a long table of very dark wood, pasting photographs into an album. She was a picture of arrested motion, one hand with a photograph between two fingers caught in midair, the mouth a little round O. Surprise again.

Why no fear? Of me, the mighty Elf, terror of the western plains? They should be scared out of their wits. They were like protected species, these two. They were like those animals explorers found on desert islands—tame because they knew not what fearful monsters we are.

My wits wandering again!

"Drop the photograph, Your Excellency," Elf took great pleasure in putting these aristocrats in their proper place, giving them their full titles, automatically dehumanizing them.

The duchess dropped the photograph on the table and rose slowly, silently, with great dignity. The duke had not stirred. His gaze, still fixed on her, had retreated into inscrutability. Not even surprise. Emotionless. Elf felt her anger rise at this coldness.

"Stand up, Your Grace." Her voice sibilant now. She'd barked the first time. Now she was lowering her voice at him, demonstrating she could outcool His Most Excellent Excellency.

In the cobbled court, Theresa stood in the blackness, the wooden key in her hand, emaciated lips moving soundlessly: Why? The great entrance door with its bronze lion was locked.

Far down the white road headlights rounded a bend. Theresa came out of her revery abruptly. Headlights! The Porsche stood there in the courtyard. Theresa had run into it, crossing the courtyard. The only other car she'd seen in the valley had been the police limousine.

Police.

Well, let them handle it.

No. The police would mess it up. Anyway, it was her responsibility. She had lured Elf onto the island, however unwittingly. Was anything unwitting? Life was the sum of one's contradictions and there was no avoiding accumulated responsibility for past submissions.

Theresa stole back up the crazy staircase. It might not work but it was the only possibility.

The action was going badly.

The duke sprang at her, courageous but foolish and above all amateur. Elf could have shot him but she didn't want him shot. She coshed him—and she didn't want to do that either. Because he had come at her with such a rush she hit him too hard and now he lay in a heap of gore at her feet. Messy. And she wanted him conscious.

"Oh!" gasped the duchess. She paled a bit. That was all. It was not enough. Elf grimaced savagely. Marvelous control, these aristos. Or perhaps just bloodless.

"Turn around, Duchess," commanded Elf, leveling the gun at her, looking for weakness in the façade, not finding any. "Stand away from that wall about two feet, legs spread. Now just lean against the wall with arms outstretched supporting yourself with your hands."

It was undignified, a duchess in that position employed by police the world over not only to immobilize their victims, but to humiliate them. Elf looked at the duchess, legs spraddled, arms splayed, infinitely ridiculous. I feel no triumph, nothing.

She tied up the duke with Theresa's bit of rope and bound him to the heavy oak table, seated upright, eyes front. It was important that he witness the business when he came to. He was out cold, still bleeding profusely. Elf tore a strip off his own shirt and bound the wound tightly. She didn't want him bleeding to death. There were things to be done.

What things? What am I doing?

Elf crumpled into the heavily carved oak chair lately occupied by the duchess, gun dangling carelessly from one hand, eyes on the floor. Who am I now—Hamlet? Self-questioning. Have I ever questioned? Questioning even my questions.

"Turn around, Duchess." Almost politely.

The duchess heaved herself away from the wall, put her legs together, and turned to face Elf—stately as a minuet. The eyes unforgiving.

When would this marbled cunt give tongue, wondered Elf. The duchess had said nothing except "oh." Not much of a sound, that. A sort of "ee-yew" more than "oh." Only the very upper classes could utter such a sound. Elf contemplated the lady, alarmed by the absence of emotion in herself. Where is my superb anger? My scorn? My senses should be exploding.

"My husband . . ."

Excellent English. A musical foreign accent.

"Your husband is okay." Elf kept her eyes on the floor, negligently, daring her to try something. Attempting by her indifference to achieve an unbending, perhaps humiliation, of this cold female.

"What do you want?"

Elf pursed her lips. "The effective end of the destructive power and repressive controls of the affluent society. The abolition of poverty. The destruction of stupefying work by the toiling masses that is both needless and demeaning to the personality."

What am I making speeches for? To this marbled cunt?

The four-letter word wakened her to the absence. Usually the gun in her hand, the bliss of domination, set her to slavering. I'm cold as yesterday's potatoes. What's the matter with me?

Elf pulled her eyes off the floor, feeling empty and ironical. "What do I want? Shall we say intelligent self-determination. I wish to free the slaves from their brainless preoccupation with empty materialism, which has brought them nothing but unhappiness. . . ."

Aah. I'm beginning to get through. This woman is not terrified by my gun; but she fears my intelligence. Elf could see the beginning of alarm in her eyes.

"I wish to free you, Duchess, from the chains of your wealth, which is seriously hampering the development of your personality." Elf smiled lazily, searching the duchess's eyes for appreciation of this gibe.

The duchess scarcely heard.

"Roberto . . ." she cried.

Elf jerked her head sidewise. The duke had come to. Dazed but conscious. Furious, too. Elf could see him strain at his bonds. Much good it would do him. That was a scorpion knot she'd tied. Nobody ever got loose from a scorpion knot.

The duchess emitted a stream of mellifluous Spanish at the duke, caressing him with sound. Fond of him, was she? That opened vistas. Or it should have. I'm not responding. It's not happening. Why? Exhausted, that's why. I must take control.

Elf coughed, ending the Spanish endearments between husband and wife, concentrating the couple's attention, which had wandered from the current center of their existence, which was she, Elf. The person with the gun occupied the center of the stage or else what was it all about? My wits are wandering.

"Take off your clothes," she barked harshly at the duchess, angry at herself now. Aimless. I have never been *aimless*.

"No," said the duchess.

Ah, this was better. Elf raised the gun, sighted down it. "Take off your clothes or I'll put a bullet right square in the middle of that aristocratic belly." Snarling it.

"Never!"

The duke interjected himself into the equation. "Do it, Francesca."

"Roberto!"

"It's important to stay alive," said the duke.

"Oh, you think that, do you?" Elf swiveled around and studied the duke with some surprise. She would have thought he might be one of those idiot aristocrats who would die defending his honor, which was not worth defending. "How very interesting. You're running against the mold, you know."

The duke ignored Elf. "Do it, Francesca."

Francesca, thought Elf. Very musical. She watched as the duchess slipped her sweater over her head. Underneath it, nothing. Very modern duchess. I would have thought there'd be a slip, bra, the whole bourgeois nonsense. Nothing at all but small round breasts—the kind Elf loved best. . . . Why don't they rouse me? Why doesn't something?

"Now the skirt," said Elf, eyes on the duke. Striptease of his duchess. Something should happen to the chemistry of that blueblooded robot with his programmed responses. Shouldn't it? A widening of the eye cavity. That was all.

The duchess stood naked now, having removed pants, stockings, shoes. Expressionless. She had, as it were, banished Elf totally. Elf had disappeared from view. She was a duchess alone in her bedchamber getting undressed. That was all.

She started to take off the single strand of pearls around her neck.

"No. Leave it," said Elf sharply. "The apotheosis of duchesshood, that pearl necklace."

The naked duchess stood there in her pearls, looking through her, around her, above her, ignoring her utterly. A very good performance.

It should have made Elf mad. It didn't. She was gazing at the duchess blankly. And why don't I devour her? In front of her husband. The sort of thing that was done as a matter of course by Roman emperors. And lesser Romans in decaying Rome. I could make that marbled lady shrink with revulsion. Or perhaps even make her come—in front of her husband—and wouldn't that make him writhe! These rich vultures living off the starvation of the peasants!

A shriek of the mind. Nothing in the cunt. Nothing.

Frigid!

The word exploded in her mind like a rocket, propelling her clear out of the carved chair to a position one yard in front of the naked duchess.

Frigid! Me!

Eyes like holes, Elf scrutinized the naked flesh

before her, devouring her with her eyes, feeling absolute emptiness. So this is what frigidity is like? No desire. No revulsion. Nothing.

Gun arm hanging limp by her side, Elf extended the other arm and let one finger trace a delicate arabesque around the duchess's left breast. She'd always had superbly tactile arousal from the tips of her fingers on naked female flesh. Not this time. It was like fingering a stone.

"Have you turned yourself off?" Elf asked conversationally. And immediately regretted it. She had never asked questions of her captives.

The duchess said nothing—exquisitely.

Theresa lowered herself slowly from the *palacio* roof, her long legs groping for the ledge. Forty feet up. Thank God for urban guerrilla training. In the darkness, she had a sudden blinding flash of recollection of the farm in Colorado, where she and the other revolutionaries had dangled from so many roofs, climbed so many cliffs, hand over hand, all to prepare for the final assault on capitalism, which now seemed so irrelevant.

One foot, then the other touched down on the little ledge outside the kitchen window. Four inches wide. Enough. Theresa crouched, one hand holding the rope, the other inserting the knife in the aperture. If it was locked, she'd have to kick in the window and she didn't want to do that. . . .

Elf had moved away from the naked duchess now

and stood, lost in contemplation of the Caravello. Christ carrying the cross. Not yet on it.

"He never existed, you know," said Elf, tossing off this ultimate impiety like a throwaway line about the weather. "It's a monstrous put-on, all this Jesus freakery." She had a personal score to settle with The Man.

Elf lifted the painting off its hook and laid it on the heavy oak table. Not even a grunt came from either duke or duchess, but the air was electric.

Elf picked up the scissors the duchess had been using to trim photographs and plunged it into the painting. This produced a sharp explosion of air from the duchess's lungs, but nothing so undignified as an outcry. Elf cut the painting out from the frame and rolled it up.

"I'm not going to hurt it," she said contemptuously. "Just use it as an exchange for a few of the good people in your jails."

Why was she explaining her actions? Elf had never explained, never apologized. Explanation was a form of apology; the confident never explained.

"I'll trade the Caravello for the freedom of Jocasta the Basque."

"She's dead," gasped the duchess.

"Oh," murmured Elf. "I didn't know." Dead! The famous Jocasta—a terrorist after her own heart. A year earlier, she'd have known about the death of a freedom fighter anywhere in the world.

"Then perhaps the Red Guerrilla." Elf looked questioningly at the duchess. Was the Red Guerrilla dead too? The naked duchess shut her lips stubbornly. She'd said all she had to say.

I have lost my powers, thought Elf sadly.

She slipped the painting under her arm, picked up the gun, and backed toward the door, gun arm outstretched toward the naked duchess. Into what part of that disdainful nudity shall I put the bullet. The round belly? The cunt itself? It would make a final splash of awesome proportions: ELF SHOOTS NAKED DUCHESS IN CUNT. No, they'd never dare use that lovely expressive word.

"I'm going to kill you, you know," said Elf, letting the words ring out, trying to induce a little panic in that marbled cunt.

In the kitchen Theresa heard it clearly.

My voice, thought Elf, has gone as dead as my cunt. Are they then interconnected—sex organs, voice box? Am I dead all over and is this scene just reflex action like a chicken with its head cut off?

"I've never before killed anyone in cold blood," she said, sighting down the gun. Talking to myself. "This is a test to see if I can do it."

The duke broke his silence. "I'll get every freedom fighter out of every Spanish jail—if you'll spare my wife."

"What a measured sentence," jeered Elf. She swung the gun now to point at the duke. "How very ducal, you titled shithead. Perhaps I'll trade her life for yours. I prefer shooting men to women."

"By all means." Very casual, a throwaway line designed to arouse Elf's fury. It aroused only her wonder at her absence of passion. Where's my rage?

She squinted down the barrel of the .38. "I'd shoot you both but I must have a witness. Otherwise who would know Elf James had done it?"

This remained a moot point forever after, because Theresa hit her just then very hard—much too hard—with the blunt end of the cleaver she'd picked up in the kitchen. She'd come down the hall almost on a run, galvanized by that line "I'm going to kill you." With Elf you had to take a line like that very seriously. She had swung hard slantwise across Elf's skull, trying to immobilize her, and even as she swung knowing it was too hard, much too hard.

Elf's gun slithered across the floor and came to rest on the throw rug to the left of the naked duchess. Theresa dove for it, headlong, came up with it, and rolled over flat on her stomach, gun leveled at Elf, elbows braced on the floor, left hand steadying the gun in her right hand. Elf stood near the door, stunned by the blow, the rolled painting still in her left hand. Blood spurted out of a triangular hole in her scalp and flooded down her cheek. She put her right hand on her cheek gently and then brought it away, looking at the blood, dazed, unbelieving.

For moments on end, nothing at all happened. Theresa sighted down the barrel in the classic pose she'd learned at urban guerrilla school, legs well spread behind her for balance, elbows firm. Eyes looking into Elf's.

Nobody said anything at all.

The duchess was the first to move. She uttered

a small sigh, picked up her panties, and slipped them on. After that, the sweater, the skirt, stockings, and shoes. It took under a minute to transform the naked duchess to a clothed duchess.

"Shoot," jeered Elf. "You'll never get a better chance. Or another one. Saint Theresa!"

I should kill her now. I should. It'll never end between her and me. Not ever.

The moment passed.

Instead she spoke, toneless: "What in hell are you doing? Undressing duchesses! It's not only insane. It's depraved. You've wound up more bourgeois than *they* are."

Elf emitted a dry chuckle: "I was liberating her sexuality into socially constructive forms. Desublimating her. The pleasure principle absorbs the reality principle, just as Marcuse says. Go ahead, shoot. You've always wanted to avenge Strick."

But of course Theresa couldn't shoot anyone in cold blood. Or in hot blood either. She'd just been freed from that shadow.

"The law is coming up the road," said Theresa. "I saw headlights on the white road ten minutes ago."

A flicker of emotion in Elf. A tremor through the muscular frame. "Give me the gun. It's no good to a Jesus freak."

"No, there's been enough killing."

"You're going to let me face them unarmed? Your comrade? Your lover?"

"Yes," said Theresa. "I am."

"You're not Jesus. You're Judas," shrieked Elf,

splitting the eardrums. She seized the scissors from the table and tore down the stairs, the rolled Caravello in her other hand. Theresa heard the great door downstairs open, and close.

The duchess was trying to untie the duke and not succeeding. Wearily, Theresa went to her aid. "Scorpion knot. It takes experience to untie them." She undid the symmetrical knot. "I'm sorry I took so long. She took my rope, you see. I had to find another. It took a little while."

"I owe you my life," said the duke.

"I'm not sure she'd have shot you," said Theresa sourly. "She was playing games."

She picked up the rope, laid down the gun on the table.

"This makes the odds a little evener," she said smiling.

She started out the door.

"Where are you going?"

"After Elf," said Theresa gravely.

She went into the little kitchen and hoisted herself out the window with the same rope on which she had come in.

CHAPTER

36

The jargon was obsolete, as out of date as yesterday's newspaper. I'm ashamed of you, Elf, thought
Hawkins.

Oppressors:
Call off the pigs or the Caravello will be destroyed.
The painting will be returned unharmed only after you
free the twelve Basque freedom fighters in El Morro
Prison.

ELF JAMES

The note had been found at the end of the audience chamber, written melodramatically in Elf's own
blood on the ducal writing paper.

The Spanish police chief was exasperated. "Three
of the Basque freedom fighters—whom we prefer
to call terrorists—are dead. Six have been released.
Two have been transferred to other prisons. And
the only one remaining in El Morro is dying of
cancer. Your Elf's information is very much out of
date."

Not my Elf, thought Hawkins wryly, Rodgers' Elf. I'm a Theresa man. Elf was floundering in her own incompetence. It wasn't at all reassuring. Elf, the sharpest girl bank robber and revolutionary of them all, at the end of her tether. The most dangerous time.

"How would she know if we freed twelve Basque freedom fighters—even if we had them to free?" asked the duke.

Hawkins spread his hands wide, expressive of total mystification. "I don't know what is on Elf's mind and, when she wrote that note, I doubt that she had a plan. She just wanted to scare us off. The painting is her only weapon. She's using it."

Three o'clock in the morning. The three men were in the sitting room. The duchess had long since gone to bed. The duke was haggard with fatigue, the bandage Elf had fastened on him still on his head. He had refused all pleading to go to bed. It was his *palacio*. He had his duties as host. Also, thought Hawkins, it was his Caravello.

"How important was that Caravello?" asked Hawkins.

The duke looked at him reproachfully. "All Caravellos are important," he murmured.

"Well," said Hawkins bluntly, "I realize that— but I've never heard of 'The Ninth Station'—or, in fact, of any of these Caravellos and I just wondered . . ."

"None of our Caravellos has been catalogued," said the duke negligently. "My family didn't wish to call attention to them."

290

Hawkins was struck breathless by the sheer ducal effrontery of it. One of the world's great painters, Caravello, and here were three of his paintings, uncatalogued and unknown, in a ruined and virtually abandoned fourteenth-century *palacio*. How very Spanish.

"In these lawless times," said the duke gently, "the best protection for art treasures is none at all."

He thinks it's nobody else's damned business, especially mine, thought Hawkins.

"I wish no publicity at all about this," said the duke. "I don't wish my name spread over the world press." A command. The Spanish police chief nodded. He understood perfectly. But did Hawkins?

The police chief directed his medieval gaze on Hawkins: "I am aware that if this had happened in the United States, already the press would be called in, the television. . . ."

"We don't call them in," said Hawkins. "They just come in uninvited." The Constitution invited them in but he wasn't about to explain the U.S. Constitution to a couple of fourteenth-century Spaniards at three in the morning.

The police chief looked at Hawkins sternly. He was a bit put out about Hawkins anyway. What had he been doing at the scene of the crime while he, chief of police, was in Palma thirty kilometers away?

"It is our belief," said the police chief as if handing down a commandment, "that the press invites and sanctions this kind of blackmail by publicizing it. In ordinary blackmail, it has been found very

291

effective to keep secret the victim's name. This has removed the weapon from the blackmailer's hand. Do you understand me?"

Hawkins nodded. He not only understood, he was way ahead of the chief. If you take the weapon out of the hand of the blackmailer, you place it in my hand, thought Hawkins.

"None of my men, not even my deputy, knows that a painting is missing. Nobody knows except the duke and myself. You wouldn't have known either if you hadn't—so fortuitously—appeared on the scene, Mr. Hawkins."

"I missed the action by half an hour—or I'd have had both girls."

The duke sipped his coffee: " 'The Ninth Station' is, I think, the greatest of all Caravellos, but its loss would be nothing next to the loss of my privacy. In these days of kidnappers, terrorists, and urban guerrillas the greatest treasure a man in my position can have is his privacy."

Hawkins blinked stubbornly. He agreed but then he had his own obsession: "What do you propose to do?" he asked the chief.

"Nothing," said the chief.

Nothing comes from nothing, thought Hawkins. Like King Lear. Nothing takes some doing. We can do anything in the United States *except* nothing. We have no gift for doing nothing.

"My men have surrounded the *palacio*," said the chief. "The girls can't get out. They have no food, no water. That will bring them out."

Hawkins thought of Oakland. All that gunfire,

292

which in the end burned down the house and presented the police with a corpse of an already dead man. That was the American way. The Spanish way was simple starvation. It would save a lot of bullets. But would it save his Theresa?

"I think we should all get some sleep," said Hawkins.

At the invitation of the chief, Hawkins drove back to Palma in the limousine and allowed his rented SEAT to be driven by a police officer.

"What were you doing at the *palacio* so—happily —after you had said goodnight?" asked the police chief. The reproach was very gentle. Nevertheless it was a reproach.

Hawkins thought it over. Should he play his card now? His only card. "I want Theresa, chief. No matter what. I wish to take her back to the United States."

"Theresa is wanted here for illegal entry and possession of narcotics."

"You do wish to keep the existence of the paintings a secret?"

Direct blackmail.

The police chief scowled a mighty scowl. They rode the rest of the way in total silence. Nevertheless Hawkins knew he had won.

Theresa was operating by instinct in darkest darkness. The first light she would see would be Elf's. Elf could hardly operate without light, because she had never been in the dungeons before, while Theresa had explored them from one end to the other. She crawled under the six-foot wall of the first dungeon level into a huge underground chamber. Was Elf in it?

No, she wasn't. I can feel her presence and it's not here. Theresa crawled through the blackness head first down a spiral stone staircase to the second dungeon level. How to outwit in the dark one of the world's great authorities of combat in the dark? Her and her scissors. Me and a rope. Oh, I wouldn't bet on me.

Why am I not gibbering with terror? Because I'm not frightened at all. I am even exhilarated by this terminal quest. Terminal? Well, yes. Flight to the final reality. My mind is extraordinarily precise in this darkness. How did Elf find her way in it? That girl with eyes like an owl—and ears like a bat. I must not even think quite so loud.

One more flight of twisting stone steps. Head first down them like a caterpillar. And as quietly. Ahead of her a glow of light no larger than a toad's thumb.

Very unlike Elf to leave a candle in the window. Some trick, probably. Expecting me, is she? Or the police? Where did she get candles? Out of my tower room, of course. But why is she exposing herself in this way. Perhaps she's not exposing herself but trying to get me to expose myself. What does Marighela say about that? Fortunate for me that I have read the same books Elf has. In fact, Elf gave them to me and may now be regretting it.

Stratagems for persuading pursuers to reveal themselves. I remember it well. A candle in a tree.

Take refuge well to the right or the left, and shoot when the pursuer steps into the circle of light—if he's that foolish. So Elf would be lying well to the right or left—except she can't be left because the wall is there. Thank God for early reconnaissance. So she must be lying to the right—listening with her bat's ears to my thoughts in this infernal cellar.

The sound came from the right and caught Theresa by the throat. Soft, familiar, old-fashioned. Glottal, liquid, faint as a butterfly's flutter. A snore. But I know it well. I have lain too long with that body not to.

Or is it an Elf trick?

How long had Elf been without sleep? I had a few hours in Antonio's bed. But Elf has had a busy night—stealing my gun, my key, my rope, and my candles. Undressing duchesses. Last night she got very little sleep. Sucking me off till all hours.

Theresa lay listening to the soft snore, evaluating its timbre, its pace, its pulse. Could anyone, even one so monstrously full of guile as Elf, reproduce her own snore? No, because no girl has heard herself snore; and especially Elf who had always indignantly denied that she did such a thing.

Theresa crawled toward the snore—softly because Elf was one of the world's lightest sleepers.

One of the reasons she was still at large.

CHAPTER

37

It was an awful three days.

Steel called four times. Three of them Hawkins contrived to be elsewhere. The fourth time—by accident because he thought it was the Spanish police chief—he picked up the phone.

"They're trapped in the dungeons underneath the palace," said Hawkins.

"Dungeons? Palace?" howled Steel. "What is this —a horror movie?"

How could he explain Majorca to Steel? He hung up.

Daily he went out to the *palacio* to talk to the duke, to watch the *Guardia Civil*, in their olive-drab costumes, their tricornered hats, patrol the walls of the *palacio*.

Twice daily he called the Spanish police chief, who was just barely speaking to him.

Mostly, though, he stayed in his hotel room, going over the record, all of it. After all, he knew the girl very well, knew her psychologically, sociologically, psychiatrically, ideologically. Her family life, school life, university life, revolutionary life. I should be able to predict what she will do or what she will try to do.

He couldn't.

Why had Theresa gone after Elf? For what purpose? Theresa had fled *from* her three times. Why then go *after* her? The duke had said the girls seemed to be enemies rather than friends—or lovers. But lovers turned into enemies, didn't they? He found it hard to believe his Theresa—he had ceased policing the possessive out of his thoughts—would do anything so . . . plausible. So basely motivated. So . . . what? . . . human. Anyway if Theresa had wanted to settle Elf, she'd had an opportunity, gun in hand. She hadn't taken it, hadn't even taken the gun along.

To even the odds. A terrible thought. Single-handed, the odds would always favor Elf.

Theresa had taken the rope.

Why?

What does a Jesus freak do with a rope—scourge herself? Scourge Elf?

Hawkins read late into the night anything he could lay his hands on in Majorca concerning religious mysticism. Hunching his long bony body over the book like a skeletal question mark, he devoured the life of Saint Francis. Imagine looking for clues in the annals of a dead saint! There were close parallels, of course. Saint Francis had been a rich wastrel who embraced poverty as a vocation.

A joyful embrace—both for Saint Francis and his Theresa.

He was in the middle of Saint Francis when Steel called for the twenty-sixth time. Hawkins was in a mood of transcendental irony and he let Steel have it—straight out of the book—without preamble:

"The Kingdom of God is at hand," trumpeted Hawkins over the transatlantic telephone. "Cure the sick, raise the dead, cleanse the lepers, drive out devils."

And hung up. It would do Steel a world of good—these medieval adjurations. A little roughage for his FBI soul.

The following night Hawkins ploughed into the life of Simone Weil, the French mystic they called "the pilgrim of the absolute"—a phrase that fit his Theresa very well indeed. A lot of parallels there, too. Simone Weil had also led a grape pickers strike, had wallowed in poverty. . . .

Steel called again and this time Hawkins fired a whiff of Simone Weil's *pensées* into the telephone to the astonished Steel three thousand miles away:

"The quantity of evil in the world is precisely equal to the necessary amount of punishment. Purity attracts evil which rushes to it like moths to a flame, to be destroyed."

It would make a nice sampler, thought Hawkins, done in needlepoint to hang in Steel's office. He listened gravely to Steel's expletives, which on the transatlantic telephone were reduced to a distant tinny squeak, taking all the menace out of them.

He hung up and went back to his religious studies. At eleven that night he read of Simone Weil's end—and five minutes later he was in the SEAT, driving toward the *palacio*.

The map was of vellum, yellow with age and stiff as old leather. At the lower left-hand corner was a spidery legend: April, 1564.

"This is the latest diagram you have?" inquired Hawkins, disbelieving.

"It's the only one," said the duke, polite but ironical. "There was no need, you see. Nothing has been done to the place since then."

Brown sepia lines showing the layout of the entire vast structure—including the dungeons.

"I explored the dungeons once when I was twelve. I haven't been down there since. Much of it has crumbled away. Nothing has been added."

Except a couple of revolutionary girls.

"The police chief won't like it," said the duke, "going in alone. They are dangerous revolutionaries. Elf has killed seven people."

"They only have a pair of scissors and a rope between them." He refrained from saying that Elf had put a police constable into the hospital with a pair of scissors.

"You'd better take this." The duke handed him a pencil-thin flashlight. "You'll need it for reading the map. What will I tell the police chief?"

"Nothing," said Hawkins. "He understands the uses of nothing better than any lawman I know."

Hawkins found the first cellar without any diffi-

culty, using the vellum map and the pencil-thin
flashlight. At the foot of the second staircase, he
stared long and hard at the vellum drawing, memo-
rizing it. Then he turned off the flashlight and proceeded on foot in pitch darkness. At the top of the
next stone staircase, he dropped to all fours. Paleo-
lithic man stood erect against the woolly mammoth.
In the twentieth century we're back on all fours,
thought Hawkins, crawling painfully over fallen
stones smelling of the fifteenth century at a speed
a snail would have considered grotesque. An hour
later a tiny light ahead glowed with the promise
of evil. Hawkins pushed toward it like a moth.

"God is the source of all good. Hell is our own
invention."

The voice was languorous, blissful, and almost
extinct. It was the first time he'd ever heard her
voice, thought Hawkins, crawling on all fours toward the candle.

Theresa was on her knees, thin as a pencil stroke,
as if engraved on ivory. Elf lay next to her on her
side, eyes closed, arms behind her back.

"His greatest gift in the end is silence." Theresa's
voice irradiated with bliss.

"Hello," said Hawkins politely.

Theresa's blue eyes opened slowly, and she contemplated Hawkins, unsurprised, as if she'd been
expecting him.

"Too late," said Theresa triumphantly.

Elf, Hawkins discovered, had died hours earlier—
and just how and why was to start many learned

arguments among forensic experts, doctors, lawyers, and even theologians for months to come.

Hawkins took custody of Theresa, a girl he had been pursuing for a very long time, reverently, both of them on their knees as if they were in church.

CHAPTER

38

The conversation at the bedside was sometimes so
lucid as to amount to revelation. Two kinds of
revelation, theological and legal. Hawkins was, after
all, a lawman, though a reluctant one.

"Our first conversation was about grape pickers
and their pay. I was indignant. Elf was enraged.
She taught me rage."

Theresa's brown face on the white hospital pillow,
the blond hair newly washed by the nurses. She
looked like a Giotto. Thirteenth-century ascetic.

"Rage was her vocation," Theresa whispered—
and slept.

That explained a great deal. Rage was Elf's vocation, love was Theresa's. The one loved the oppressed, the other hated the oppressor. The eternal
opposites, the law of contradiction.

In the intervals away from the hospital bed, Hawkins temporized with the Spanish police chief, a man

he respected and was beginning even to understand
a little.

Elf was beyond the reach of law, but there was still
Theresa. The Spanish police chief was ready to over-
look illegal entry, narcotics. But not murder.

"Even if you could persuade yourself it was murder, you could never persuade a jury, not even a
Spanish jury. Elf died of loss of blood. The wound
was caused by Theresa saving the life of one of
your great noblemen."

The Spaniard looked at him with his hooded eyes.
"Elf was bound to an iron ring that has not been
used for that purpose in six hundred years. She
died struggling against her bonds—and she was
bound to the ring by your Theresa. That makes
her as guilty of murder as if she had pulled the
trigger."

"She didn't pull the trigger. She had a chance.
She didn't take it. Anyway . . ."

Anyway, the experts were not at all sure that
Elf had died of loss of blood. Possibly it was shock
that changed everything. The legal complexities
were infinite.

Theologians argued about whether Theresa was a
saint or a lunatic—most of them arguing lunacy,
of course. Saintliness is always lunatic while the
perpetrator still breathes.

Hawkins managed to fend off a murder charge,
at least while Theresa was still in the hospital, by
brandishing the Caravellos. The one Elf had fled
with had been recovered, damaged but repairable.
The Caravellos were safe only so long as their

whereabouts, indeed their very existence, was un-
suspected by art thieves.

If Hawkins told the newspapers about three un-
suspected Caravellos . . .

The threat gave the Spanish police chief pause.
But for how long?

The duke and duchess paid their respects with
flowers and their gracious presences. Theresa smiled
a benediction—and slept.

The duke stared at the emaciated face on the
pillow as if it were an art object. "What possessed
you," he asked Hawkins, "to make a dash to our
place on that night? What made you think . . ."

Hawkins shrugged. "I've been chasing the girl
for years. I . . . know a great deal about her."

He didn't want to tell the duke or anyone about
the end of Simone Weil. Simone Weil had died of
many things but self-induced starvation was promi-
nent among them. She had refused to eat more than
the rations given her French countrymen under the
Nazi occupation, and it had killed her.

"Theresa," he explained as best he could, "was
always dramatic even when she despised herself
for occupying the center of the stage, for committing
—as she called it—vaudeville. She had a great gift
for starvation anyway. It induced the kind of exaltation she sought to clarify her mind."

But, of course, great strides had been taken in
the practice of force feeding, in the art of keeping
people alive who didn't want to stay alive. Theresa
refused all food, but there were ways of inducing

calories and vitamins and nutrients, many of them very unpleasant.

Antonio came to visit the hospital—but the police wouldn't let him in, of course. A peasant, even if he was *her* peasant, didn't have the same privileges as dukes and police.

Theresa slept on.

Steel called from Washington, mollified—at least on the telephone.

Hawkins read the news story in the *International Herald Tribune*. The pursuit in Majorca had, he discovered, been Steel's idea all along. Steel had dispatched Hawkins there as the culmination of a bit of brilliant sleuthing. Steel's, not Hawkins'.

Hawkins chewed the inside of his cheek wryly. Possession, he thought, is nine points of the law. He had Theresa; they didn't.

Eight days after the capture, Theresa began getting better—to her great indignation.

"Very unkind," she whispered to Hawkins at her bedside.

"Martyrdom is obsolete," observed the FBI man.

"It's not!"

"Today they give them airplanes and let them escape to Yemen."

Their conversations were always laconic. She hadn't much breath.

She'd sleep and then, if he was still at her bedside, resume. Hawkins waited for days before asking the question that still bothered him. "Why did you

go after a girl you feared so much? Why not take
to your heels?"

"I'd fled three times. She'd have just come after
me again."

"We'd have got her this time."

"You'd have shot her down, unforgiving and un-
forgiven."

Hawkins chewed his cheek, eyes on the waiflike
white face on the pillow. He had to slow himself
down because she hadn't much strength.

After a bit, he said, "Was she in the end . . .
forgiving?"

Theresa's blue eyes clouded. She remembered
Elf's implacable black eyes. "She snapped at me
with her teeth like a piranha," she whispered.

They both grinned at that.

"I didn't kill her. She simply died. There was no
place else for her to go. The Movement is finished.
Elf died of irrelevance."

"I don't think the law recognizes irrelevance as
a cause of death," said Hawkins.

Theresa managed a faint smile—and slept.

Later Hawkins asked, "Why did she want to pin
a murder on you?"

Theresa's blue eyes were clearer now and the
voice stronger: "Elf had studied the teachings of
the Montañeros in Argentina very closely."

"We all have," observed Hawkins dryly.

"Then you know the Montañeros trained girls
as assassins to liberate them from their traditional

roles as chattels. A girl wasn't truly liberated until she killed someone."

"Or thought she had."

"I never killed anyone," whispered Theresa.

That'll take some proving, thought Hawkins. Aloud, he said: "But if you thought you had, that's all that mattered. Things spoken can never be unspoken."

"You're a very peculiar FBI man—to have read Wittgenstein."

Hawkins had read Wittgenstein only because Theresa had. Her books were his orientation course. She has educated me—this skeletal object with the blond hair and blue eyes. "She was trying to possess you altogether, wasn't she?"

Oh, she possessed me altogether all right, thought Theresa—but she wasn't going to say *that* to Hawkins, this shambling Quixote who had been pursuing her for five years. Unbeknownst, thought Theresa, chewing happily on the Victorian word. To be pursued unbeknownst by this nice, quiet loose-limbed man. I'm already falling in love with him because who else is there and anyway I always fall in love with the loose-limbed lanky ones—like Strick.

"I thought you all looked like J. Edgar Hoover," she taunted him. "Bulldog homosexual types."

"I'm not very typical," said Hawkins, apologetically.

I fall in love too easily, thought Theresa. My vice. Loving people.

She fell asleep.

The next day he walked in on her devotions, on her knees on the bed, hands clasped, eyes heavenward: "Contradiction is what holds us together," she was praying, "what animates our deepest selves. I am capable of any crime and equally of all degrees of saintliness. That is my sin and my fulfillment, all of it your gift, thrice blessed."

She sighed—and saw him standing at the door.

"My prayers are getting too complicated—and much too long. They put God to sleep."

Three days later she was walking. To the end of the corridor and back.

On Hawkins' arm.

"We're causing quite a stir," she whispered.

The other patients were staring—blatantly, in the European way.

"I'm afraid you're quite a famous lady."

Theresa was exasperated. "I'm not a lady. I've been many disreputable things—revolutionary, arsonist, bank robber, *religieuse*. Never a lady."

Hawkins wouldn't let her get away with that. "I think you're a very great lady. You remind me of your mother."

"Oh, dear God!"

She wouldn't speak to him for an hour after that.

Our first quarrel, thought Hawkins. We're getting on.

She was now altogether his prisoner. The Spanish police chief had awarded him total custody, holding Spanish charges in abeyance. (Without quite quashing them. A policeman always likes to have a charge handy in case he needs it.)

A *Guardia Civil* man guarded the hospital room at all times. Except for him—and the doctor—there was no one.

The doctor was a precise, pince-nezed Spaniard, who was enormously positive about everything. The less doctors knew, the more sure of themselves they were, thought Hawkins, who trusted this one not at all.

"When can she travel?" he asked the doctor.

"Tuesday," said the medico with immense assurance.

"Tuesday?" said Hawkins, flabbergasted. It was then Friday. "She will be precisely ready for travel on Tuesday. Not before." The fussy little man was putting all his fussy little implements back into his case. "Good day."

He left without further explanation.

"Tuesday," observed Hawkins.

They were alone together in the room.

"Not much time," said Theresa.

No, thought Hawkins. Not much time. What do I need time for?

"I'll miss it."

"Miss what—the hospital?"

Theresa laughed, almost a taunt.

"How old are you?" she asked.

"That's very unfair."

"Prisoners don't have to be fair to their captors. Come on—how old?"

"Fifty-six—this year," said Hawkins, making it worse than it was.

"Sometimes you act about four and a half," said Theresa.

Hawkins rubbed his chin. "You're getting better all right."

Theresa sat in her wheelchair, arranging the heavy white robe around her feet. "How many girls have you captured?"

"Dozens."

"I don't believe you."

"None."

"I don't believe that either." She smiled. "Does this always happen between captor and captive?"

"What?"

"Oh, come on," she said irritably. "You know very well."

He knew very well. But he wasn't a member of her outspoken generation.

"Relationships usually spring up between . . ." He broke off, and stared down at the square. "I don't think of you as my captive," he said. "It's more the other way around."

She was dazzled by the confession. He'd never unbent this far before.

"I've never had a captive of my own. I am one of nature's born captives," she remarked. "And you, I had assumed, were one of nature's born captors."

Hawkins lowered his scarecrow body on her bed. "Are you disappointed?"

"Hardly."

Then he told her something he'd never told

Amanda or, even until very recently, himself. "I got into the Bureau by economic accident and I stayed in out of inertia and cowardice."

He smiled boyishly. "So now you know."

Theresa laughed. "I already knew that—or most of it. If you hadn't told me, I'd have told you." She rose from the wheelchair and sat down next to him on the bed, waving her long legs under it.

The night nurse paid her first visit at 8 P.M., when she came on duty, and after that not until 12. That gave Theresa four hours. She attacked with words because she sensed that was the way through his particular thicket.

"You'll never really know me otherwise. You might say it's part of your continuing investigation."

"I don't need to continue the investigation," said Hawkins. "You have been apprehended."

"Well, then, part of your continuing apprehension."

"Apprehension is a good word for it," said Hawkins. "I'm exceedingly apprehensive."

"I'm in love with you."

"You're in love with the whole world," said Hawkins.

"What's the matter with that?"

"We belong to different generations in every sense." But he couldn't explain his generation, nor could she hers.

"You admire sexual forbearance," said Theresa. "I find it unnatural."

"I have certain loyalties," said he. Amanda.

311

There were long silences in this duel. The garish overhead light went off and in its place came the soft night light. Theresa climbed into the bed, folded her arms across her breast and looked demure.

In the end he succumbed partly because here was the more elementary truth but mostly because he was three thousand miles from the disciplines of home, from Amanda, from the Bureau—a classic case of alienation.

Afterward, they lay silent, listening to the hospital sounds in the corridor, the rubberized hiss of the wheelchairs, the heel tapping of nurses, the Spanish murmurings.

"I feel like something out of *A Farewell to Arms*," said Hawkins.

"Out of *what*?"

"Never mind." Hemingway was clearly not her bag.

"How about Camus?" he asked.

"Sentimental bullshit," said Theresa.

We're not a generation apart; we're *two* generations apart. I'm her spiritual grandfather, thought Hawkins.

The night nurse, still with disapproval, looked in at midnight, to find a fully dressed Hawkins, seated in the bedside chair, the patient asleep. (Genuinely asleep. Sex had blown her out like a candle.) The nurse took the pulse, felt the brow, scrawled a hieroglyphic on the record at the foot of the bed. And departed without a word.

Hawkins remained for an hour, eyes on the sleeping girl—thinking solitary words. Hunter. Hunted. Pursuit. Chase. Capture. End.

No, not the end. Next came punishment. In 1849, the Austrian General Julius Haynau ordered the wholesale flogging of women after putting down the Hungarian revolt against Austria—blaming the whole thing on the ladies. Way ahead of his time, that man. Next came James Thurber's *The War Between the Sexes*—history repeating itself as farce. After five years' obsession, she's mine, all mine, and what do I do with her—eat her? Hawkins was shattered by the anticlimax of capture.

They have no barrier reefs, these children. But what about the likes of me, who have spent our lives in quiet lagoons, in protected harbors?

I'm in open ocean now. The Philosopher.

What do you do in open ocean?

Pull up the sails.

The thought scared the wits out of him.

The Spanish police chief made a ceremonial visit on the last day. Theresa was dressed—in jeans with a black turtleneck sweater over her thin body. Hawkins was leaning against the radiator, looking as insubstantial as a piece of string.

A skeleton and a scarecrow, thought the police chief. Aloud he was all police business. "There are some charges that will remain in abeyance—in perpetuity," he warned Theresa sternly.

"A long time," murmured Theresa.

"It would be unwise to return to Majorca."

"I had no plans . . . to return." She thought

regretfully of her *palacio*. The chickens. The mule. Antonio. Out of reach—in perpetuity.

The Spanish police chief shook hands with Hawkins. Crisply, ceremonially, as always. He had not quite forgiven Hawkins for his betrayal of trust. But almost. He had his intuitions, his small dark suspicions that this was not altogether a police matter. He didn't pursue them, being the man he was.

"I trust it has been instructive, our island," he said.

"It's been an education," said Hawkins. The Spanish police chief had himself been almost a four-year history course from the Moors to the Armada. "I'm very grateful . . . for your assistance, your . . . wisdom."

The Spanish police chief permitted himself a small laugh. "Oh . . . wisdom," he deprecated. "Just old age."

Still he tarried, taking his time to say it.

Finally: "I would greatly appreciate it, *Señor* Hawkins, if you would send me a little letter, at the end, telling me how it all . . ." he waved his hand in a peculiarly Spanish arabesque . . . "comes out."

"Oh, of course," said Hawkins, astonished.

The Spanish police chief looked at him with his hooded glance. "I don't understand what is happening in America." He sighed deeply. "But I have a strong suspicion that what is happening there will be happening here—in about twenty years."

EPILOGUE

"How it all comes out?" said Theresa bitterly. "He thinks it's a fairy story. The princess with the long blond hair."

"Well, perhaps he's right." Hawkins poured her some wine from one of those little airline bottles. He'd managed to procure one of the two-seat rows on the jumbo, which gave them some privacy. "You *are* a fairy story—all you young revolutionaries from the sixties. You're in danger of becoming mythologized—like the Wild West, which has produced movies that run ten times longer than the Wild West itself ran."

"How many charges," whispered Theresa, "have they preferred against me?"

"Twenty-two."

"I'll be sent to prison for a million years."

Hawkins shook his head. "You may not be sent to jail for twenty minutes."

"Ho!"

Hawkins smiled at her in a proprietory way. "You're very innocent."

That made her laugh boisterously. She thought *he* was the innocent.

"I'm talking about law, not sex now. I shouldn't be telling you this. It would be better if you remained innocent."

"Why are you telling me then?"

"I have my reasons. Now listen: about law it's impossible to predict anymore what a law court will do. In England a streaker got ninety days—exactly the same sentence meted out to an IRA assassin. A man who admitted raping two women got off scot free because he told the court he thought they were enjoying it."

"Madness!" said Theresa primly.

"I know," said Hawkins. "Trials are political to a degree unknown since the sixteenth century. We once had political convictions—Sacco-Vanzetti, that kind of thing. Now we have political acquittals—anyone with a black skin, for example, is forgiven the rules of evidence altogether."

"You shouldn't say things like that."

"Law," said Hawkins—with a bitterness that surprised even himself—"has very little to do with law anymore. Law cases are won with money—and publicity. Your parents are very rich and your father is already preparing a defense in which you will be considered both physically and mentally incapable—not of committing the crimes but of being responsible for them."

Theresa was outraged: "I don't want their money!

316

I don't want political acquittal! I don't want any special privileges!"

"Ssh, hold it down."

Her outcry had been loud enough to disturb the other passengers, watching *The Great Waldo Pepper* on the silver screen.

Theresa's voice sank to an indignant whisper: "I don't want to escape punishment because my father's rich."

"It'll be your punishment to escape punishment," said Hawkins. "A very ironical ending to the saga of Saint Theresa."

But she was in something close to despair: "I don't want to be defended by my father. Don't you see?"

He did indeed. Better even than she did because he had spent more time studying her than she had in studying herself. The whole charade had started as a revolt against her parents.

"My goddamned parents and their goddamned money," said Theresa. "They'll keep me out of one prison by delivering me right back into the original one."

"You have an alternative," said Hawkins carefully.

"What alternative?"

Hawkins let her wait for it. He'd spent a largely sleepless night thinking about it. It was risky as hell but it was about time he took some risks.

"I'm a lawyer," he said, "who has never practiced law. But I have been admitted to the New York Bar." He smiled at her. "Of course you'd be out of your wits to take me in preference to your father. I'm totally untried in court, whereas your father is one of the most brilliant trial lawyers in America. Also . . ." He shrugged. "He would be taking the safest course too—pleading your incompetence. I would take the opposite course."

"What opposite course?"

Hawkins hunched his eloquent shoulders: "It's not easy to explain."

Theresa took his left hand in both her hands. "I'm a lawyer's daughter."

"That makes it even harder."

"Try."

"I'd say it is the English law itself that is incompetent to stand trial. English law is a holdover from the seventeenth century as irrelevant in the twentieth century as thumbscrews. Law as it is practiced today protects the Mafia, the hoodlums, the rich, the powerful—and persecutes—persecutes is the right word for it—the helpless, the idealistic, the admirable. The whole legal system is a perversion of justice from one end to the other."

"Marvelous!"

"Insanity," said Hawkins briefly. "The judge will tear me apart. But it'll make headlines. And, in the end, that's where trials are fought now, in the newspapers. You aim the arguments at the higher jury— the populace itself."

One of life's turning points, thought Hawkins, of which there had been far too few. At least in his life. Far too many in hers. "If you want to be a martyr,

Saint Theresa—and I know that you do—hire me as your lawyer. You'll be crucified."

Theresa laughed: "I'll never get a better offer."

Had an FBI agent in charge—or, for that matter, any pursuing officer of the law—ever become defense counsel? Hawkins didn't know. That, too, would make headlines—his own crucifixion. He had a horror of personal publicity. He was in open ocean, all right.

"And Amanda? How about Amanda?" asked Theresa.

"One crucifixion at a time," said Hawkins. "Amanda will have to wait her turn."

Theresa was very quiet then until the jumbo started letting down for Kennedy. Then, quite unexpectedly, she burst into tears. Appalled, Hawkins handed her his handkerchief. He had hoped to avoid this.

"What are you crying for?"

"Elf," sobbed Theresa.

THE BEST OF BESTSELLERS
FROM WARNER BOOKS!

MORE LIVES THAN ONE? by Jeffrey Iverson   **(89-372, $1.95)**
More Lives Than One? reads like a detective story and is the most thorough attempt to authenticate experiences of "previous incarnation." 8 pages of photographs.

DARE TO LOVE by Jennifer Wilde   **(82-258, $2.25)**
Who dared to love Elena Lopez? Who was willing to risk reputation and wealth to win the Spanish dancer who was the scandal of Europe? Kings, princes, great composers and writers . . . the famous and wealthy men of the 19th century vied for her affection, fought duels for her.

THIS LOVING TORMENT by Valerie Sherwood   **(89-415, $1.95)**
Perhaps she was too beautiful! Perhaps the brawling colonies would have been safer for a plainer girl, one more demure and less accomplished in language and manner. But Charity Woodstock was gloriously beautiful with pale gold hair and topaz eyes—and she was headed for trouble.

A STRANGER IN THE MIRROR   **(89-204, $1.95)**
by Sidney Sheldon
This is the story of Toby Temple, superstar and super bastard, adored by his vast TV and movie public, but isolated from real human contact by his own suspicion and distrust. It is also the story of Jill Castle, who came to Hollywood to be a star and discovered she had to buy her way with her body. When these two married, their love was so strong it was—**terrifying!**

 A Warner Communications Company